I0546078

Alien Secrets
Flight of the Kestrel book 2

A M Thomas

Alina Publishing
Swansea

Published by Alina Publishing
45 Rhondda Street, Mount Pleasant
Swansea SA1 6ER

ISBN: 978-1-9996781-1-1

Printed by Kindle Direct Print

Available from Amazon
Also available from Amazon for Kindle and on
Smashwords.com in 2019 for multiple ebook formats

Kestrel artwork by Brett Buckle
http://brettbuckle.co.uk/
Cover design by Steve Jones

Dedication

To my husband Michael who has encouraged me all the way, even though he doesn't like science fiction

Acknowledgements

I want to thank my editor Gail Williams (https://thewriteroute.wordpress.com/), and Swansea & District Writers Circle (http://www.swanseawriters.co.uk/) for all their advice and support.
I am grateful to Brett Buckle (http://brettbuckle.co.uk/) for the Kestrel artwork and to Steve Jones for designing the cover.

Among the stars
Who knows what friends we'll find
What mind
Will reach us from afar
And teach us things
Like how the universe sings?

About the author:

Writing poetry and making up stories since she was a child, she only started to write seriously when her children were grown. Her main ambition was to write science fiction, but along the way she got fascinated by local history and distracted by a major stroke. However, she wrote poetry about her stroke and spent her recovery writing a local history book. Taking early retirement gave her more time to concentrate on her writing.

Connect with the author online:
Website: www.annmariethomas.co.uk
Email: amt.tetelestai@gmail.com
Twitter: https://twitter.com/AnnMThomas80
Facebook: http://on.fb.me/1P9OkCu
LinkedIn: http://linkd.in/1MUdsAv
GoodReads: http://bit.ly/21nG4Jv

FREE BOOK!
Join her mailing list and receive this free book and monthly updates
http://eepurl.com/bbOsyz

Chapter 1

Shom Reuel's wrists were secured to the table. Like most interrogation rooms, this room had only a table and two chairs. No decoration, no contrast of colour in the room at all. The stone walls and floor were grey-brown, even the table and chairs were grey-brown.

It was strange, they hadn't removed his hat. They seemed to assume he was human, like the men he'd been arrested with, despite his bright pink skin. Not that that gave him much advantage, since humans would be stronger and faster in the lower gravity here on Boka. But Reuel grew up in what humans called low gravity, for him this planet's "low" gravity was normal. At least he didn't have to wear his back brace, an annoyance on board Kestrel and any other 1G planets they visited. On higher gravity planets he could barely function at all.

He understood only a little of the Bokan language, and his captors understood only a little Standard, so there was an uncomfortable wait for someone more fluent. He hated the waiting, not knowing what they were going to do to him was unnerving. He wished they would hurry up and get on with it. He was used to violence, that was part of everyday life in the poor region of his youth. He could defend himself or his family, stand up to bullies and thugs; but he hated waiting.

The two Bokan males who brought him in paced restlessly around the room. They didn't seem to like waiting either. The Bokans were reptilian humanoids with scaly skin, a wider jaw and a broad, solid physique. Their metre-long tails stood straight up their

1

back through a hole in their trousers. They looked strong, even though their gravity was lighter than on Earth. Their planet was quite warm and they could regulate their body temperature, so they had no need for thick clothing like other reptilian species.

The interrogator arrived, a youngish Bokan in a smart black uniform. Reuel imagined he had just graduated from training school, and had to stifle a smile. Still, the thought eased his tension a bit.

The interrogator asked him the usual things: who he was, where he was from, why he was here, and made notes on a tablet screen. Reuel stuck to his cover story: his group were sociologists studying the Bokan culture. He acted as if he was a lowly ignorant assistant. He let some of his nerves show, since he thought a lowly assistant would be nervous. But he watched everything, trying to prepare for what might be to come.

His interrogator rose and left the room. Reuel tensed, every sense alert. He noticed now how clean the room was, and his mind rushed to the conclusion that it had needed cleaning after the last interrogation. What did they do? What bodily fluids had been spilled?

He watched the face of the man left to guard him - though he couldn't think what they expected him to do, with his wrists strapped to the table. The man, in a grey jacket and trousers without any badges, stood to attention near the door, staring at Reuel. No, not staring - studying. Bokan first contact was recent, so it was likely the man had never seen a non-Bokan before.

The idea that they were not alone in the universe was new to the Bokans. When they developed warp drive and were able to explore further than their own system, meeting other species was a shock. The Planetary Alliance for Cooperation and Trade (PACT) was an alliance between the species with warp drive technology, so when they were alerted to the Bokan emergence, a delegation was sent to invite them to join. Initially the Bokans were suspicious, and jealously guarded their technology, but they soon realised the other species were further advanced than they were. Negotiations for Boka to join PACT were proceeding with cautious optimism.

Reuel wondered how the guard would react if he lowered his head to his hands and took his hat off. Like all Altairians he had no hair, but a row of soft spines ran down the centre of his head. The spines moved in response to emotion, at that point Reuel was having trouble keeping them calm under his soft hat.

The thought of the guard seeing his spines writhe made him smile, which made the guard look away. That made Reuel smile even more. On reflection, he decided to keep his hat on, not introduce unnecessary complications. If the Bokans used violence against him, they would find out he wasn't human soon enough.

The guard, whose curiosity was getting the better of him, snapped to attention at the sound of the door opening. The interrogator entered and waved his tablet at Reuel.

'We have been unable to find any reference to your expedition,' he said, walking round the table to stand over Reuel.

Reuel refused to take the bait. 'I do not know about that,' he said, putting a worried look on his face. 'I was hired by Mr Parks directly. He does the paperwork, I do what I'm told. As long as he pays me.'

The interrogator paused to consider. Reuel felt the tension gathering and his spines stirring. The man's sudden movement startled him.

'Very well,' he said, and turned to the guard. Reuel understood the gist of the Bokan instructions: 'Put him in a cell with the other one. We must speak to the leader.'

Reuel had been holding his breath and let go. He was relieved for himself, but concerned about Parks, though there was nothing he could do.

***

Reuel was put in a cell with Daniel Hoy, a crewmate, and he was glad to see Hoy was unharmed. Hoy had a yellower cast to his skin compared with most humans Reuel had met, and his eyes were more pointed. This was because he came from "the East" on Earth.

The cell door clanged shut and the bolt shot home. Reuel looked around. The cell had dirty stone walls and floor. The ceiling was metal sheeting, with a fluorescent light in a cage in the centre. There were no windows. Hoy signalled Reuel to check the room for monitoring devices. It didn't take long.

'Clear.'

'So much for a covert mission,' said Hoy. 'Parks and his bright ideas, he had to rush into things.'

Reuel was relieved Hoy wasn't criticising him. This was the first clandestine mission he had been on since joining the crew of the Kestrel six months ago, and he wanted to do well. The three of them, Parks, Hoy and Reuel, had been sent to validate intelligence that the Bokans had developed a secret weapon.

Reuel watched as Hoy checked out the door. It was heavy metal, the hinges were on the outside, and there were no electronics, no key pads or hand print recognition systems. It seemed the security systems were mechanical and on the other side.

'We're not going to get out of here in a hurry.'

'Hanging about in the street was not a good idea either,' said Reuel. 'I think that man was already suspicious of us.'

'So Parks went and asked him for directions! It's his fault we're in this mess!' Hoy said.

Reuel's head snapped round. He wasn't sure how to read Hoy's reddened face. These humans with head hair instead of spines were still difficult for him to read. At home on Altair the nuances of someone's cranial spine quivers were there for all to see. None of his species would dream of speaking so harshly of a senior officer, such behaviour would be unthinkable.

'How is Commander Parks?' Reuel asked.

'Reuel!' Hoy snapped. 'No ranks. We're sociologists, remember? We've come to study a new alien society.'

'Sorry, sir. They took him away as soon as we were arrested, and that must have been an hour ago. Did they say anything when they questioned you?'

'No, they just asked questions. I said nothing, of course. What did you say when they questioned you?'

'I stuck to the story, told them I was the junior member of the team and did not know the details of our expedition.' He struck an exaggerated humble pose. 'I am here to fetch and carry. You should ask Mr Parks.' He stood straight again. 'Where is Parks?'

As if in answer to his own question, the bolt rattled and the door opened. Parks' face was a mess, his clothes crumpled and his knuckles bleeding. A knot clenched in Reuel's stomach as he feared the Bokans would probably do the same to him. A guard pushed Parks in the back and he stumbled forward, while the door was bolted behind him.

Nathaniel Parks was a human of, Reuel had been told, Scandinavian descent. He believed that meant Parks was from the north of the northern hemisphere of Earth. Tall, with blond hair, cut short, and blue eyes. A look of relief crossed his face as he saw his two crewmates unharmed.

'Are you two all right?' Parks asked, sitting on the floor. He ran a hand through his hair and then explored his bruised face with his fingers.

'Yes.' Hoy knelt beside him. 'Are you OK?'

'I'll live.' Parks gave a wry chuckle and rubbed his knuckles. 'I gave as good as I got, but Bokan skulls are hard.'

'Can I recommend, sir, you concentrate on the lower chest in future?' Reuel said. 'Their ribs are not substantial. Also the eyes are a good target...' he paused, seeing their surprised faces. 'I looked it up in preparation for this mission.'

He went over to Parks with a container of water. 'I found this by the door, sir. It looks all right.' He bent to give Parks a drink and spoke in a low voice. 'I cannot find any cameras or microphones, the walls are solid. We might even be underground. There is nothing here but those mattresses along the wall.'

There were four of them, two either side, but to call them mattresses was a compliment. They were thin and lumpy, the dirt giving no hint of their original colour.

'It's a shame,' Parks whispered, 'because I thought we were doing quite well up to then. That contact we were given pointed us in the right direction, and there's definitely something going on. This building being partially underground explains the lack of obvious security measures from outside, which is where I made my mistake. If only you two hadn't joined in the fight, you might have escaped, to rescue me later. Still, it is what it is.'

'We'll have to hope our cover story holds,' Hoy muttered. 'Let's hope this secret weapon we're looking for isn't a new interrogation device.'

The door opened and two guards came in, all but dragging a prisoner who could hardly walk. When the guards let him go, the man, possibly a human, fell to his hands and knees, his head drooping, his face covered by his long dark hair. Hoy and Reuel moved to assist him.

One of the guards pointed at Parks. 'You! Come now.'

Hoy jumped between him and Parks.

'I'm in charge. Talk to me.'

'No,' said Parks, 'it's my responsibility.'

Parks dragged himself to his feet and approached the guard. At two meters tall, Parks was taller than both guards, but the other drew his weapon, so there would be no arguments. The first guard grabbed Parks' arm and they took him away, and the door clanged shut behind them. Hoy and Reuel exchanged a worried look.

'There's nothing we can do for him for the moment, let's see to this guy,' Hoy said. 'Help me get him onto a mattress.'

The man had been badly beaten. His bare arms were covered in bruises and there was what looked like blue blood on the back of his tunic. They rolled him onto his side. His face was bruised and there was a lump in the centre of his forehead with fine red lines radiating from it that looked like a particularly nasty wound. They carried the man over to the nearest mattress. Reuel fetched the water while Hoy tried to make the man comfortable.

'Can you hear me? How do you feel?' Hoy asked.

The man groaned and opened his eyes. 'I can't, I can't.'

'It's OK. We won't hurt you. We're prisoners too.'

Reuel lifted the man's head and helped him to drink. 'I am Shom Reuel, and this is Daniel Hoy. I am from Altair and he is from Earth. We did not intend to end up as a guest of the Bokans, but we spoke to the wrong person. How about you?'

'Tanu,' the man gasped, 'of the family of Pe'Rod. I'm... an explorer.' His voice was soft, speaking took a great effort.

'Well, there is little to explore in here,' said Reuel. He tore off the bottom of Tanu's long tunic. Using the rag as a swab, Reuel pushed back the man's long dark hair and washed dirt, blood and sweat from his almost-white skin. His high cheekbones and grey eyes made him look fragile, and his arms and hands were so thin, they were skeletal. Reuel himself was slim, being from a lower-gravity planet, but he thought the man looked human enough.

'I suggest we all try to get some rest,' said Hoy. He pulled Reuel close and whispered. 'Don't be so free with the introductions. We can't trust anyone.'

'Sorry sir, I will be more careful.'

Hoy settled down on a mattress across the room. Reuel lay down on the adjacent mattress, but after only a few minutes, sat up again.

'Sir, how can you rest in this situation?' he whispered. 'What are they doing to Parks? If they do the same to him as they have done to this poor man, who knows what state he will be in when they bring him back. What will he tell them about us? We could be in even worse trouble!'

'Don't be such a cry baby, and don't underestimate Parks. He's a hard nut to crack.' Hoy dropped his voice and leaned closer. 'He worked security in the past. Remember your training. What we need to be doing is planning how to get out of here and resting so we're ready when the opportunity comes.'

Reuel lay down, affronted at being called a baby. The hat he wore to hide his cranial spines was uncomfortable when they were writhing, so he tried to calm himself, but a thought occurred to him and he sat up again. 'So how *are* we going to escape from a solid room with no electronics in the door, and two guards outside?'

'Looks like we'll have to do it the old-fashioned way, and jump the guards next time they come in,' Hoy said. 'Now pipe down and try to get some rest.'

Reuel opened his mouth to speak, but Hoy got there first. 'That's an order.'

Reuel stared at the ceiling. He felt out of his depth, but he trusted Parks and Hoy. They were First and Second Officers on the Kestrel.

Part of PACT, a non-military organisation created to assist trade, research, and the sharing of culture and technology between the different species who had developed warp capability, the Kestrel was a Fast-Response ship with a crew of eleven. The Fast-Response Fleet was almost an independent police and diplomatic force, able to operate between planets, where jurisdiction may not be clear. They offered investigation and assistance wherever needed.

Reuel had been so proud when Captain Darrow picked him for this mission. There were not many low gravity planets in the Kestrel's region of responsibility, and his physical limitations meant he had to stay on board when they were at higher gravity planets. He wanted to do well, and reminded himself that he had been in bad situations before, growing up back home. He reflected that dreaming of adventures in space was not the same as being in one.

This was not what he had expected.

When he closed his eyes his senses concentrated on the rank smell of their cell. It reminded him of the changing room after an exercise session, with the added scent of mildew on neglected fruit boxes. Foul as it was, it also made him just a little homesick for the back alleys and cramped houses, though he was glad enough to escape when he joined the Academy. He lay there thinking of home.

Chapter 2

Reuel's mind wandered to his first ship, The Rart. It was an Altairian Fast-Response ship, and he had managed to upset someone. The first few months were fine, but one day he turned away from the food dispenser and bumped into a lieutenant, spilling hot stew all down the front of the officer's uniform. Not only did it make a mess, but it burned the man's chest, made worse by Reuel's vain attempts to mop it up.

It was a mistake anyone could make, and the lieutenant's fault for standing too close. That was why the captain decided not to charge Reuel with assault, but the lieutenant would not accept the decision. Altairians are skilled at the art of feud-craft, making an enemy suffer without resorting to violence or even personal encounters. From then on, the lieutenant made Reuel's life a misery, though not a single incident could be traced to him. From missing personal items to double shifts, every day there was something.

Everyone knew who did it, but the lieutenant was skilled, and no official action could be taken. The lieutenant was skilled at his job too and the captain was reluctant to lose him, so Reuel had to go. He learned later that the man had started feud-craft against someone else in a spaceport, and been killed for it. Reuel felt vindicated, but sad it had come to that.

This vengeful, violent side of Altairians was not well known and rarely seen. Soft-spoken and graceful in their movements, Altairians appeared to be gentle people. They were courteous and kind, both among themselves and with other species. But push an Altairian too far, and the darker side will show.

The whole of Altair had once been violent, with warring overlords and roaming gangs. Eventually there was a devastating war and the victor had wiped out the leaders of every other clan and enforced peace. Somehow, it had worked, and modern Altairian society shows no trace of that deadly past.

Most of the Kestrel's missions consisted of settling disputes, transportating passengers or supplies, and giving emergency relief. Consequently Reuel's violent side had never been seen.

While less violent, Altairian society was not egalitarian. There were deprived areas, and people without work, without credits, and with time on their hands easily became violent, especially the young. Reuel grew up in such an area. His one parent died in an accident at work and he was raised by a lone grandparent. Money was short, but education was free, and Reuel excelled. That was his means of escape.

When he was offered the chance to join the Kestrel, Reuel was not only glad to escape the Rart, he was grateful for the chance to interact more closely with non-Altairians. He had always been interested in the other species, and almost went into research rather than joining the PACT Academy. He might still go into full time research in later life. But now he had the opportunity to travel, to help people, to research in his spare time, and to meet the other species in person.

Most of the Kestrel crew were human, but that was a species in which he was particularly interested, and there were two other species on board: the Zoan, Balitoth and the Kohathi, Nefar.

Reuel and Balitoth shared a cabin and discovered a

shared interest in learning about humans and their culture. The human tribal ritual of "football" seemed a good subject of study, and they began watching recordings of matches together. They soon found it was indeed a bonding experience, and became good friends.

***

In the Bokan cell, their fitful rest was disturbed by the rattling of a flap at the bottom of the door. A plate of something that looked like bread and another flask of water were pushed in. Then the flap rattled shut again, waking Tanu.

He started thrashing about. 'Please, don't, I can't!'

'It is well,' Reuel tried to reassure him as he stretched, got up and fetched the water. 'Here, drink. Can you sit up?'

He helped the man sit and Hoy brought over the bread, which he divided in quarters, keeping some back for Parks. It was dry and tasted like fungus, they had to wash down every mouthful with sips of the water. Hoy took the water away from Reuel.

'Don't drink it all, we don't know how long it'll be before we get more.'

With each mouthful Tanu became more aware. 'Who are you?' he asked at last.

'Fellow prisoners,' Hoy said, with a warning look to Reuel. 'We asked the wrong question of the wrong person. Why are you here?'

Tanu considered before answering. 'Because I refused… to cooperate.'

Reuel asked, 'How long have you been here?'

'I don't know, seems like weeks. They were nice to me at first, but then they lost patience.' He trembled at the thought and fell silent.

Reuel thought about the prospect of being here for weeks. Being locked up was bad enough, the bread was worse, but he dreaded to think what was happening to Parks. The Bokans might decide to interrogate himself and Hoy the way they had interrogated Parks, and apparently Tanu, to see if they would reveal more. He wasn't sure if he could withstand torture. He shuddered, his cranial spines writhed under his hat.

The door opened and one guard came in supporting Parks, the other stayed in the doorway, his weapon at the ready. The guard dropped Parks, grabbed Tanu and dragged him out, kicking and screaming.

Hoy and Reuel rushed to take care of Parks, thoughts of overpowering the guards forgotten. Parks' jacket was missing, and there was blood on the back of his shirt. He was shaking and could barely stand. As they helped him to a mattress, Tanu's cries echoed in the corridor until the other guard slammed the door.

'Take it easy, sit down and let me look at you,' Hoy said, stooping down with Parks. 'What did they do?'

Parks choked on the water Reuel was giving him and took a minute to recover.

'They used what they called the "pain-giver". I've never felt anything like it.' He started to shake.

'Take your time, sir,' said Reuel. 'Sip more water.' He helped Parks drink.

'I need to lie down,' Parks said, and sank back onto the mattress.

Reuel leant towards Hoy and whispered, 'He must have told them everything! They'll execute us!'

Parks reached up and grabbed Reuel by the shirt. 'I'm stronger than that, keep it together.'

Reuel went a brighter pink than usual, sat back on

his heels and pushed at his hat, which wriggled as his spines moved.

Parks dropped his head back on the mattress. 'We're OK for now, but we've got to get out of here before they decide to do that again.'

'We've already worked out the only way out of here is to jump the guards,' said Hoy, cleaning the blood off Parks' face with the fabric ripped from the hem of Tanu's tunic. 'They've taken Tanu away, so our next chance is when they bring him back. You're in no fit state to fight, so you'll have to distract them, and Reuel and I will take one guard each.'

Parks reached for his right trouser pocket and winced. He beckoned to Reuel. 'There's a small knife in my pocket. It's not much, but every little helps. I managed to palm it when they were fitting the pain-giver.'

Reuel reached into Parks' pocket and pulled out a scalpel.

'We must be careful, surely,' said Reuel, eyeing the scalpel. 'If we kill the guards it will cause an even greater diplomatic problem than our spying.'

Parks saw the darkness in Hoy's eyes, reflecting his own distasteful reasoning. When Hoy spoke, Parks wasn't surprised.

'It's true, becoming murderers won't help us or our mission, but if we stay here how much of this -' he pointed to Parks' injuries '- do you think we can withstand? We have to escape. If we only disable the guards, how long before they recover enough to raise the alarm? We don't know. What we do know is knocking them out was extremely difficult when we were arrested. As abhorrent as the idea is, killing the guards is our only hope of actually getting out of here.'

Parks could see Reuel was shocked. His cranial spines jumped under the hat and he grabbed his head in pain.

Parks forced himself to raise his head again. 'I don't take this decision lightly, but to have Alliance people spying is a much bigger diplomatic incident than to have unknown individuals kill guards during an escape. Now, do you want the knife or not?'

Reuel sighed. 'I can kill better with my bare hands,' he said, handing the scalpel to Hoy.

Chapter 3

'What's this pain-giver?' Hoy asked Parks.

'Did you see the blood on the back of my shirt?' said Parks with a shudder. 'They fit a device over the top of your spine where it directly attacks the nervous system. The bastard just plays with a little button and the results are excruciating.'

Reuel gasped. 'Tanu had blood on his back too, they must have used it on him,' he said. 'We must take him with us, sir.'

Hoy shook his head. 'We'll need to help Parks as it is. We can't possibly take Tanu - who knows what state he'll be in when they bring him back?'

'I'm stronger than I look, I will carry him,' said Reuel.

Parks spoke up from the mattress. 'Who is this Tanu guy - did you learn anything about him? I wouldn't be happy leaving anyone to the tender mercies of the Bokans.'

'He only said he was an explorer,' said Reuel. 'We really must help him, sir, if we can.'

Parks understood Reuel didn't want a life on his conscience.

Reuel looked around. 'This water container is quite flimsy, but the bread plate is metal. Maybe we can hit one of the guards with it while we stick the knife in the other one. If we put them out of action and take their weapons, then you can help Parks and I can carry Tanu.'

'Now you're starting to think clearly,' said Hoy, 'but you're taller than me and I'm stronger. You help Parks and I'll carry Tanu.' He turned to Parks. 'Eat some of this disgusting bread and then get some rest. We need you as fit as possible for the escape. Reuel and I will sort out the details.'

'Listen,' said Parks, 'these Bokans may look humanoid, but they have different anatomy. Their rib cage is deep, so it's easier to reach the heart from the back, up under the rib cage and across in front of the spine.'

'Thanks, sir. Now will you rest? I'm hoping you can help Tanu while we're dealing with the guards.'

Parks pulled a face and turned on his side, his back to the wall, while Hoy took Reuel to the other side of the cell to make plans.

As he watched them, Parks thought Hoy and Reuel made a strange looking pair. Hoy, from Earth, was slim, wiry and short, like his Asian ancestors. Reuel was born on Altair, where the lower gravity made people tall and slim. His skin and cranial spines were bright pink.

According to their files, their fighting styles were very different too. Hoy took great pride in mastering the martial arts of his ancestral heritage. He often took opponents by surprise, and the grace of his movements belied the power behind them. Unlike Hoy's disciplined grace, Reuel learned to defend himself in the back streets where he grew up. He fought low and dirty, so he could be just as surprising in a fight - especially in low gravity.

At two metres tall, Nathaniel Parks towered over both of them, but he wasn't going to do much towering in his present condition. Parks' stomach clenched with worry. He didn't know the Kestrel crew well, so he hoped Hoy and Reuel were good fighters, because he was too weakened by the torture.

The beating was bad enough, but the pain-giver had

finished him. His nerves felt as if they were on fire, and he couldn't stop trembling. The mattress wasn't comfortable, but he closed his eyes and forced his tense muscles to relax. He needed to rest.

***

It was hard to tell how much time passed, but it seemed to Parks like quite a while later when the door bolt rattled. Instantly Hoy was on his feet and standing by the door, leaning casually against the wall on the side where the door opened. Reuel leaned down and helped Parks to sit up, holding the metal plate behind Parks' back.

The guards entered, carrying a barely conscious Tanu between them. As they came through the doorway, one guard became suspicious and let go of Tanu to reach for his weapon, putting the other guard off balance. At that moment Hoy jumped behind the guard nearest the door, grabbed his mouth shut, and slid the scalpel into the guard's back and up under his ribs.

Reuel swung round and caught the other guard in the throat with the edge of the plate. Reuel grabbed his opponent around the neck with one arm and covered his mouth with the other hand. He twisted the guard's head so hard they heard the crunch of his neck breaking. Both guards went down with barely a sound. Unfortunately, one guard fell on top of Tanu. Reuel dragged the guard off, grabbed the weapon and went to guard the door. Hoy was investigating outside.

Parks staggered to his feet and roused Tanu, who moaned and looked around wildly.

'It's OK,' Parks reassured him, 'we're escaping, but I need you to get up.'

Parks tried to help Tanu up, but Tanu struggled. He trembled violently, and Parks couldn't get him to his feet.

Hoy came back into the cell. 'It's clear, and we're not far from an exit. Come on!'

Hoy grabbed a security badge from the nearest guard and lifted Tanu over his shoulder. Parks went to Reuel, who slotted himself under Parks' shoulder. Hoy closed the cell door behind them and pushed the bolt home.

The corridor was bare and dirty, of similar construction to the cell. Parks looked left and right. To the left were two more cell doors ending in a blank wall. To the right were a handful of doors on either side sloping up towards the rooms at the entrance where they had been brought in. That end of the corridor was closed off with swinging doors.

Hoy eased one door open and checked, the space beyond was empty. They pushed through and turned left into another corridor which also sloped up, towards a rear exit. This one was much better appointed, with a beige tiled floor and walls painted light green. It was strange to have offices and cells so close to each other.

As they moved along they heard voices as someone opened an office door but was still turned towards the person he was talking to. Hoy pushed open a door on the left and led them through, the door closing quietly behind them as the voices came out into the corridor.

They found themselves in a dark room. There was just enough light from the frosted glass window to see it was a kitchen, with ovens and hobs. Parks sat down with a soft groan and signalled to Hoy to put Tanu down.

'Looks like the kitchen is closed,' Parks hissed. 'See if you can find food and water. We don't know when we'll get more.'

Hoy moved to investigate.

Parks' mind raced with possibilities and unknowns. *Stay here a while or go? How long before the guards are missed? Why is the kitchen dark?* One of the voices in the corridor called out.

'They're saying "Goodbye,"' Parks whispered. 'If it's the end of the day, the building might soon be a lot emptier. If it's the end of a shift, there might be a whole lot of new people coming. Which is it?'

Parks couldn't focus his thoughts beyond questions.

Meanwhile, Tanu was flailing about on the floor, trying to get up. Reuel went to help him.

'No!' Tanu cried and pushed him away.

'Keep him quiet,' Parks whispered. 'Knock him out if you have to.'

Reuel leaned across Tanu, with his hand over his mouth, and looked into his eyes. 'It is me, Reuel, remember?'

Tanu was too far gone to think straight and was trying to scream behind Reuel's hand.

'I am sorry, my friend,' said Reuel, and hit him.

Hoy returned. 'Everything's locked away, but I found some fruit and more fungus bread.' He pulled a face and handed it out. 'Put it in your pockets, we don't have time to eat now. There's nothing to carry water I'm afraid. We'll have to move you and Tanu to the tap.'

Reuel turned his body to show a large wet patch down his left side.

'What!?' Hoy exclaimed.

Reuel grinned and pulled the crumpled water container out of his jacket pocket. 'I thought we might need this. There was no way to stop it spilling, but there is quite a lot left.'

The three Kestral crew drank, then Reuel refilled the container and squeezed it back into his pocket.

Hoy looked at Parks and frowned. 'Are you fit to command, sir?'

Parks shook his head. 'Proceed.'

Hoy listened at the door and then opened it a crack. The corridor was silent. There was no way of knowing when the next person would pass. He closed the door and came back to pick up Tanu over his shoulder again.

'Now's as good a time as any. Let's go.'

Reuel helped Parks to his feet and ducked under his shoulder. With Hoy in the lead they slipped out and made for the exit, twenty metres away. The door opened at a touch of the security badge against the panel.

Chapter 4

They found themselves in an open parking area, with a few vehicles, most with wheels. Only one had hover capability, and it was in a specially-marked parking space. Unfortunately the car park was enclosed by a high chain link fence, but at least they could see there was no one about. They moved away from the lit doorway and crouched down between two vehicles parked close together.

They were surprised to find it was dark, and glad to see the lights were widely spaced, although the vehicles were too. Parks struggled to focus and keep his concentration on what was happening. He had come closer to breaking than he cared to admit. The temptation to stop, to let his mind and body shut down was strong, but it was vital he keep it together, not jeopardise their escape.

'Can we steal a vehicle?' said Reuel.

'It would take too long, and we've no tools,' said Hoy. 'Now, how are we going to get out of here?'

The car park exit was a heavy sliding gate with a card reader on a post, and an obvious security camera. Hoy and Reuel scanned the fence, looking for gaps. Reuel signalled to wait and slipped off to where the fence joined the building. He had found something.

'The fence has been damaged, and there is a small gap near the wall,' he reported when he returned.

It took some time to reach the side of the parking area. Parks was weak and suffered bouts of trembling.

'Sorry sir,' Reuel said, as he stopped to adjust his hold on Parks for the third time.

'Carry on, Ensign,' Parks said.

Hoy was also struggling carrying Tanu, because Tanu was taller than Hoy.

They moved from the shadow of one vehicle to another, and manhandled Parks and Tanu through the gap. They crossed the road and went into a side street. They had originally approached the security building from the front, so they were surprised to find it was in an urban area. Four-storey apartment blocks stretched in both directions along the road. Square, flat-roofed, and built of grey concrete blocks, they were ugly and looked to Parks like something out of Earth history.

Reuel turned to Hoy. 'Not very modern, are they? I know the Bokans have only just discovered warp drive, but it seems only the city centre has been developed. Perhaps these are accommodation for those working in the security centre. I would hate to live here.'

'But have you noticed how large the windows are?' said Hoy. 'They obviously like a lot of light. Let's hope they've all got their curtains closed, we don't want to be spotted.'

Lights were on in most windows but no one was about outside.

'Looks like early evening,' Hoy continued. 'Everyone's home from work. We need to get away before people start going out for the evening - if that's what they do here.'

'Which way?' asked Reuel.

Hoy shifted Tanu on his shoulder and looked up at the stars, trying to shade his eyes from the street lights' glare. 'We hid the shuttle south of the city. This way.' He set off to the left.

They made slow progress as Parks needed to rest every few minutes, and after a while Tanu began to come round again, and struggle in Hoy's grip. After turning a couple of corners they came to a small area of open land like a park, with trees and bushes and paths laid out. The plants looked spikey, but the spikes turned out to be soft.

Hoy hurried them in and ducked his head behind bushes growing against the wall of the neighbouring apartment block. He backed out again and signalled for Reuel to help Parks scramble in and sit down. Then Reuel came out to help Hoy to get Tanu in. Tanu cried out as they manhandled him behind the bushes, and Reuel ran back to the street to check for alarm or pursuit. Hoy was trying to calm Tanu when Reuel returned and climbed into the space.

'It is quiet here,' Reuel said, 'but there are lights and vehicles at the far end of the street. It could be a patrol or a search party.'

'I need some water,' said Parks, and Reuel passed him the container from his pocket.

Hoy spoke quickly. 'We'll never make it like this. Sir, you rest here and look after Tanu. Reuel and I will be much quicker on our own. We'll go for the shuttle and come back for you. Hopefully we'll also draw them away from here, but you must keep Tanu quiet.'

Parks nodded and moved closer to Tanu. 'Go, go!'

Hoy and Reuel disappeared into the darkness. Parks lifted Tanu's head and helped him to drink some of the water. He leaned close to Tanu's ear and spoke softly.

'I know how you feel, but you're going to be all right. My friends have gone for help. You must stay quiet.'

For the first time, Tanu managed to focus on him, and realise he was not a guard. Tanu frowned in confusion and paused for thought. Finally, he swallowed and said, 'Safe?'

'Very nearly, pal, just hang in there.'

The ground was hard and dry but under the bushes it was softened by a thick layer of fallen leaves and the soft spines. It smelled musty and woody. It reminded Parks of the forests back home. He adjusted their position to be sure they were out of sight.

Soon they heard the passing patrol. Parks covered Tanu's mouth but smiled to reassure him. He could hardly breathe while he waited to see if they would enter the park. He strained his ears for sounds of tracker animals, but there were none, and the patrol passed by.

Once the noise faded, Tanu relaxed. He seemed to go to sleep. Parks checked he was breathing, just to be sure. He felt exhausted himself, but had to stay awake and on watch.

His thoughts turned to the mission. What a mess! He couldn't see anything they did wrong in their investigation since they arrived - up to the point where they asked a plain clothes policeman about the security building. That was a mistake and could have been better handled.

And now, they were hiding from the security services under a bush and no idea about the secret weapon they had come to investigate. Still, it looked as if they might escape after all, and the Bokans didn't know who they were. Thankfully.

***

When Hoy and Reuel slipped away from the park, Hoy cautioned Reuel to slow his walk.

'We mustn't run or look furtive, because it makes us look suspicious,' he said. 'Walk at a normal pace and chat, like friends out for a stroll. If anyone speaks to us, I'll reply - your Bokan isn't good enough.'

'What should we talk about?' Reuel whispered.

'Reuel, whispering's not normal,' Hoy said. 'Talk about anything.'

Reuel sighed. 'Well, suppose you explain to me what the plan is.'

They turned another corner into the shadow of a building, Hoy pointed to the sky. 'See that group of stars? They're in the south, so we follow them out of the city. I'm hoping we can circle round and pick up where we came in, that'll make it easier to find the shuttle.'

'Let us hope we did not camouflage it too well,' Reuel said with a grin.

Hoy pulled a small item out of his boot. 'Don't worry, I brought this. Once we reach the right area, this button will make the shuttle respond. It'll tell us where it is.'

There weren't many people about, but those who saw them, frowned and kept their distance. Then a vehicle passed them, turned round and came back. Three young Bokan men got out and approached them.

Hoy said, in Bokan, 'Can we help you gentleman?'

One of the men came forward and stood close, towering over Hoy. 'Who are you, what are you doing here, and what is that?' he said, pointing at Reuel.

Reuel saw the pointing but didn't understand all the words.

Hoy signalled to Reuel to stay calm and replied evenly, 'He's my friend. We're part of a team of sociologists, come to study your culture.'

'You won't find much culture round here,' he said, laughing with his friends.

One of the friends said, 'Look, his hat is moving!' He

made a lunge for Reuel's hat and Reuel reacted instinctively and parried the arm. The man yelled and cradled his arm. 'What did you do that for?'

While Reuel was distracted the third man reached out and pulled Reuel's hat off, revealing his cranial spines, moving. They all recoiled in horror.

Reuel said in broken Bokan, 'Do you want to see my powers?' and pointed his hands at them.

They decided they didn't want to, and hurried back to their vehicle, throwing Reuel's hat back to him. Hoy dragged Reuel round the nearest corner and burst out laughing.

Reuel was puzzled. 'Did I not do well? I made them think I had strange powers.'

'Very strange indeed. Do you know what you said? "Do you want to see my electricity?"'

Reuel laughed. 'They went away, so it worked. Let us go before they find their courage.'

They picked up the pace, came to the end of the road and looked left and right.

'Does this look familiar to you?' Hoy asked.

Reuel looked again. 'This way,' he said, pointing right. 'I remember the broken gate over there.'

They turned right and found the road ended in open country. They crossed a field, over a gate and headed for a clump of trees. They were away from the street lights now and had only the light of the Bokan moon to see by. Luckily it was full and cast a ghostly light over everything. Hoy pressed his button and the shuttle beeped and flashed a light. They hurried over and began removing the branches covering the ship. Under the branches was a camouflage tarpaulin. They had just begun working on it when they were startled by a voice behind them and the beam of a torch.

'What are you doing?' A Bokan man with a small two-legged furry animal on a lead had been crossing the field, and was coming towards them.

Hoy thought quickly. 'Come and see what we've found,' he shouted. 'There's something hidden here.'

The man came over and tied his pet's lead to a tree. 'What is it?' he asked.

'It looks like a shuttle. Help us uncover it.'

Reuel kept his head down and moved away to help pull off the tarpaulin.

'This isn't one of ours,' the man said. 'We need to inform the authorities.'

Reuel picked up the word for "authorities" and looked at Hoy in alarm, but Hoy smiled.

'Definitely,' Hoy said, 'but there's no rush. After all, the people can't escape - we've got their shuttle. Let's see if we can open it.'

Hoy "found" the door release and the man rushed forward to look inside. At which point Hoy hit him with a broken tree branch and knocked him out.

'Quickly,' Hoy said to Reuel, 'help me move him out of the way.'

***

It seemed a long time before the sound Parks was waiting for reached his ears: the low hum of a shuttlecraft's engines. He thought it got too loud as the shuttle came in to land. Parks was sure the noise would attract the neighbours, and probably the patrol.

He began to drag Tanu out of the bushes, but the man was unconscious and Parks was too weak to make much progress. Each time Parks fell his level of panic rose. The wind from the engines whipped the bushes and rattled the nearby windows. Parks had to pause and take a calming breath.

Keep it together, you're even more of a liability if you panic.

There was a shout and Parks looked up to see a figure running back into the adjacent building. They had come out to see what the noise was and were going to report it. Reuel appeared and heaved Tanu over his shoulder and disappeared with him back to the shuttle. Parks staggered to his feet as Reuel returned and ducked under his shoulder.

'Quickly, sir,' Reuel said. 'We could see the patrol lights in the next street as we came in to land. They will be here at any moment.'

'We've been spotted by a neighbour too,' said Parks.

Parks and Reuel reached the shuttle, where Hoy was trying to strap Tanu into a chair. Tanu had come round and Hoy tried to restrain him without frightening him any further. Tanu was too weak to do much about it. Hoy handed over to Reuel and ran for the controls, as a shot from a laser pistol grazed the doorframe. The patrol had arrived. Parks ducked and lost his balance, falling out onto the ground. With Hoy intent on the controls, the shuttle began to lift.

Reuel screamed, 'Wait! He is not in yet,' and leaped out after Parks. He threw himself down to cover Parks.

The shuttle settled again and Hoy appeared at the doorway giving covering fire. The patrol ducked and Reuel scrambled up, dragging Parks to his feet. As they struggled to the doorway, Parks cried out and stumbled.

'My arm! I'm hit.'

Hoy fired again and rushed to help. They almost fell into the shuttle. Hoy slammed his hand on the door control and ran for the controls. The shuttle took off, even before they found their seats. They stumbled about, and managed to get strapped in. Parks was distracted by pain, but saw Tanu was crying, and Hoy was concentrating on flying. Reuel had snatched off his hat to free his agitated cranial spines and ran his hands along them.

After a calming breath, Reuel reached over to the injured alien. 'Tanu, it is me, Reuel, you are safe, trust me.'

As they broke orbit, Tanu gave a watery smile.

Chapter 5

They were glad to be back in safety on the Kestrel. Doctor Sebu Nefar and Medic James Tomos entered the shuttle as soon as they were secure in the hanger. Bewhiskered Nefar was Kohathi, a lot younger than he looked. Young Tomas was human but born and raised on a cargo ship. Their uniforms were white rather than the standard dark green. Nefar took a quick biological scan of Tanu, who became hysterical, and had to be sedated.

'You'd think he'd be grateful,' said Hoy.

'Put yourself in his shoes for a moment,' said Parks, fumbling with his harness as Tomos began scanning him. 'He's been tortured at least twice, then dragged out through the streets, shoved under a bush, bundled into a shuttlecraft and strapped down. He probably thinks this is the next round of torture.'

Hoy looked shamefaced. 'I didn't think of it like that, sir. He doesn't really know who we are, does he?'

'I may have to keep him sedated until he is well enough to understand,' said Nefar. He continued to scan Tanu while he spoke. He turned to Parks. 'And what about you?'

Parks was reticent, so Hoy interrupted. 'He's had a good dose of what Tanu's had, and he's been shot in the arm. He's barely able to stand.'

Tomos had been checking Parks over, and nodded in agreement in response to Nefar's questioning look.

'Right,' said Nefar, 'that one can wait, now he is sedated.' He pointed to Parks. 'You are having a full medscan, initial treatment, and then straight to bed.'

To everyone's surprise Parks gave in without protest. Tomos and Nefar transferred Tanu to a hover stretcher outside the shuttle, while Hoy helped Parks onto a second stretcher. As they moved away from the shuttle the captain arrived.

Captain Joseph Darrow was unremarkable to look at. British, with average build, brown eyes and curly brown hair, in the standard dark green PACT uniform, he could be mistaken for one of the crew by those who didn't know the yellow armband colour that signified his rank. Only Hoy, Reuel and Tomos saluted, Nefar continued working and the others were on stretchers.

'How bad is he?' Darrow asked Nefar.

'I shall let you know in half an hour, sir. Report in your office or mine?'

'Yours - I want to know about this guy too.' He gestured at Tanu. 'And some answers from the rest of you.' He frowned at Hoy and Reuel. 'It's evening, ship's time, so we'll debrief tomorrow morning.'

'Make it an hour for the report then,' Nefar said. 'If you want to debrief the away team tomorrow, you should meet in Commander Parks' cabin. That is, if I decide he is fit to talk at all.'

Parks sighed. 'No need to throw your weight around, Doc. I'll be OK.'

'That is for me to decide. Let us not waste any more time.' He turned to Tomos. 'Help me get these two to sick bay.'

***

As soon as they reached sick bay, Nefar helped Parks to a bed and activated the privacy screen. 'Undress please - completely. But don't stand until I return to help you.'

'What?' Parks protested. 'It's only my arm and my back.'

'I once had a patient with an unnoticed insect bite. We treated all the obvious injuries, he died from the bite which was found postmortem. I will examine all of your body, Commander.'

'When you put it like that…'

Nefar helped Tomos transfer the other man to a bed. 'Undress him and do some basic medscans while I treat Commander Parks.'

'Yes sir,' Tomos said, and activated the privacy screen when Nefar left.

Sick bay was an L-shaped room with the Doctor's cabin completing the rectangle. There were two treatment beds in the main part and a stasis unit, pressure cabinet and other equipment around the corner. The walls were lined with drawers of varying sizes, and scanners and regenerators hung from the ceiling on rails. Nefar and Tomos wore a badge on their uniforms which allowed them through the privacy screens. When Nefar turned back, Parks was undressed and lying on the bed under a sheet.

'Now,' Nefar said as he switched on the medscanner, 'lie still please. You said your main injuries are your arm and your back. What happened?'

'Laser shot to my arm. As for my back, the Bokans have a device they fit across the spine between the shoulder blades which causes intense pain through most of the body…' Parks choked and began to tremble. 'Sorry Doc.'

'That is quite all right. Do not distress yourself. We can make you well.' Nefar's brow furrowed and he examined the medscan.

'This is incredible. I have never seen such…'

He realised he was mumbling to himself and glanced down at Parks to see if he had heard. Parks was still trembling and there were tears in his eyes. Nefar reached for and administered a relaxant to his suffering patient. He didn't want Parks unconscious, but he wanted to ease the pain, physical and emotional.

He treated and bandaged Parks' arm and worked on the lacerations and bruises from the beating. Then he turned him over and examined Parks' back.

There were eight puncture wounds between the man's shoulder blades: three on each side of his spine about a centimetre apart and two centimetres either side of the spine, and two straddling the vertebrae in the middle. It seemed the six outer wounds were where the device attached to his back, and the two in the centre actually went into the spinal column. The wounds themselves had bled, but were not serious. It was what he saw on the medscan that worried Nefar.

The stimulus or shock, whatever it was, had travelled through all the major nerves in Parks' body, and caused deterioration in some of the nerve sheaths. This would require bed rest and several intense regenerator sessions. Nefar had never seen anything like it. If that had been done to the other man, a less robust figure, the damage could be permanent. But then it was designed for the Bokans, and the intricacies of their nervous systems were not something Nefar was familiar with.

He used a hand-held regenerator to start healing the wounds on Parks' back and then checked his whole body. Finding nothing else, he helped Parks into a sleepsuit and positioned the tissue regenerator over the bed. He switched it on and set it, then went to see to the other patient.

'Sir, this scan can't be right, surely?' Tomos said. 'I don't know what I did wrong.'

Nefar examined the scan. There were the same signs as on Parks' scan, only the condition was more advanced, and Tanu's brain appeared to be affected. The patient was humanoid in most aspects, but the brain had some differences. It was hard to work out whether the differences were natural or injuries caused by the pain-giver device.

'Do not be concerned, Tomos,' said Nefar, 'your only error is in assuming this man is human. These readings, and his blue blood, prove he is not.'

Nefar examined the lump on Tanu's forehead. It was triangular in shape, raised half a centimetre, and a blotchy red in colour, not blue and purple as a normal bruise would be. Fine red lines radiated out from the lump like thread veins. There didn't appear to be any skull damage underneath, but it must have been quite a blow to raise that lump.

Tanu had also been beaten, and Tomos had started with a handheld regenerator on some of the bigger bruises. Nefar wasn't sure Tanu's more severe nerve damage would respond to a regenerator. Once Parks' initial treatment was complete, he would try it on Tanu and see if he responded.

Nefar did a full-body examination and found no other injuries, but he was concerned at the lack of muscle tone. This man was tall and very slim, much like Reuel, he must be from a low gravity planet, but his body didn't show any of the low-grav adaptations. Nefar hoped Tanu would pull through, it would be interesting to discover more about him.

Chapter 6

Parks woke with a start at the sound of a red alert. He had been sent to his cabin but had only been in bed half an hour and was groggy. He struggled to consciousness, wondering if he was getting too old for this. He went to jump out of bed and his injuries reminded him he couldn't. At least his instincts were still sharp.

He carefully pulled on his uniform and shoes, grabbed his breather and tether, and went out into the corridor. John Blackwell was passing.

'Commander, wait!' Parks grabbed the engineer's arm. 'What's going on?'

'Pursuit,' Blackwell said as he hurried away, 'looks like you brought some company with you.'

Parks headed for the bridge. Unfortunately for him the way to the bridge led past sick bay, and the door was open.

'Commander Parks!'

The voice of Doctor Nefar came through the open door. 'You are not fit for duty. Return to your quarters, and I recommend you strap yourself into bed and keep your breather at hand. I do not want to treat any new injuries.'

Parks started to protest, but the doctor came out and escorted him back to his cabin. The Doctor was after all one of only two men on board the Kestrel who had the right to give Parks orders.

Sebu Nefar was new to the Kestrel. He was Kohathi. Parks had utmost respect for the race, on their last mission another Kohathi doctor, Tofi Dathan, had bravely sacrificed his life to save others. The Kohathi take apprentices to continue their work, and Nefar had been Dathan's apprentice. He volunteered to join the Kestrel in Dathan's place.

Sebu Nefar might have appeared to be a genial be-whiskered old man, as all Kohathi did, including the females. He was young for his race at a mere 82, and much stronger than he appeared. Parks knew better than to argue with Doctor Nefar.

***

'What have we got, Lieutenant-Commander?' Darrow asked as he stepped on the bridge.

'Captain on the bridge.' Hoy and Balitoth both saluted from their chairs.

Hoy sat to the left at the helm, while to the right at the scanners and weapons console sat Lieutenant Balitoth, the Zoan communications specialist. Zoans were reptilian too, but with a shorter jaw than Bokans, and they felt the cold. Balitoth wore a padded waistcoat over his uniform. Both were strapped in and had breathers attached to their chairs. Darrow clipped his breather to his chair and strapped in.

'Two Bokan pursuit ships, sir,' Hoy said. 'At current rate of closing they'll be within firing range in five minutes.'

'Any chance we can outrun them?'

'No sir, they're built for speed.'

'Have you attempted to communicate?'

'Yes, sir,' Balitoth said. 'No reply.'

'Why would the Bokans attack us?' Darrow asked as he took the central chair behind them and looked up at the viewscreen. 'Negotiations between the Bokans and PACT are already fraught with difficulties, this could finish them.'

'Perhaps they did not recognise the ship, sir.' Balitoth suggested. 'The Bokans do not have the PACT ship recognition database and have not been out in space for long, so they would not have met many ships.'

'So they're just chasing an unknown ship who picked up some escaped prisoners,' Hoy said.

Could it have anything to do with the man they brought with them? Darrow had a sudden idea. *This mission is turning out to be more dangerous than I expected. I have to defend my ship, but if we destroy the attacking ships, that will no doubt cause trouble for the negotiations too.*

He checked the encounter was being recorded. At least he could prove the Bokans attacked first. So much for a clandestine mission.

Darrow didn't like fighting. He was fully trained and had been in a few space battles through his career, but he didn't like it. He was more of a diplomat. He believed there was always a peaceful solution, you just had to find one and persuade the other party.

Not always possible of course, and what could he do here if the Bokans wouldn't even talk to him? He felt the full weight of responsibility for the lives of his crew.

Darrow turned to Balitoth at the weapons console. 'No offence, Lieutenant, but I wish we had Parks on weapons.'

'None taken Captain, but you know, communications can be a weapon too.'

'What are you going to do?' laughed Hoy. 'Insult them?'

Balitoth bared his pointed teeth, but ignored him, and spoke to Darrow. 'I have been monitoring their communications, sir: they are not encoded. If we can survive their first pass I can pick up their attack commands and rebroadcast an edited version to send them in the wrong direction.'

'What's to stop them coming at us again after?' Darrow said.

'I believe I may engineer a collision.' Balitoth looked pointedly at Hoy.

'Sounds like a plan,' said Darrow. 'I need clear heads now. Hoy, this is where you get to demonstrate your flying skills. Try to keep us out of trouble. Balitoth, give us your best shooting and maybe we won't need your plan after all.'

He flipped open the comm channel. 'Ensign Reuel to the bridge.' He turned back to Balitoth. 'Once Reuel arrives you can concentrate on the comms and he can man the scanners and weapons.'

Darrow watched his crew. Despite their fear, they would be professional. Reuel was skilled on weapons but seemed shaken after Boka. Unfortunately no one else was available. Balitoth never showed emotion anyway. Hoy had been on Boka too. How had he ended up with Hoy and Reuel on duty?

He racked his brains to think who he could call on, but that was the problem with a small crew, there wasn't much choice. Chambers was a better pilot than Hoy, but he had just pulled an 18 hour shift in Hoy's absence, and would probably have to be woken from a very necessary sleep.

The Bokan ships opened fire as soon as they were in range. Hoy swerved and banked the Kestrel and Balitoth returned fire. The ships were rocket-shaped with a huge engine at the rear and small wings down their length. One of the ships suffered minor damage to the nose but they managed two direct hits as they passed the Kestrel, flying in close formation across from starboard to port.

Reuel arrived at a run, his cranial spines raised in agitation, and almost lost his footing as the Kestrel was hit. He saluted and immediately reported from the scanners, as Balitoth moved to the rear of the bridge and flipped down a wall console for comms.

'Direct hit on the engines, sir.'

Blackwell's voice came over the comm. 'Captain, they hit the regulator. I can give you maybe half an hour at this speed, then the engines will fail, unless we slow right down or stop for repairs.'

'Do your best Commander.' Darrow's tension was a tight knot in his stomach.

'Coming round for a second pass,' Reuel reported.

'Now's the time,' said Darrow to Balitoth.

'I am prepared Captain.' His fingers flew over his console.

As the pursuit ships came in to attack, suddenly they broke formation and one swung in towards the port side as the other swung towards the starboard side. Hoy dived the Kestrel and the two ships manoeuvred frantically to try to avoid colliding.

Their wings touched and buckled and the engine of one gouged a hole in the other. Both ships spun wildly apart, out of control. The Kestrel shot away as the whole bridge crew cheered. Darrow noticed both Hoy and Reuel drop their heads for a moment as the tension passed.

Darrow said, 'Well done, all of you. Reduce speed to one quarter.' He contacted Engineering. 'How bad is it, Commander Blackwell?'

'The damage is not extensive, but we can't nurse the

regulator for long, especially at full speed.'

'We're slowing down, we don't expect additional pursuit. Any injuries?'

'Only minor, sir.'

'Good. Work out some figures for how far we can get at what speed and feed them through to Lieutenant-Commander Hoy on the bridge.' The captain turned to Hoy. 'We're not far from Caspar by my reckoning, but I'd rather not go there if we can help it.'

Balitoth said, 'In my study of other races, I try to seek out all the best things about each race. I find it extremely difficult with the Casparans.'

Hoy looked up from his console. 'What you're trying to avoid saying is that they're an arrogant lot who are only in the Alliance for what they can get out of it. I've never met anyone who annoyed me as quickly as the Casparans I've met. Remember Desmar Barok? He was not an exception. He nearly started an interstellar war.'

Darrow smiled as he turned to leave. 'Well, see what alternatives you can find and call me when you're ready.'

***

Darrow went to sick bay. The man named Tanu was on one of the beds, still sedated, under a regeneration canopy. Tomos was monitoring his vital signs. The other bed was empty.

'Where's Parks?' Darrow asked.

'Resting in his cabin,' Nefar said.

'How is he? What did they do to him? He looked awful when they got back.'

This was more than a captain's concern for his crew. Darrow and Parks had been friends for many years, having met at the PACT Training Academy. After a serious injury to his shoulder, Parks had been reassigned from shipside duty to a land based security team. Darrow had known how that chafed for the man, and requested him as emergency replacement for First Officer.

Their first mission together had led to the discovery of the Prin, energy beings with advanced technology. When the Prin healed Parks' shoulder, he couldn't wait to get back out there. That Darrow needed a new First Officer and Parks was then perfectly placed to step in, hadn't hurt either. Darrow still worried about him though.

'Commander Parks will live, Captain. He is going to be indisposed for a few days,' Nefar said in his careful way. 'He took quite a beating, but lacerations and contusions I can deal with. What concerns me is what the Bokans call a pain-giver. It has been used on both Parks and our mystery guest.'

He switched on a display showing the punctures on Parks' back. Darrow stepped forward to look more closely.

'It fits over the spine,' Nefar continued, 'and directly affects the nervous system through the spinal column, causing more than pain. I found a lot of nerve damage. Maybe not to Bokans, perhaps they do not realise the difference for other species,' he switched off the display and sighed.

'I can repair Commander Parks with a few regenerator sessions, then check out any longer term medical implications. This other one I am not so sure about.'

Darrow walked over to the bed where the man lay sedated. Nefar continued.

'His brain is affected and he has started having fits. I am not happy about the lump on his forehead - I cannot work out what it is, and it seems to be linked into his brain.'

'What do we know about him?' Darrow asked, frowning.

'Nothing. You will have to ask the mission team what they know. All I can tell you is he is humanoid, but not from Earth. His blood is blue - copper based not iron based like ours.' Nefar lifted the man's arm. 'His muscle tone is poor - he is either not a physical sort of person, or he comes from a planet with low gravity. Any more than that will have to wait. If I can get him conscious and lucid we might find out, but he is in a bad state.'

'Can you help him?'

'Not with the facilities here, I am afraid. That pain-giver device has affected his central neural system, which is still deteriorating. The stasis chamber will not save him - the neural degeneration will continue. I believe we can save him if he gets treatment soon, but I do not think he will make it back to Earth.' He shook his head. 'Even if I can stabilise him, he will be in a coma. Is there anywhere nearer with up-to-date medical facilities?'

'We're looking for somewhere to make port: that attack damaged the engines. Caspar is probably nearest, but I was hoping we could find somewhere else.' Darrow ran his hand over his unruly curls.

'Caspar would have the facilities we need, Captain. I know they are difficult people to deal with but I believe it is Tanu's best hope.' Nefar paused. 'Is the attack over, I noticed the change in the tone of the engines?'

'Yes.' Darrow smiled. 'Balitoth came up with a

clever comms trick and the two pursuit ships collided. They'll take some repairing. I also came to see if there were any casualties.'

'Ensign Stubbs got thrown out of bed and broke his wrist. He will be one-handed for a short while, which will not please Commander Blackwell, when there are repairs to be done. Commander Blackwell received minor burns when the regulator blew. The most serious problem is Tanu here.'

Darrow thumbed the comm channel. 'Captain to the bridge. How soon can we get to Caspar?'

'Hoy here, Captain. Commander Blackwell says if we cut power to twenty percent we can nurse the engines to get us there in 18 hours.'

The doctor winced. Darrow spoke into the comm channel. 'Anything closer?'

'No sir.'

'Very well then. Proceed to Caspar. Notify Engineering to give us best speed. Out.'

Chapter 7

With the crisis over, Reuel returned to his cabin. Not that he was relaxing. He shared with Balitoth, who remained on duty, so Reuel had no one to talk to. He dreaded the debriefing, but as he thought over the events, he couldn't see anything he had done wrong. It wasn't his fault they got arrested, and he *had* been vital in their escape.

He was disgusted with himself for getting so scared, since back home he was considered tough. There is always the possibility of violence in poor urban areas, especially among young males. Reuel knew how to handle himself in a fight, even before he received formal training at the Academy.

Ever since he became an adult, Reuel had not been afraid. Tense, prepared, nervous, yes. Worried about his friends. But not afraid. He knew what to expect, and he had won enough fights and skirmishes to be confident. But anticipation of agony was something else. This was new.

Back in the cell, as Parks described his experience with the pain-giver, a cold weight had settled over Reuel and he shuddered. This was not a danger you could square up to and do battle with. Physically, you were helpless. Tied down, unable to protect yourself or retaliate. Reuel knew pain. He had been hurt before, sometimes badly. Pain could be endured. Pain was temporary. Pain was soon forgotten. But this…?

It wasn't just the severity of the pain Parks described, it was the anticipation. What if the Bokans decided the servant might know more than he said he did? What if they thought he was the weakest of the team? How certain was it the pain-giver would be used on him? He had felt the horror growing in his mind, paralysing him. Even his cranial spines grew stiff. This was new. He wasn't prepared.

How could you prepare for something so extreme? His mind had begun to freeze, unable to cope with the thought of what they might do to him. At the same time there was a little corner of his mind watching this happen and wondering at it. He was watching himself lose control and analysing it.

He felt ashamed. He had been defeated by the mere thought of something that might never happen. He understood for the first time how people could become paralysed by fear. Tensed for fight-or-flight, but no one to fight and nowhere to run to. He should be better than that. What chance of promotion if he was afraid?

A couple of hours later, Balitoth came off duty and returned to their cabin. It was late, ship time, but Reuel was still awake.

'How was your shift?' he asked.

Balitoth shrugged. 'Uneventful, after the attack. It was unfortunate you and Hoy were called on so soon after Boka. How are you?'

'Troubled, my friend.' Reuel did not hesitate to confide. 'I am not happy about my … performance.'

'Did they interrogate you? Were you not strong?' Balitoth paused in undressing for bed.

Reuel shook his head, as much to get his cranial spines under control as to deny the question.

'The interrogation was not a problem, they merely asked questions and made threats. They concentrated on Commander Parks, once they established he was our leader. It was when I saw what they did to him that my courage failed. It is different in a fight, where the anger rises and you can be proactive. Sitting waiting for my turn to come was a different thing all together.'

Balitoth sat on the bed to take off his shoes. 'But your turn did not come, did it?'

Reuel shook his head. Balitoth raised his hand to stop Reuel's answer.

'So you do not know what your performance would have been under torture. Thinking of the future and feeling fearful is not at all the same as dealing with that future when it comes. You have told me a little of your time as a youngling, how dangerous the gangs were. You must have been fearful anticipating what would happen if they got hold of you. But when they did, you acquitted yourself well, did you not?'

Reuel nodded slowly, thinking the words over. He felt a weight drop from his shoulders. Balitoth always had a more reasoned way of looking at things.

'Now,' Balitoth continued, 'let us not let concerns for tomorrow rob us of our sleep tonight. Agreed?'

Reuel smiled. 'Agreed.'

***

Tomos shared a cabin with Roy Stubbs, the Assistant Engineer. Tomos was clean-cut, open faced, with sandy reddish hair that flopped over his forehead. Stubbs was slimmer, rough-looking, his dark hair cut close to his head. Tomos was younger than Stubbs, but had more in-flight experience, having grown up on his parents' cargo ship.

With Tomos having only just joined the crew, Tomos and Stubbs were still getting to know one another. 'Another shift over,' sighed Tomos, coming into the cabin and falling on his lower bunk. 'Dr Nefar is reorganising sick bay. I thought it was fine but he wants to put his own stamp on it. "New broom sweeps clean", as they say.'

'What are you talking about?' Stubbs looked up from his console.

'Oh, sorry, haven't you heard that one? It's an old saying. How's your wrist? I saw you with Dr Nefar.'

'Compound fracture apparently.' Stubbs displayed the splint on his wrist. 'It's a long way to fall from the top bunk, I should've strapped in. Blackwell was not pleased.'

'Hey, what's that on your hands?'

Stubbs examined his hands. His nails were outlined in blue. 'It's lubricant. I should've worn gloves. This stuff never washes off, you have to wait for it to wear off.'

'You could bleach it, at least it wouldn't show so much. I can get you something from sick bay that'll fade those stains, but I'm not going back there now, I've only just escaped.'

'Thanks.' Stubbs turned back to his console and they were silent for a while.

'What are you working on?' Tomos asked.

'Particle distribution inside the exchanger. It's a tricky one.'

'Not if you use a germanium diode.' Tomos got up from the bunk and came to look over Stubbs' shoulder. 'It makes it easier to track, see?' He pointed to the diagram on the screen.

Stubbs batted his hand away. 'Do you mind? I'm concentrating.'

'Sorry, only trying to help. I'll go and eat and get out of your hair.'

***

The next morning, ship time, Hoy and Reuel were summoned to Parks' cabin, where Captain Darrow waited. Parks was propped up on pillows in bed (senior officers didn't have bunks). Darrow sat in a chair by the bed. There was another chair, but Hoy and Reuel looked at each other and came to an unspoken agreement they were better off standing to attention. They weren't sure how much trouble they were in.

'Stand easy,' said Darrow. 'I want a full written report from you all as usual, so give me the key points for now. First of all, what went wrong?'

There was an awkward silence.

Parks coughed. 'It was my fault, sir. We managed to find out there was a stir on at a security building and went to investigate. There was definitely something going on… but I asked the wrong person. He turned out to be an off-duty security guy. That's how we got arrested.'

'Did you find out anything at all?' Darrow asked.

'Nothing concrete, sir,' Hoy said, 'but I would say the rumour the Bokans have got something is true. Whether it's a weapon, I don't know. They were shipping in all sorts of people. I recognised Jernatha, the chief Bokan scientist, and I overheard some talk about a psychologist.'

'Psychologist?' said Darrow. 'Why would they need a psychologist for a weapon?'

'Something to do with our new guest Tanu, I think,' said Parks. 'The guy who questioned me was talking about a psychological report when they took me in the second time, and they had just been interrogating him.'

He shuddered, and Darrow laid a hand on his shoulder.

'We'll talk about that later. What do you know about this Tanu?'

Reuel spoke up. 'He told us his name was Tanu, sir, of the family of Pe'Rod.' He frowned. 'I would guess that makes Pe'Rod his surname. He said he was an explorer. That is all I am afraid. He was in quite a state. He did not understand what was happening most of the time.'

He paused, remembering something. 'Oh Captain, I do not know if it is important, but I think the Bokans were trying to get him to do something. He kept on saying "I can't".'

'And why did you bring him with you? What do you expect me to do with him?'

Now it was Reuel's turn to look uncomfortable. His spines trembled. 'I am sorry, sir, it did not seem right to leave him behind. You saw what they did to him. And Lieutenant-Commander Hoy had no trouble carrying him, sir, he did not slow us down. Leaving him behind would have been cruel.'

'I agreed, Captain.' Parks added. 'After getting a taste of their treatment, I couldn't have left him. Once he's better we can drop him off somewhere.'

'That might not be so easy.' Darrow muttered. He looked up at Hoy and Reuel. 'OK, you two can go. I want those reports by 1300 hours - and I want individual accounts, not a combined collusion.'

'Yes sir.' They both looked relieved. They saluted and left.

Darrow turned back to Parks, and his voice softened. 'I'm sorry old friend, but I need to know what you told them under questioning…'

Darrow put through a call to his commander, Commodore Michel. When Michel answered, the video feed showed a human in his late fifties, with sandy hair that had yet to turn grey, and a slim build. Moving to a desk job had not blunted the edge of his fitness.

'Captain Joseph Darrow reporting, sir. Request a secure line.'

'One moment.' Michel set up the security. 'Line secure. I assume this is a report on your mission to Boka?'

'Yes sir. My men were captured but revealed nothing under interrogation. They escaped and made it back to the Kestrel, but we were pursued. Our story is that we were only at Boka to drop off a party of sociologists, which was the landing party's cover story. The pursuing ships didn't even contact us, they just attacked. We succeeded in crippling the ships and escaping, but I don't know if Boka will track us and attack again.'

Michel frowned. 'That is unfortunate to say the least. But there was always the risk your men might be discovered. We need to do some damage limitation. The Alliance talks are precarious enough as it is, these Bokans are a suspicious lot. Now they know we've been spying on them.'

'Not really, sir. They know we dropped off some sociologists and suspect we helped them escape after they were arrested. There is no evidence otherwise. It seems to me there might be some truth in this rumour about a secret weapon, for them to react in such an aggressive manner. My men feel there was definitely something going on, which is possibly why they were arrested so quickly, because they were strangers.'

'Thank you, Captain. I will instruct the negotiators to stick with that story and challenge the Bokans over their extreme reaction.'

'There is one other thing, sir. Our engines were damaged in the attack and we're heading to Caspar for repairs.'

Michel winced. 'Not a good idea. Is there nowhere else you can go?'

'I'm afraid not. The Casparans will want to know how the damage occurred. I can't mention the Bokans - the Casparans are almost as touchy as the Bokans. Can I tell the Casparans it's classified?'

'No, Captain. There can't be any hint of your mission. You'll have to be creative. Stray space debris, perhaps. Thank you for your report.'

'Yes sir. Darrow out.'

Darrow cut the connection and scowled. *Get creative, indeed. Space debris? Now who do I know on Caspar,* he thought, *who might be able to pull some strings?* He had an idea. He searched through his old incoming messages until he found the one he wanted. A personal request from Prime Minister Barok to call on him if he was ever on Caspar. The Prime Minister's son had died on the Kestrel's previous mission. He replied, and hoped he was doing the right thing.

***

Tanu screamed. Dr Nefar came running, dishevelled from sleep. Tanu was scrabbling to reach between his shoulder blades. He twisted and turned, desperate to reach his back. Dr Nefar took hold of his arms and held him down.

'Tanu! Tanu! Wake up! You are safe!'

Tanu opened his eyes and looked wildly about. Then he focussed and looked at Nefar. He relaxed and started to cry.

'I know what they did to you, but you are safe now. They will never come near you again.' Nefar reached over to a nearby cabinet where he had a sedative prepared. He pressed it to Tanu's neck and helped him get comfortable. 'You need to sleep to regain your strength. Be calm, all is well.'

Tanu closed his eyes and Nefar headed back to his own bed in his cabin off sick bay. He must talk to Tanu tomorrow about his experiences with the Bokans. Teach him to deal with it and put it behind him. As he climbed back into bed his mind went to Commander Parks. He still had a haunted look, though physically he was well on the way to recovery. He must talk to Parks too.

Chapter 8

When the Kestrel reached Caspar, Darrow said nothing about their needs. He simply asked to land. A landing beam guided them to a berth at the spaceport.

The Casparans were small, green-skinned people living on a small orange planet with lighter gravity than Earth and slightly less oxygen in the atmosphere. Fully grown, they stood a metre and a half tall, and looked like children. They had also been in subjection to the Ochrans, human-sized copies of the Casparans, until only a few decades ago. Consequently, they were very careful about dignity and respect.

'Everyone sit tight until I return,' said Darrow. 'I might be several hours.'

'Aye aye, Captain,' Parks saluted.

Darrow left the Kestrel and hopped on a shuttle-bus from the spaceport into the centre of Caspar - their capital city was named the same as their planet, which often caused some confusion. He didn't take much notice of what was passing outside the window, he was preoccupied with the task in hand. He was going to try to see the Prime Minister, who might just as easily lock him up as help.

Getting off the bus in the city centre, Darrow went to the large government building on the main square. He hadn't had a reply to his message, so he wasn't sure what reception he would get, but he had brought a copy of the original message with him.

Inside, up the grand entrance steps and between the pillars, he was struck by the high ceilings and ornate decoration. Every surface was carved and painted, and not a hint of green, the Casparan's favourite colour.

No doubt left over from the Ochran occupation, he thought.

He took a deep breath and approached the reception desk, which only came just past his knees. The man behind the desk was wearing a plain light green uniform. Darrow bowed low in the Casparan manner, with his arms outstretched.

'Excuse me, I've come to see Prime Minister Barok.'

'Do you have an appointment?' the man said, turning to his computer screen, ready to look it up.

'I haven't received an appointment, but I contacted the Prime Minister and he has asked to see me.'

Darrow handed over his tablet with the message displayed. The man glanced at it and handed the tablet back.

'I will have to check if the Prime Minister is willing to see you today without an appointment. Please take a seat.'

Darrow turned away from the desk and noticed there were two sizes of chairs - Casparan size and Ochran/human size. He was glad he didn't have to try to sit in a small one. The chairs were padded and covered in blue fabric and stood in groups of six around the reception area. He took a larger seat and started some work on his tablet while he waited.

And waited.

And waited.

He began to feel hungry and checked the time. He had been waiting two hours! He approached the reception desk again.

'Excuse me, but I'm waiting to see Prime Minister Barok.'

'I have passed on your request, I will contact his

secretary again.'

Darrow decided not to sit down. He didn't want to cause a fuss, but he wanted them to know he was waiting and not keeping out of the way. He continued to stand at the desk, towering over it, until the receptionist put through a call. A discussion followed, in Casparan, which unfortunately for them, Darrow understood enough to follow.

The Prime Minister wanted to see him, but they were having trouble clearing space in his calendar. That was good news for Darrow, but he didn't show he understood. The receptionist was asking them to take Darrow off his hands and eventually it worked. The call ended and the receptionist turned to him.

'Someone is coming to fetch you sir.'

Darrow bowed again. 'Thank you for your assistance.'

A man in a bright green uniform with much orange braid appeared and bowed. 'Please come with me.'

Was this a policeman come to arrest him or an official come to take him to the Prime Minister? Darrow followed him up a flight of stairs to the next floor, down a corridor and into an office. A man came from behind the desk to shake his hand.

'Greetings Captain Darrow. I am Tiras Accad, Liaison Officer to the Prime Minister. Do sit down.'

Darrow's heart fell, but he was also relieved. Not prison then, but this was still not Prime Minister Barok. Hopefully this was one step closer.

Accad had some lines on his face and grey in his long green hair, which was tied at the nape of his neck. He was dressed in the traditional Casparan clothing of narrow trousers and a long tunic split up the sides, but unlike the usual bright colours, his clothes were of a dark green material, almost black, and he wore a heavily embroidered sash across his chest.

The office was expensively furnished, with a patterned wood floor and a soft seating area to one side. It didn't have human-sized chairs and Darrow had to choose between remaining standing, which felt aggressive, or sitting on a little chair, which felt ridiculous. He looked at the chair, looked at Accad, and moved the chair to stand in its place by the desk.

'I apologise for the seating, Captain,' Accad said, 'but we will not be long. Now, why do you want to see Prime Minister Barok?'

'He asked to see me,' Darrow said, and handed over the message. 'And I have a situation of some urgency I'm hoping he can help me with.'

Accad read the message and stroked the screen, but Darrow had locked it. Darrow put his hand out for it to be returned, which Accad did with a nervous smile.

'What is the matter?' Accad asked.

Darrow considered. He didn't want too many people knowing his business, but decided to tell this man in the hope it would get him some progress. 'My ship needs repairs and I have a medical emergency, which is becoming more urgent the longer you keep me.'

'These are not matters you need the Prime Minister for, surely,' Accad said. 'I could ... pull some strings, I think you say.'

'That would be very good of you, but there is also the matter of the Prime Minister's request to see me,' Darrow said with more patience than he felt. There was something going on here, he was sure of it.

'I am sorry but that will not be possible.'

As Accad was speaking the intercom on his desk buzzed. Accad answered and there was a short conversation in Casparan, which Darrow found hard to follow. The man on the intercom wanted something and Accad didn't want to give it to him. Eventually Accad said, 'Yes sir,' and closed the intercom with an angry look on his face.

'If you will follow me, the Prime Minister will see you now.'

Darrow followed Accad to an elevator and up to the top floor. Prime Minister Barok was waiting outside the elevator and greeted Darrow warmly with a human handshake. He was dressed in a similar way to Accad except he wore a large ornate orange and green badge on his chest. Accad stayed in the elevator and went back down.

'Captain, welcome! My apologies for the delay, I was unavoidably detained.' He scowled briefly then smiled. 'Thank you for coming to see me.'

Darrow was surprised to see he was a younger man than Accad, with light green hair that hung loose to his shoulders and warm brown eyes. He led Darrow to a comfortable seating area, once again with seats of two different sizes, in shades of russet and mustard. Like Accad's office, this one was wood panelled, but seemed less ostentatious.

Darrow felt awkward towering over the most powerful man on Caspar. Would he be able to answer the man's questions about his son's death in a way that would satisfy him? He guessed what Barok wanted to know, but didn't want to upset him. He wanted his help in return, but wondered whether the man would actually want to help him after he heard the answer.

Barok clasped his hands on his knees and leaned forwards. 'I expect you know why I want to see you, I want to know about my son.'

Darrow swallowed hard.

'What can I tell you about your son, sir?'

Barok thought for a moment. 'I want the truth, Captain. I read the mission reports, and I am grateful for the way they were written, but I knew my son. He did not make friends easily, shall we say. I want to know what really happened.'

Darrow had expected this, but still felt the knot in his stomach. He spoke gently.

'Your son tried very hard to be respected and listened to. He was upset when we brought the Prin intruders on board the Kestrel. He felt he was being ignored and we were too trusting. He was right, though we didn't find that out until later.'

Darrow paused and took a breath. 'He took matters into his own hands and attempted to kill the Prin. He killed one and the others killed him. They can fire a bolt of energy, you know. Before he died Ser Barok fired a second time. Dr Dathan tried to save the other Prin by diving into the path of the shot. The impact pushed him backwards into the Prin, and their energy, plus the shot, killed him.'

Barok was silent for a time. Then he sighed. 'Thank you Captain. I guessed it was something like that, but I didn't know he killed Dr Dathan as well. That is most regrettable.'

'His action also made the breakthrough we needed, sir,' Darrow said quickly. 'When the Prin saw Dathan's sacrifice, they changed their opinion of us and agreed to talk. We were all betrayed by a rogue faction in the Prin government. The breakthrough your son won for us will one day bring contact with a new species.'

'But my son … was a murderer.' His voice broke and he looked away.

The knot twisted in Darrow's stomach and he didn't know what to say. His heart sank. How could he ask this man to help him after that?

Barok smiled. 'But you made the best of him, which saved me too, from shame. Thank you, Captain.' He rose and offered Darrow his hand. They shook hands and Barok sat back down. 'Now, what can I do for you?'

Darrow was so surprised he couldn't reply for a moment. He collected his thoughts. 'My ship has been damaged, we need repairs. We also have a seriously injured man who needs medical treatment.'

'Consider it done,' Barok said, returned to his desk and made a call giving authorisation for repairs and medical treatment.

He stood and shook Darrow's hand again. 'If you have any problems, refer them to me. I do still have some authority here.'

'Thank you, sir.'

Darrow left, in a daze. He headed straight back to the Kestrel, and within half an hour they were contacted by a maintenance team and a medical team. Doctor Nefar was asked for medical records, but not allowed to go with Tanu when he was taken away.

The following day Darrow granted half the crew shore leave while the other half stayed to help the Casparan maintenance team with the repairs. He warned them all not to be provoked and to cause no trouble.

'And no one is to stay out tonight,' he announced. 'I want you all back on board by sunset. Tomorrow the two teams can swap over. Parks, you're to report to Dr Nefar in six hours for another regeneration treatment, so take it easy.'

Chapter 9

Stubbs and Tomos were both given the first shore leave shift. Sick of Tomos seeming to know everything because on his cargo ship he'd been everywhere and knew most cultures, Stubbs decided to separate from his ship mate. His wrist itched in its brace as it healed. He hadn't been everywhere and didn't know Casparan, but Caspar was part of the Planetary Alliance and most people spoke Standard. Stubbs figured he'd be fine on his own.

The overcast sky reduced the tinge of Caspar's two red suns, and he was glad of his thick jacket. If not for the orange leaves on the trees and the oddly sharp scents, he could almost be at home in Ireland on Earth.

He wandered into the town and strolled past little houses and big shops, not in width - in height, which seemed incongruous. Casparans were shorter than humans, so that would explain low ceilings in the houses, but why the higher ceilings in the shops, when they didn't encourage visitors?

The houses were unpainted light grey stone, but the shops were rendered and brightly painted too. It was about midday, and there were a lot of people about, mostly dressed in the traditional brightly-coloured long tunic and slim trousers. He saw few non-Casparans, which made him feel conspicuous. He was more than a head taller than everyone else. Most people ignored him, but there were one or two who scowled at him, just for being an off-worlder.

After a while he got hungry and approached a couple of women to ask directions to a café. He came up behind them and touched one woman on the arm to attract her attention. He was not prepared for the reaction. When she turned round and saw him, she screamed and clung to her companion, trembling. He tried to explain.

'It's all right, I won't hurt you. Please.'

A crowd gathered, and the men were angry, gesticulating and shouting. They spoke their own language, and he didn't understand. He started to panic. The captain had told them not to get into any trouble, and he didn't even know what he'd done.

'Hey!' The shout stopped the babble of voices and everyone turned to a figure behind the crowd. Tomos gave a deep bow and opened his arms, palms up. He said a word Stubbs didn't catch and bowed again. The people smiled and moved away. Stubbs gave a huge sigh.

'What did you do? More to the point, what did I do?'

'Did you touch her?'

'I only touched her arm to get her attention. I was looking for somewhere to eat.'

'You didn't read the briefing, did you?' He raised a hand to still the reaction. 'It's all right. We all do it the first time. Come with me and we'll find a café.'

Tomos put his arm round Stubbs' shoulder and led him away. Stubbs wanted to be angry with him, but couldn't. He was being really nice about it and had rescued him from a situation that could have got nasty. They found a café that catered for non-Casparans, and Tomos helped Stubbs order food suitable for human consumption. They sat in the larger chairs, then Tomos explained.

'Their height makes them belligerent, not wanting to be belittled, but it also keeps them from causing too much trouble, as they can't easily fight a much taller man. It was taller men that conquered Caspar many years ago, taller men who otherwise looked exactly like them - Ochrans. When Ochrans discovered Casparans they believed that since they were smaller, they should be treated like children and servants.' Tomos scowled.

'Caspar only gained independence about 70 years ago. Consequently, they stand on their dignity and can seem stuck-up and haughty, but it's just a self-preservation mechanism. The way the Casparans kept their pride was to develop a high regard for dignity and manners. You have to be careful to be polite - lots of bowing and gestures.'

He demonstrated the bow again. 'This is a sign of respect. It's safer to do it with everyone you meet. And don't touch the women, nobody touches the women.'

'But what did you say?'

Tomos grinned. 'I told them you were an ignorant off-worlder.'

'Oh thanks.' Stubbs pulled a face. 'You just know everything, don't you?'

'Hey!' said Tomos, frowning. 'And you make snap judgements. Is that why you've been offhand with me?'

Stubbs reddened. 'Well, you're always showing off …'

'And here I thought I was getting you out of a sticky situation. On board I was offering to help, not showing off. It's good to know you're not the only one the engineer can call on. Still, if that's the way you feel …' Tomos began to get up.

Stubbs grabbed his arm. 'No, I'm sorry James. I do get prickly. Before you came, I was the youngest of the crew and I'm always trying to keep up.'

Their food and drinks arrived as Tomos sat back

down. They barely started their meal when Tomos put down his cup and motioned to catch Stubbs' attention. Two female Casparans approached their table and bowed. Stubbs looked to Tomos for guidance. He could see another row coming. Tomos stood and bowed and Stubbs followed his lead.

'Good day, sisters,' Tomos said, 'how may we be of service?'

'Will you talk with us,' the one in front said, 'about … out there?' She swept her hand over her head, and the other girl giggled.

'Would that not be frowned on?' Tomos asked carefully.

'We frown on being frowned on,' the first girl said, and both girls giggled again.

Stubbs was nervous, but nodded to Tomos' questioning look.

'Very well,' Tomos said, 'we would like to talk with you when our meal is finished, but I do not think it appropriate here. If you will wait for us under the tree across the road, we will follow you to somewhere where your … integrity will not be compromised.'

Stubbs took the initiative and bowed as he asked, 'Please, what are your names?'

The girls giggled again and looked down as the first girl said, 'Birsha,' pointing to herself, 'and Emim,' pointing to her friend.

'My name is Roy,' Stubbs said, 'and this is James. We will see you soon.'

They left and Tomos and Stubbs sat down and quickly finished their meals.

Stubbs brightened. 'Well, I'm glad I have you to look after me. Talking to girls is another thing I'm not very good at.'

Tomos laughed. 'Just one thing Roy, please, don't tell them any details about the ship, just generalities.'

'Okay, okay, I'll be careful. Now what shall we do with them?'

'We don't do anything - remember, you can't touch the women. They only want to talk to us.'

'Oh well,' Stubbs said, 'that'll be a first.'

They met the girls under the tree, keeping watch on passers-by. They didn't want to attract attention.

'You are either brave or foolhardy,' Tomos whispered. 'Where can we talk without being seen together?'

Birsha took Emim's arm and beckoned them to follow. They walked a short way from the town centre, to a park with pretty flower beds and paths shaded by trees. The orange foliage was not as soothing to the eye as the green that the boys grew up with, but there was an air of tranquillity about the place. The girls led them to a bench in front of some bushes and signalled them to sit. The girls walked on and turned a corner.

'I wonder where they're going?' Stubbs said.

Tomos smiled. 'I think I know. Look through the bush behind us.'

As Stubbs peered through the leaves the girls came into view and sat down on the grass.

`Good day again,' Tomos said quietly. 'What would you like to know?'

Birsha began. 'Since independence, women have gradually been allowed a wider role in society, but it is still a fight. We want to join the PACT Academy and work in space -'

'But we want to know if it is worth it,' Emim interrupted loudly, to be shushed by Birsha.

'It depends what you're expecting,' Tomos said.

'Space is immense, and even with warp drive it can take a long time to get to places, so there's a lot of routine.'

'That gives you time to study, though,' Stubbs said, 'so you can get more qualified, or do research, or pursue a hobby.'

'If you've never been out there though, it can be amazing,' Tomos said. 'Different planets, different people. Space stations, scientific research ships, cargo ships.'

'He grew up on a cargo ship, you know,' Stubbs said. 'How weird is that?'

'Do you not have a home planet then?' Birsha asked.

Tomos laughed. 'Well, my parents are from Earth, and the rest of my family's there, so I always say I'm from Earth.'

'Is it dangerous in space?' Emim asked.

'Not if you're in a good ship and properly trained,' Tomos said.

'Unless you get sent on missions,' Stubbs said. 'I was shot on the last one.'

'Oh, you poor thing!' Emim said, and both girls made a keening sound in sympathy.

A man in a dark green uniform approached Tomos and Stubbs along the path. Tomos cleared his throat in warning. The man strode up to them.

'What are you doing here?' he demanded.

Tomos nudged Stubbs and they both rose, bowed and sat down again.

'We are on shore leave while our ship is being repaired,' Tomos said, 'and came to enjoy the scenery.'

One of the girls gasped, and the man heard it. He bent down and peered through the bushes. 'Who are you talking to?'

'We were talking to each other, sir,' Tomos said. His

mouth dried, he pressed his hands on his legs to stop them shaking. He stole a look at Stubbs and hoped he wouldn't react.

The man called out, 'Sisters, were you talking with these aliens?'

The girls jumped up and Emim said quickly, 'Oh no sir, but they were talking about their lives in space and we stopped to listen. Out of sight, of course.'

Tomos' heart clenched. *Out of sight? That does it.*

Birsha must have realised too. She said, 'It would not be appropriate for us to speak to the aliens, so we listened to their conversation from here. They had no idea we were listening.'

'I think it's time we returned to our ship,' Tomos said, getting to his feet.

'Yes,' Stubbs said, joining him. 'Thank you for allowing us to enjoy your beautiful city.'

They bowed and, at a nod from the official, quickly left.

Chapter 10

The following day it was Reuel's turn for shore leave. He'd been to Caspar once before. He could walk unhindered, since the gravity was similar to Altair. The Casparan spaceport looked like spaceports everywhere, except for the predominance of green. The control tower in particular was highlighted by a lurid lime green paint.

The spaceport concessions were generic and expensive, so Reuel headed towards the city centre. There were one or two things he wanted to buy. The overcast sky was a good thing, as the presence of the two suns could be overpowering. The weather was pleasantly warm and dry, so he rejected the spaceport shuttle bus and chose to walk. He remembered it took him less than an hour on his previous visit.

There was no open countryside: businesses and houses stretched all the way from the city to the spaceport, although those nearer the spaceport were at a disadvantage. They endured all the noise and smell without getting the benefit from the passengers. Most people jumped straight on the shuttle bus when they disembarked.

He passed several children playing with a ball, the same scene you would see on most planets in some form or other. What made this scene strange to him was the size of the children. Altairians were two metres tall on average, whereas Casparans were at most a metre and a half fully grown, and their children were proportionately smaller.

Reuel thought they looked like dolls, or the

miniature robots some people used because they were less conspicuous around the house. He slowed down to watch their game, but they noticed him and stopped playing to stare.

Oh dear, he thought. *Perhaps I should have worn my hat.*

He decided to press on. Away from the spaceport, orange vegetation and multicoloured flowers with orange leaves started to appear in front of the houses and in strips outside businesses. He decided the Casparans must like everything tidy and neat, as the plants grew in regimented lines.

There was little individuality in people's gardens, except for the occasional new plant. Otherwise they were all the same, as though manufactured *en masse*. It was the same in the city centre: formal flower beds and patches of orange grass, all in strict order.

The people were a little like that too. All very formal in their movements, bowing to one another as they met. No one appeared to wander about but followed each other in lines. Reuel joined a line to see where it went but stepped out because of the disapproving looks. He bowed, arms out with his palms up to apologise, even though he didn't know what for.

He remembered a particular white fluffy sweet he tasted last time he was here. He looked around the shops to see if he could find it again, but couldn't remember the name. He got on well because his manners were impeccable - he bowed to everyone he met and flattered everyone he spoke to. He found his sweets and bought enough to last a while and allow him to share.

After finding his sweets, Reuel found a café selling food he could eat and sat down for a snack. He watched the passers-by with interest. The men's tunics were shorter than the women's and of brighter colours. To his surprise, no one wore green. It was the Casparan's favourite colour, so much around them was painted green, but not the clothes. The waiter arrived with his order.

'Excuse me for being an ignorant tourist,' Reuel bowed, 'but why does no one wear green clothes? I thought it was the Casparan's favourite colour.'

The waiter laughed and bowed back. 'No sir, you have not understood. Casparans are green, everything that belongs to Casparans is green, but Casparans belong to no one. No green on them. Except the officials, who serve the people.'

Reuel smiled. 'How wonderful! I like that very much.'

'You are welcome, sir. Most people from outside do not understand. We are amused when they wear green.'

'It is well then that I did not wear my uniform, which is dark green.' The waiter laughed with him. He continued, 'I only have an hour or two here. What would you recommend as places to see?'

The waiter paused in thought. 'Caspar has many beautiful places, but they are away from the spaceport. Perhaps you would like to admire our beautiful buildings. If you take the street to the right and turn right at the next corner, a short walk will bring you to the main square. The buildings are nothing like this,' he waved to indicate the local buildings. 'The government buildings, the art gallery, Independence Hall, even the new hospital behind, they are a showcase of Casparan achievement. We are very proud of them.'

Reuel bowed again and slipped the waiter a few coins. 'I thank you for the advice, and will certainly go when I have eaten.'

The mention of the hospital made him think of Tanu. Once he saw the square he could go and see how he was getting on.

***

The nurse at the reception desk looked bored and harassed. She wore white, with a motif like a coiled green ribbon on both shoulders. Reuel bowed.

'Excuse me, I am sure you are busy, but I would be grateful for your help in locating my friend, who was brought in yesterday.'

She looked up from her screen and her eyebrows rose as she saw his skin colour, height, and his cranial spines. Reuel smiled and raised a hand to his spines.

'I hope my spines do not alarm you, sister. I am from Altair, and delighted to be on your lovely planet once again.' He decided to try flattery. 'As I passed through the main square on my way here I was impressed by the magnificent buildings, and by this hospital too. I have been on many planets and seen many sights, but none like this.'

She eyed him suspiciously. 'What impressed you the most, kind sir?'

'Oh, the carvings of course! Such detail, such intricacy. In places, it looks like lace. Have you seen the human fabric lace? It is fine threads woven together with knots to make a delicate trimming or a sheer covering on a garment. Tell me, what is the scene depicted over the entrance here?'

'It tells of the hero Shomestry who found the lifeweed plant that kills infection. It was the foundation of our modern medicine.'

Her work forgotten, the nurse was clearly captivated in her tale.

'He was injured in a battle and left behind when the army moved on, hidden beneath a bush. He stopped his bleeding with the leaves of the bush, packing them into his wounds as a dressing. When his wound did not fester and began to heal, he gathered as much as he could carry and dragged himself after the army.' She paused to wipe away a tear.

'When he caught up with them they were almost defeated. The next engagement would be the end. But with the lifeweed they found strength to evade the enemy for a few days while their wounds healed. The next battle was the end - but for the enemy!' She finished with a flourish and smiled at Reuel.

Reuel bowed deeply and put his hand on his heart. 'Dear sister, a truly moving story. Especially so for me, for my given name is Shom.' He showed her his identity badge. 'It is an honour to bear the name of a hero.'

The nurse bowed back and smiled. 'I am honoured to meet you, sir. Now let me see about your friend.'

He followed up her smile. 'My friend's name is Tanu and he came here from the PACT ship Kestrel.'

Her smile turned into a frown when the results of her search came up on her computer screen.

'There is something wrong here,' she said. 'There is a gap where his records should be. Not an omission, but a deletion. There was a record under the name Tanu but it has been removed rather inexpertly.' She sniffed. 'Very sloppy work indeed. I shall refer this to the quality control department.'

She bustled off down the hall and went into an office. A few moments later she returned. This time she was puzzled. 'There seems to be a problem with this Tanu's registration, and the people responsible are reluctant to cooperate. I will see to it myself. If you can come back tomorrow morning, I will have the information for you then.'

Reuel's face fell. 'Sadly I must leave this evening. May I leave my contact details with you for when you find him?'

Reuel gave her his contact details and moved away. He had no idea how to enquire further, and his shore leave was limited, so he headed back out to the street. He was thinking about where to go next when he heard a shout. Outside the hospital three people were getting into a large brown vehicle. One of them was Tanu, who had shouted when he recognised Reuel.

He waved, but the two men with him tried to push him inside. Wearing a grey jumpsuit, he was unsteady on his feet and grinning like he was drunk. Reuel waved back and started walking over, but one of the men intercepted him.

'I am sorry, but this man cannot see anyone now,' he said with a curt bow of his head. 'You can see him later.'

They all jumped in the vehicle and drove away. Reuel decided they seemed to know what they were doing, and Tanu seemed happy, so it was best to leave it there. He could make further enquiries when he returned to the Kestrel. Maybe that was where the men were taking him, as he seemed to have recovered.

***

By the afternoon of the second day repairs were almost complete. Darrow contacted Nefar from his office and asked him to find out when Tanu would be released. He came back with sad news.

'I am sorry Captain. The Casparans informed me Tanu died.'

'What? I thought you said we got here in time.'

'I thought we did. I asked to see the medical records, but there seems to be some difficulty. I also asked for the body to be returned to us, but they said it is their custom to cremate the dead immediately.'

Darrow was shocked. After the escape, rescue and space battle, Tanu was dead. There would be time for regret later, but for now he dismissed the thought.

'Never mind, doctor, you did your best.' Darrow switched the comm to broadcast. 'All hands prepare to leave in one hour. Recall all those on shore leave.'

He went to the bridge.

***

Parks was in sick bay when the doctor broke the news to the captain. As soon as Nefar came within reach, Parks grabbed his arm.

'Doc. Tell me straight, am I going to end up like Tanu?'

'No, no, Mr Parks.' Nefar shook his head and pulled his arm away. 'Your condition is not so serious. Your brain was not affected. His physiology was different to yours and his brain more susceptible to the damage.' Nefar paused for thought. 'Even so, I had managed to control the fits and slow the deterioration of his condition. I cannot understand why he should have died.'

'Maybe it was just one of those things. Can happen to anyone,' said Parks. 'Am I clear to go, Doctor?'

'Yes, you may go. And you may return to light

duties. But no more adventures for a while, please.'

'OK, I'll be good.' Parks smiled and headed to his cabin to get back into uniform.

Within minutes he was on the bridge, reporting to Darrow. He could have reported over the comm, but he wanted to see what was going on. He was surprised how much he had missed it. He often wished he could have time off and laze around, but when he got it he found it was never as good as he imagined. He was a man of action, and inactivity didn't suit him.

Reuel came onto the bridge to speak to the captain. 'Sir, can I ask how Tanu is?' he said, saluting. 'Is he back on board yet?'

Darrow laid a hand on his arm. 'I'm sorry Ensign, Tanu didn't make it. He died this morning.'

'But sir, that's impossible. I saw him only two hours ago.'

Darrow frowned. 'What do you mean?'

'I went to the hospital to see if I could visit him and they told me he had been transferred. Then as I left, I saw him being helped into a brown vehicle. He saw me and waved. I assumed they were bringing him back here.'

Parks chipped in. 'Doctor Nefar said there was no reason for him to die. He said his condition was under control. Can we get a post-mortem?'

'I'm afraid not,' said Darrow. 'The information I received said they cremated him, according to their custom.'

Balitoth spoke up from the communications console. 'Excuse me Captain, but the Casparans do not use cremation. Their custom is to preserve the body. Each family stores their dead in underground vaults, and there are public vaults for those without family. They would never consider cremation, they think it dishonours the dead.'

'Are you sure?' Parks said.

Balitoth nodded.

Parks looked at Reuel and saw the deep concern in the movements of the other's cranial spines. 'Wait! Suppose the Casparans are trying to find out the same thing the Bokans were? What is it this guy knows that's so important? Captain, I trust Reuel more than I trust some voice over the comm channels, we've got to go after him.'

Darrow held up his hand. 'Now wait a minute. This man has given us enough trouble already. We've got clearance to leave. We don't want to go upsetting the Casparans, you know what they're like. They can turn the slightest thing into a major incident.'

'Sir, I think Tanu might *be* a major incident,' Parks insisted. 'We were sent to Boka to follow up a rumour they'd got hold of something new, a secret weapon. And there was certainly a stir. And what did we find? Tanu. Then we bring him to Caspar, and there's another stir. I don't believe in coincidence, I think he's important.'

'Captain,' Reuel said, 'let me go back to the hospital. I spoke to a nurse there when I tried to visit Tanu. Perhaps she knows where they took him.'

Darrow considered a moment, and made his decision. He flipped open the comm. 'Commander Blackwell? Do you think you could do one more *very thorough* check on the engines? And if you found something else that needs fixing, it might just be the cause of us delaying our take-off?'

'Aye, aye, Captain.' Blackwell said. 'We can't be too careful, can we?'

The captain turned back to the bridge crew.

'Lieutenant Balitoth, notify the authorities we are one crewman short and are sending out two people to find him. Lieutenant-Commander Hoy, go with Ensign Reuel. You both know Tanu. If anyone asks, you're looking for a missing crewman on shore leave. And keep open comms, both of you. I want you in constant contact. Don't come back until you hear from me, we might be hard pressed to find an excuse for you to go out again.'

Chapter 11

Hoy waited outside the hospital while Reuel went inside. After what he'd learned about the colour green, Reuel felt awkward in his dark green uniform, but this visit was official so he had no choice.

Reuel's hope of charming the nurse he had spoken to before fell when he entered the hospital reception and she wasn't on the desk. He approached and began asking the nurse on duty, when "his" nurse came out of a corridor wearing a coat and headed for the door. Excusing himself, Reuel rushed over and attracted her attention with a cough, being careful not to touch her.

'My dear sister,' he said, with a bow. 'I hope you remember me, Shom, named like the hero Shomestry. You were so helpful to me earlier.'

She stopped and smiled. 'Yes, I remember. I have been looking for your friend in our records.'

'I have news!' Reuel said. 'When I left, my friend Tanu was outside being helped into a brown van. He waved to me. I was so glad he was all right. But now I cannot find him. Can you help me?'

Her face brightened. 'A brown van, you say? Come with me.'

She went to the reception desk and sat down at the console.

'I have not, so far, traced your friend,' she said, 'but I may be able to trace the van. The brown vans are used to transfer non-emergency patients. I can check the log of transfers made today. They may have failed to record your friend for some reason, but they should record all transport movements, to enable us to book transport when we need it.'

Reuel edged round the end of the desk to see the screen she was working on, but he couldn't read the script and the duty nurse hissed at him to get back.

'Here it is! The only transfer this afternoon was one male patient to the psychiatric hospital.'

***

Reuel came out of the hospital looking pleased with himself. 'They took Tanu to a psychiatric hospital a few miles away on the coast,' he said to Hoy. 'The nurse gave me directions.'

They couldn't find any transport so they had to walk. As they moved through the suburbs of the town, the buildings became low and all shades of green. Once the houses ended, the scenery was similar to Earth and Altair, except for the foliage being orange everywhere.

'I am surprised the Casparans have not managed to get all their plants green as well,' Reuel joked.

It took over an hour to reach the complex, which was perched on a cliff top. The thinner atmosphere meant Hoy couldn't walk too fast, but the weather was cool and dry, so it wasn't a chore.

They kept in contact with the Kestrel. They were almost at the hospital when Darrow contacted them.

'Go to secure channel.'

They switched their comms over. 'Secure,' Hoy reported.

'The Casparan authorities contacted us to ask why we haven't left,' Darrow said. 'They aren't convinced about the engine malfunction. Unfortunately the Casparan maintenance team was thorough and kept detailed records. They're not prepared to allow us to wait for the supposed missing crewman either.'

'Does this mean we have to call off trying to find Tanu, sir?' Reuel asked.

'Captain,' Hoy suggested, 'couldn't you leave and come back for us? Hopefully we will find Tanu by then.'

Darrow said, 'Stand by.'

Hoy and Reuel reached the hospital and looked around the outside. Darrow came back on the comms.

'Chambers suggested we need to test the engines after such extensive repairs. We're going to take off and do some trial runs. We'll take the last run down towards the coast. We informed the authorities and they agreed.'

'We've reconnoitred the hospital, sir,' Hoy reported, 'and we're in luck. It doesn't have the security that a detention centre would. They must have decided they needed the psychiatric facilities for Tanu. There may be some guards inside, but the building itself has minimal security. I don't think we'll have any problems getting in, but we'll have to play it by ear once we're inside as we don't know what we'll find.'

'Proceed,' Darrow said. 'We'll be heading your way in twenty minutes. We want to be able to pick you up as soon as you're back outside.'

The psychiatric hospital was a long, single storey, L-shaped building, in the favoured Casparan shade of light green. They managed to check the outside of the building without challenge. There were bars on the windows, and a high fence at either end.

One fence had a locked gate, but Hoy lifted Reuel up to see over. The fence enclosed a lush garden, but there was only one entrance. That might be a problem getting out. Reuel was tense, but glad to have a chance to redeem himself, if only in his own eyes.

This time it was Hoy's turn to take the lead. He decided to brazen it out and go straight in and ask to visit their friend. Behind the reception desk was an old man. He smiled a welcome and didn't seem suspicious. There was no sign of any guards.

'Can I help you?'

Hoy gave the Casparan bow of respect. 'Good day, sir. Our friend was admitted today and we've had no news of him. His name's Tanu. Can we see him?'

The man checked the records. 'I do not have that name here, but maybe his records have not been processed yet. We only had one admission today. Let us go and see if it is him.'

They couldn't believe their luck as they followed him down the corridor. Reuel reminded himself not to be lulled into a false sense of security. The old man knocked on a door and went in. Hoy and Reuel were close behind. Tanu lay on a bed, his eyes closed. In a chair next to the bed sat a man who was clearly not a nurse. He wore leather clothes and a sidearm.

'Excuse me, these men would like to visit their friend--'

As soon as the guard saw the PACT uniforms he reacted. He reached for his weapon, but Hoy took two quick steps and kicked it out of his hand. The guard threw a punch, Hoy side-stepped the blow, the follow-through caught Reuel on the shoulder. He staggered back against the doorframe, almost knocking over the old man as he ran away.

Hoy punched the guard in the ribs, put one hand on the floor, and slammed his foot into the man's knee. As he went down, Hoy grabbed for the guard's weapon, and they struggled for it. Reuel recovered his balance, and his wits. He grabbed Tanu from the bed and slung him over his shoulder. He headed for the door and despatched the guard with a kick in the head on the way out.

'That should keep him down for a while,' Hoy said.

A shout echoed in the corridor as the old man reappeared at the far end with three other guards. Hoy and Reuel headed in the other direction at a run. Hoy gasped out a commentary over the comm, finding it hard to breathe in the thinner atmosphere. A male nurse came out of a room just ahead of them. Hoy chopped his hand to the side of the man's neck, and the nurse went down.

Reuel was having trouble with Tanu. Though drugged he was starting to regain consciousness, struggling in Reuel's grip. Hoy dragged them into an empty room and triggered the lock on the door before he closed it. Not a moment too soon, as an alarm sounded and a series of clicks signalled the lockdown of all the doors.

Hoy signalled to Reuel to put Tanu down and move the bed to block the door. The door was heavy, presumably to prevent patients from getting out, but it wouldn't buy them much time and they were trapped.

Reuel sat Tanu on a chair and Hoy grabbed him by the shoulders.

'Tanu, listen to me! Remember us? We've come to rescue you. Focus now!'

Tanu shook his head. There was a shout from outside the door, the guards calling for a key. There was a thump as one of the guards tried the strength of the door. It held.

Reuel helped Hoy move the bed, came over and stooped down in front of Tanu. 'It is me, Reuel. We got you out before did we not? Trust me.'

Tanu's vision cleared and he smiled. 'Reuel!' His face fell. 'I can't run, I'm sorry--'

Hoy interrupted him. 'Don't worry about it, just co-operate will you? We've got to get out of here.'

***

On the bridge of the Kestrel, Chambers was panicking.

'Captain, please don't ask me to do this.'

'Lieutenant, it's the only way, there's nowhere to land.'

'But last time…'

'You can't ruin your life for one mistake. I believe you learned from it, and have become a better helmsman. You can do it.'

'I don't know…'

'Well, I do. Prepare yourself and wait for the signal.'

***

The room was bare except for the bed, the chair, and a small cabinet. The window looked out on a flowerbed and an orange lawn, which ran from the back of the building down to the cliff edge, with a safety fence. Reuel opened the window and Hoy fired the captured weapon at the bars outside. There was a bright light and a crackle - it was some kind of electrical charge, no good for cutting metal.

Hoy swung himself up and launched his feet at the bars. There was a clang, but no movement. Reuel produced a small knife from an ankle scabbard and dug at the plaster around one of the bolts holding the bars. As the plaster came away it revealed the bolt was held by mortar, not drilled directly into the stone. Reuel worked harder and removed more mortar. He started on a second bolt.

There was a shout from the corridor - apparently the lockdown could only be released by the supervisor, who was out. One of the guards cursed and his footsteps could be heard running away. Hoy launched himself at the bars again, and they moved a little. Reuel continued to dig into the mortar. Hoy's fourth attempt managed to push out the bars.

Using the cabinet as a boost, Reuel climbed out, then helped Hoy to get Tanu through. As Hoy joined them on the lawn, a guard stepped through the gate in the fence at the far end of the building and gave a shout when he saw them. Hoy fired the weapon, but its range was too short. The other guards were unlocking the room door, and would be outside in seconds. Unless there was a way down the cliff, they were trapped.

Reuel was carrying Tanu, so Hoy ran towards the cliff edge and looked down. He turned abruptly.

'Reuel, get down here now!'

As Reuel started to run, a shot crackled by them. Hoy went down on one knee and returned fire. Two guards were climbing through the window and soon the three guards were running towards them. In all the rush, Reuel was impressed Hoy was so calm, when he was so tense: his stomach knotted and his spines rigid. He didn't see how they would get Tanu down the cliff. Besides, hanging off a cliff they would be easy targets.

He realised the roaring in his ears wasn't just his pounding blood. Their pursuers stopped and stared. He turned towards the cliff edge, and saw the Kestrel rising into view, hovering like the bird of prey she was named for. The Kestrel fired a warning shot, which scorched the grass between the fleeing trio and their pursuers. It was a brilliant piece of flying, the ship held steady a few metres from the cliff.

The shuttle bay doors under the nose opened and the ship slowly rotated and lifted up over the edge of the cliff, flattening the fence. The wings were folded in to keep them out of the way. Hoy and Reuel bundled Tanu into the ship, which immediately climbed through the atmosphere and away, the wings deploying and the bay doors closing as she rose.

Parks met them in the shuttle bay. Tanu seemed to recognise him. Reuel leaned against the wall and took some deep breaths to help steady himself. He looked across at Hoy, who only now allowed himself to relax and show the strain. Reuel admired that control.

Chapter 12

Parks looked up from Tanu. 'Get him to sick bay and then report for duty. We're going to have the Casparans on our tail.'

Within minutes battle stations sounded. Everyone scrambled for their breathers and tethers, in case of a hull breach. The bridge crew: Darrow, Parks, and Chambers all strapped in. Reuel arrived at a run and strapped in.

'Tanu is in sick bay, sir,' he reported.

As Reuel took over the scanner station Chambers told him two Casparan pursuit ships had been detected. Immediately a third ship registered.

'Captain, the Bokans have found us again,' Reuel said. 'One ship coming on screen now.'

'Damn!' Darrow said and opened the comm channel. 'Commander Blackwell, can you give us any more speed?'

'Negative, Captain, we're flat out.'

Darrow closed the comm and turned to Reuel. 'Ensign, any PACT vessels in the vicinity?'

'Negative, Captain, and the nearest base is ten hours away.'

'Shout as soon as the ships get within firing range. Lieutenant Chambers, stay on course until the last second, then evasive manoeuvres. Commander Parks, make sure you have weapons lock. Polarise the plating.' Darrow opened the comm channel for general broadcast. 'Attention all hands. Brace for evasive manoeuvres and possible impacts.' He turned to Parks. 'No chance you can pull Balitoth's comms trick?'

'Not with two separate enemies I'm afraid, Captain.'

'Kill the alarm,' Darrow ordered.

The bridge became silent as the crew poised for action. Darrow was sure he could hear his own heart beating.

The comm channel beeped. 'Captain, this is Doctor Nefar. Tanu has gone.'

'What do you mean, gone?'

'He seemed to be semi-conscious. When you gave the order to brace, I turned away to secure my equipment. When I turned back, he was gone.'

'You'll have to deal with it yourself, Doctor, we've got our hands full up here.'

Reuel called from the scanner station. 'Firing range in five seconds.'

'Fire at will,' Darrow said.

The Casparan ships were spherical, hard to identify the front until the guns deployed. They had two pairs of forward facing guns and only one pair to the rear. They were highly manoeuvrable, rolling about like manic billiard balls.

They came in hot and fast, side by side, raking Kestrel from nose to stern with laser fire. Kestrel banked sharply and dodged most of it, but not all, and scored two hits on one of the ships but missed the other. The Bokan ship kept its distance, letting the Casparans do the work.

Parks succeeded in locking the plasma cannon on one of the Casparans, trying a short burst allowing for deflection. The sphere fired forward retros coming almost to a dead stop, Kestrel's plasma burst wasted on empty space. Parks hissed in frustration. The two spheres reversed course, rapidly accelerating, streaking under Kestrel's hull, their lasers blistering her plating.

Parks fired a spread of six torpedos. The Casparians separated, rolling away and launching counter measures to confuse the guidance systems. Nevertheless, two torpedos locked on.

'Yess!' cheered Parks, but too soon.

One struck a glancing blow, the detonation throwing the Casparan ship to one side, but an EM Pulse fried the other's circuits sending it spinning useless into space.

Darrow's fingers twitched as he watched the fight, willing his men to succeed. He thought of the rest of the crew: anyone not on the bridge was preparing for damage control, including being tethered in case the inertial dampers failed. So far, polarising the external plating had coped with everything.

The Casparan ships came round for another fast pass, lasers tearing and scorching the hull, blasting the sensor array, Kestrel's eyes and ears. Parks locked on and fired forward cannon. Plasma flares lit up the blackness around Kestrel's agile attackers as they pulled out of range, turning to resume their attack.

'The long range scanners are out of action,' Reuel reported.

'Starboard plasma cannon's hit,' said Parks. 'Still fires, but no targeting.'

'Chambers, move us away from the Bokan ship as you manoeuvre,' said Darrow. 'We don't want to be a sitting duck for them too.'

As the Kestrel moved, the Bokan ship moved with her, out of the fight but ready at a moment's notice. The Casparan ships came round again. Parks kept firing, and there was jolt after jolt as the Kestrel was hit. Although larger with greater fire power, the Kestrel was still one against two, and the nimble Casparans were proving hard to hit. And whoever won, the Bokan ship was waiting.

Reuel called out, 'We can't take many more hits, Captain. The thrusters are hit. Aft plating is buckling.'

The bridge door opened and Tanu come to stand beside the captain's chair. Darrow only became aware of him as Tanu leaned towards the view screen, his face creased with concentration and his fists clenched. Darrow opened his mouth to send him away, but his throat constricted and his vision went red. There was a roaring in his ears, then nothing.

***

When Darrow regained consciousness, the first thing he saw was Chambers on the floor and Tanu slumped over the helm console.

Darrow gasped, 'G… get away from there!'

Tanu lifted his head. 'It's all right, Captain, I was only bringing the ship to a halt, so there wouldn't be an accident.'

Darrow found himself staring at Tanu's forehead, where the central triangular lump glowed bright red. Tanu's eyes were bloodshot and his face was so pale it matched his grey jumpsuit. Darrow shook himself to clear his head.

'The ships…'

Darrow turned to the scanner station, where Reuel was recovering and checking the readouts.

'There is nothing there, sir, only debris.'

Tanu bent to help Chambers up, and nearly fell out of his seat. Chambers got up in time to catch him as he passed out. Reuel looked over at Tanu, at the glowing triangle, and paled with shock. He got up, the scanners forgotten, and backed against the wall muttering 'Rayt, Rayt.'

'What happened?' asked Parks, getting up from the floor.

'We'll discuss it later. Is everyone OK?' Darrow opened the comm. 'Doctor, Tanu is here - you'll need a stretcher, and bring your medscanner, we all need checking over.' He turned to Parks. 'Are you OK?' Parks nodded. 'Check all sections, get a damage report and see who else was affected.'

***

Parks reported that injuries were restricted to bumps and bruises from the loss of consciousness. Everyone on board was mentally affected to some degree by whatever had happened, but the bridge crew got the worst of it. The effect was weaker further away from the bridge. Balitoth was called to duty on the bridge so Darrow, Parks, Reuel and Chambers could meet in the captain's room.

'Lieutenant Balitoth,' Darrow said before they left, 'a sweep of the area looks safe, but keep a careful watch. Stay in touch with Commander Blackwell about the state of the engines, we may need to move fast and at short notice.'

'Aye, sir.'

'Did the scanners show up anything in the last seconds we remember?' Darrow asked Reuel once the door was shut.

Reuel blinked several times to focus. 'Er, nothing Captain. No other ships, no anomalies.'

'What about weapons damage? We scored a good many hits.'

'One Casparan ship was crippled, minor damage on the other. No ship showed any sign of being about to explode. Certainly not all three.'

Chambers said, 'The Bokans were not even in the fighting.'

Darrow turned to Chambers. 'Anything to add, Lieutenant?'

'No, sir.'

'There must be something out there that caused it, and whatever it was affected us too. Any word from Dr Nefar?'

Parks frowned and waved a data pad. 'I've got initial med reports on all crew members. It was some kind of brain seizure, apparently centred on the bridge. Most of us are recovered, but Tanu took it badly - probably because he was already weak. The scanners didn't register any kind of beam or force field that could have caused it.'

Darrow sighed in frustration. 'Well, keep on digging. If there is some phenomenon out here, this region will have to be flagged as dangerous to all shipping. In the mean time, collate the damage reports and what repairs are needed. We'll meet in an hour. Dismissed.'

Chapter 13

Nefar and Tomos guided the hover stretcher off the bridge and down the corridor to sick bay. *What now?* Nefar thought. *Is this more of the brain injury I hoped the Casparans would heal?*

'What do you think would make everyone pass out, Doctor?' Tomos asked. 'Should we ask Engineering to check for a coolant leak? I know inhaling coolant fumes can cause loss of consciousness, but I don't see how it would get all the way around the ship.'

'Good thinking Tomos,' said Nefar. 'Any other ideas?'

'Some kind of anomalous field in the space we passed through? A sound beyond human hearing? Would that be a question for Engineering too?'

'Let us leave those questions to Engineering and see if medical science can tell us anything. Try hard to remember what you experienced and record it as soon as you can.'

They eased Tanu onto a bed and Nefar switched on the medscanner.

'What's happened to his forehead?' Tomos asked. 'Why is it so red?'

Nefar sighed. 'Take the medkit and see each member of the crew, including the captain - use my authority to insist. Check for anything unusual and treat any contusions. I can manage here.'

'Yes, sir.' Tomos left.

Nefar studied the medscan. The Casparans had indeed healed Tanu's brain. He must have been affected by the same phenomena that caused the rest of the crew to pass out. Nefar couldn't find anything wrong with him. Then he gasped.

'Right in front of my face!' he said.

The triangular lump on Tanu's forehead was bright red, but the scan showed him as fully healthy. The glow of the lump was natural.

'Now where have I seen that before?' he muttered.

He went to his console and searched the database. Nothing. He searched the historical database. Nothing. He was sure he had seen it referred to before. Then he searched the mythological database. He couldn't believe what he read. Was it possible? Nefar reached for the comm channel and a sedative.

***

'Captain, I need to speak with you urgently about Tanu.'

'Not now, Doctor, the ship is badly damaged. Speak to me after the meeting.'

'Sorry Captain, but this will not wait. The whole crew could be in danger. I am coming to your office now.'

A minute later Nefar rushed into Darrow's office and dropped into the seat across the desk.

'There is something you should know, Captain.' Nefar leaned across the desk and spoke softly. 'The lump on Tanu's forehead is not a wound, it is part of him. When I realised, I started a search through the databases to see if it is a characteristic of some species with which I am not familiar. The result was surprising. Have you ever heard of Cerebra?'

Darrow frowned. 'Something to do with the brain, isn't it?'

'Well, that is where we get the word from, but it is a

place.'

'A place? Oh, do you mean the legend about a planet of people with incredible mental powers?'

Nefar sat back and smoothed his beard. 'I do not think it is a legend any more, Captain. I think that is where Tanu is from.'

For a moment Darrow considered in silence. 'But Cerebra's a myth, it's not real.'

Nefar shook his head. 'I am as certain as I can be. Do you know, every species has a similar word? Where do you think it came from?' He paused to let it sink in.

'Think about it,' he continued, leaning forward. 'You decided to rescue Tanu from Caspar because he seemed important. He caused a commotion with the Bokans and the Casparans. I think they both recognised the lump on his forehead and were trying to make him work for them. And this latest incident happened immediately after he arrived on the bridge.'

'Now wait a minute,' said Darrow, running his hand through his curly hair. 'He's got mental powers? Are you saying he destroyed those ships with his mind?'

Nefar nodded slowly. 'Exactly, and if so, it raises a lot of questions.'

Darrow's mind reeled with the implications. He got up and paced the short distance between his desk and the door. 'You've spent most time with him, but what do we really know about him? He's been semi-conscious most of the time. How do we know he won't use his powers for his own gain? Is anyone safe around him?' He shook his head. 'I can't risk my crew or my ship.'

Nefar placed a hand on Darrow's arm. 'You have already risked both to rescue him, twice. I would hope he would be grateful. He is here now, we cannot just get rid of him. He is sedated now, but that will not help us discover what his plans are.'

Darrow nodded. 'At least it will give us some thinking time. Any indication he might be hostile?'

'Not so far, but he has been too weak to do anything. He was mentally impaired too, And traumatised by his treatment at the hands of the Bokans. I cannot say what his mental state is now.' Nefar shook his head.

'Even if he co-operates,' Darrow said, thinking out loud, 'we have to consider what we're going to do with him. If we report this to the Alliance, they won't pass up such an opportunity. If we let him go, where will he go? Everyone will want him. We've opened a whole can of worms, haven't we?'

Darrow sank down on his chair and as Nefar looked puzzled, apologised for the colloquialism.

'Sorry, an unmanageable situation with lots of variables and unknowns. Keep him sedated for now, and see if you can find out any more about his people.'

After the doctor left, Darrow sat for a long time in thought. This was a tough one. He could hardly believe it was true. Nowhere in the known galaxy was there any species with proven mass mental abilities. Telekinesis and telepathy were theoretical, consigned to folklore and fringe studies. This man could be the greatest danger they had ever faced, or their greatest ally.

How can I keep my crew safe and be fair to Tanu? Having rescued him twice, can I now deliver him up to another government who will want to use him for their own ends? Where does loyalty to the Alliance end? Are there some things you can't be asked to do?

***

The horror of what he had seen and felt lay like a lead weight in Reuel's stomach. He sat on his bunk, his cranial spines limp as he thought about what happened. Tanu came through the bridge door and stared at the viewscreen. Then he frowned and the triangular lump on his forehead began to glow red.

Every Altairian knew what that glow meant - Rayt!

But surely not.

The Rayt had not been seen for a thousand years. They came to Altair and used their mind control powers to enslave everyone. Over the generations the story faded into legend and many people no longer believed such a species ever really existed. But now Reuel knew the truth. In the moment before he blacked out, he felt the force in his mind and saw the Bokan and Casparan ships start to break apart.

Tanu did it, he was certain. The shock of the revelation made him sick.

Did that make Tanu a monster of legend?

He had seemed to be a gentle soul, so traumatised by his mistreatment at Bokan hands. Reuel felt sorry for him. But then he had been badly treated, broken down. Now he was recovering. Now his powers were manifesting. Reuel got up and paced the few steps to the cabin door and back. His spines began to tremble. Had he really seen what he thought he had seen?

His forehead lump glowed, I am sure of it, he thought. *Does that make him Rayt? Maybe there are other species whose foreheads glow. None that I have ever found in my species research. His forehead glowed and the ships broke apart. I felt it too, we all did. We all lost consciousness.*

Reuel stroked his spines.

Why did he do that to us? A subject is of no use if they pass out when you try to control their mind. Maybe he was not trying to control our minds, maybe he was destroying the ships and the mental force affected us somehow.

He sat back down. The pacing agitated him. He needed to think carefully.

What but the power of the Rayt could explain the ships disintegrating like that? What other cause could there be for the crew's loss of consciousness? After all, Tanu lost consciousness too.

Reuel's mind grasped at straws. *Maybe we passed through some type of cloud in space. I was on scanners and nothing registered, though I was concentrating on the other ships, rather than space. Could some unknown phenomena have affected the structural integrity of the ships? Ah, but Kestrel was not affected, so that idea will not work.*

Tanu was trying to save us, it had to be him. Does that sound like a monster? Yes - he was not saving us, he was saving himself! If the Kestrel was destroyed, he would perish along with us, and if she was defeated, the Bokans or the Casparans would take him away. He is using us, and what will he do next?

What should I do about it? Would anyone believe me if I try to warn them? The idea is fantastical.

We should have left him on Boka, he thought, *the next round of torture would probably have killed him. Why did he not use his mind control on them? Why did he let them torture him? Suppose he suddenly released it and got away?*

He paused as a thought struck him.

We rescued him! I rescued him - twice. I thought he was harmless, I was sorry for him - was that mind control?

He got up and paced again.

Well, whatever the reason, his power is working now. He is a monster. It is only a matter of time before he enslaves the crew and controls the ship Then he can get to PACT HQ, take control of the whole of PACT, the whole of the Alliance - the entire galaxy - we'd all be slaves. I've got to stop him before he appoints himself Emperor of the Known Universe. The captain will not believe me. I must take action alone. I rescued him, I identified him, I must stop him.

Although he was used to violence around him as he grew up, Reuel had never killed or even hurt anyone in cold blood, only defended himself and his family. He swallowed hard at the thought.

Tanu had to die.

Chapter 14

'We need to discuss two things,' Darrow said to his senior officers. 'Battle damage and this man Tanu. Commander Blackwell, your report please.'

Blackwell raised an eyebrow at the unexpected mention of Tanu. 'Aye sir. Kestrel sustained some serious, but not critical damage,' Blackwell said. 'Most of the damage has been quantified and repairs have begun internally on non-critical systems. Without landing somewhere we will have to suit up and go outside to repair the thrusters and the sensor array, but the rest we can fix from Engineering. The hull plating will have to wait. I've got Stubbs checking the inventory for spares, but I think we have everything we need. Engine output is reduced to half power, but we need to shut down all engines at some point.'

'Any idea when we'll have full warp drive?'

'We're carrying out a full survey of the engines now. I'll have the results for you in an hour.'

'Can we fix it ourselves?' Darrow asked Blackwell. 'Or do we need to find a friendly planet again?'

'We should be able to fix most of it ourselves,' said Blackwell. 'Even if we have to jury-rig some of it. The engines seem to be fine on checks we've done so far, and there's no damage to environmental systems or the inertial dampers, so nothing critical.'

'That's a relief. At least it postpones the need to call in anywhere until we can reach a more welcoming maintenance yard.'

Darrow opened the comm to the bridge. 'Captain here. What's our location? Is there anywhere nearby we can land for repairs?'

'We are still in the Casparan solar system, sir,' Reuel replied, 'but no longer near Caspar itself. There is a gas giant with a large moon that might serve our purposes. No atmosphere, but a rotation good enough to give 0.75G. It's in the planet shadow now, but by the time we arrive we should have daylight for sixteen hours.'

'Helm, set course, contact Engineering for advice on speed.'

'Sir, landing might be tricky with the damage to our thrusters.' Parks said. 'The VTOL engines are still operational, but manoeuvring is going to be difficult.'

'Lieutenant Chambers, is that going to be a problem?'

Chambers said. 'Nothing I can't handle, sir.'

'Captain out.'

Darrow turned to Parks. 'Commander, we'll make the trip to this moon overnight, minimal crew on duty, everyone else to get some sleep. We'll need all hands on deck tomorrow.'

'Aye sir.' Parks made some notes on his data pad.

Darrow paused and looked round at the four faces, wondering what their reactions would be to his next subject.

'Now, the man Tanu: Dr Nefar has discovered the lump on his forehead isn't a wound, it's a natural structure for him, and his race. Doctor?'

Nefar spoke. 'I believe Tanu is a Cerebran and has telekinetic capability and possibly other mental powers.'

Hoy whistled. 'So we found the Bokan secret weapon after all! No wonder everyone wanted to keep him.' He turned to Parks. 'And we thought our mission failed.'

A M Thomas

Parks rounded on Hoy. 'Tanu is not just a piece of merchandise. Now we know what he is, do you want to hand him over to the Alliance? Do you think he'll be any less tortured into submission by them than the Bokans and the Casparans?'

Hoy reacted. 'Now wait a minute! I didn't mean...'

'That's what it sounded like.'

'All right, Commander,' Darrow said. 'The question remains - what are we going to do with him? If his powers are what they seem, we could be completely at his mercy. I've told Doctor Nefar to keep him sedated, but we can't keep him like that forever.' Darrow sighed, the dilemma weighing on his mind.

Blackwell leaned forward, frowning. 'Are you saying this man Tanu destroyed those ships with his mind?' he asked. 'That's incredible telekinesis.'

Darrow nodded.

'Do we know what his powers are?' Parks asked. 'We didn't see any evidence of them when we rescued him.'

'We know he can destroy up to three ships with a single thought,' Blackwell said, waving three fingers. 'Isn't that enough? Do any of us stand a chance against that?'

'The problem is,' said Nefar, 'Cerebrans are legends, there is little hard evidence about them. The legend talks about telepathy, telekinesis, teleportation and such.'

Hoy sat up. 'If he controlled our minds, would we even know? He could be controlling us now and we only think we're having a meeting.'

'He has not been able to use his powers because of his mental and physical state of health,' said Nefar, 'but now he is much recovered, and his mental powers are obviously available to him.'

'That's why we need to talk to him, to see what his attitude is,' said Darrow, 'but we can't risk him using his powers.'

Nefar leaned forward. 'I've looked at Tanu's physiology, his body chemistry. I believe I have developed an alternative to sedation, Captain, and I want your permission to try it out. It would also enable us to talk to him and see what he has to say. Tanu was not able to use his powers when he was in pain…'

'What are you proposing to do to him?' interrupted Parks, leaning across the desk. 'You're not going to torture him?'

Nefar looked down his nose at him. 'I would ask you to remember, Commander Parks, that I am a doctor. I do not torture people, I relieve their pain. If you will let me finish, I will explain. I have worked out which part of his brain was affected and developed a suppressant. The dosage may take a little adjusting to reach optimal, but I believe he will be able to function normally, but without his mental powers.'

'Are you sure about this, Doctor?' asked Darrow. 'If it doesn't work, I don't want to think about the consequences.'

'I think you are over-reacting, Captain. He has never been at all aggressive towards me, or any of us.'

'He was friendly because we were rescuing him,' said Hoy. 'Who knows what powers he can exercise? He might be able to read all our minds!'

'May I remind you there was one ship in that skirmish he left unscathed?' Parks said.

They were all leaning forward now.

'Calm down, gentlemen,' Darrow said. 'Doctor, you may proceed - with caution. When you wake him, have him restrained, just in case.'

Parks was looking worried. 'Just a minute, aren't we forgetting something? This is a first contact situation now. I don't remember any protocols that recommend suppressants and restraints.'

Everyone spoke at once, protesting, explaining. Darrow called for order.

'Commander Parks is right, but we have to protect ourselves. It may be first contact, but it might be hostile contact, and different rules apply. We will treat Tanu well, once we confirm he is safe. If he is dangerous, we will take whatever measures we need to take.' He looked at each of them. 'For the time being, this information must go no further. Dismissed.'

When they left, Darrow leaned back in his chair and put his hands behind his head. He thought back on all the meetings this room had seen. This could be the most serious one yet.

***

Nefar arrived back at sick bay to find a strange symbol painted on the door; a mis-shaped skull with a horn, and a line across it. Alarmed, he rushed into sick bay to check on Tanu, who was unharmed and unaware. There was no sign of anything being touched in the room. Nefar got on the comm.

'Captain, there is a marking on the sick bay door. Someone else knows about Tanu. It cannot be any of the senior officers, we were meeting with you.'

'Is Tanu all right?'

'Unharmed, Captain.'

'Check out the symbol against the database, and let me know.'

Nefar closed the comm and went back to take a

picture of the symbol on the door, feeding it into the database. Then he cleaned it off. Hours later he could still find no match in the database to tell him what the symbol meant.

Chapter 15

Late that night, Tanu tossed in his sleep as the sedation wore off. Once again he was faced with the hostility of a universe unused to his powers. The low rumble of the engines and the hum of the machines in sick bay intruded and woke him.

The sick bay door opened and a figure slipped into the room. Machines on standby gave enough light to see, but not enough to identify who it was. Tanu kept still and watched with half-closed eyes as the man worked his way silently around the room to the drawer where the scalpels were kept. Although lasers were most often used, scalpels were still needed on occasion. He opened the drawer and removed one.

The figure came to the side of the bed with the scalpel raised. Tanu instinctively tried to stop him mentally, which didn't work, so he only managed to turn over as the blade came down, and the scalpel entered his arm instead of his chest. He cried out and the assailant ran. Nefar didn't hear him, and slept on. The attack was so unexpected that Tanu lay for a minute, gasping with the pain. He was groggy with sleep and couldn't think straight. Was his attacker still about?

His arm was bleeding badly. He struggled to his feet and staggered. Reaching the door of Nefar's cabin, he banged on it with his good arm. As Nefar opened the door, Tanu fainted.

***

Nefar's urgent message left Parks wide awake and uncertain what he was going to walk into. By the time he ran into sick bay Nefar was calmly standing over Tanu bandaging his arm.

'What happened? Are you all right?' He took in the scene. 'Is Tanu all right?'

'Someone stabbed him. In the arm,' Nefar indicated the scalpel in a dish. 'I think it was meant for his chest, but he must have moved. Check the crew for bloodstains - blue bloodstains.'

Parks reeled. Why attack Tanu? Only the senior crew knew his identity. Parks stepped out and contacted the bridge.

'Parks here, has anyone left the bridge in the last few minutes?'

'Hoy here, sir: no one has left. What's happened?'

'Later, Hoy. Lock down all doors, they open to my command only.'

'Aye, sir.'

Parks heard the buzz of the nearby doors being locked. He contacted Darrow, confirmed his authorisation to investigate, and began to make a systematic search of the cabins.

Parks headed first for Engineering, since Blackwell was the only other senior officer, Parks thought he should be informed first. Blackwell was not pleased to be woken and, when Parks shook him it was obvious he had been sound asleep. Parks explained the situation and Blackwell insisted on proving his innocence, on being checked. Having cleared him, Parks left, locking the door behind him.

Next Parks went to Chambers' cabin. Since Chambers was on duty and they were one crewman short, the cabin was empty, but he wanted to check no one was hiding there.

In the cabin he shared with Stubbs, Tomos was awake. When Parks came into his room, Tomos sat up in the bottom bunk.

'What do you want? What's happening, sir?'

'I want to know why you're awake,' Parks said. 'What have you been doing?'

'W-what do you mean? I've been in bed. I just can't sleep.'

'Let me see your hands.' Parks approached the bed.

'My hands? Why?' Tomos put his hands under the covers. Parks grabbed them. There was blood on Tomos' hands. No, his fingertips were bleeding. Red blood.

'What is this?' Parks couldn't believe it. This wasn't the blood he was looking for.

Tomos looked shame-faced. 'Please don't tell anyone I bite my fingers. Doctor Nefar patches them up every morning.'

'But why?'

'I-I'm homesick.'

Stubbs looked down sleepily from the top bunk. 'What's going on?' He caught sight of Parks. 'Oh, sorry sir.'

'Show me your hands,' Parks said.

'What?'

'Your hands, Ensign. Show me your hands.'

Stubbs frowned and pulled his hands out of the bedclothes. Parks checked his hands and sleeves for blood spatter. They were clean and he had obviously been asleep. Stubbs couldn't have done it.

Parks sighed. 'Never mind, go back to sleep. The ship is on lock down, don't attempt to leave your cabin.'

Parks locked the door and lent against it. He dropped

his head and took a slow breath. *This is crazy,* he thought.

He had one more cabin to check - the one shared by Balitoth and Reuel. He paused outside the door, and unlocked it. Both appeared to be sleeping. He woke Balitoth on the top bunk first, stepping back out of reach. Zoans tended to attack first, think after.

'It's all right, Lieutenant, it's Commander Parks. I need to confirm neither you nor Reuel have been out of your cabin in the last few minutes.'

'I was asleep, sir, as you could see. I do not know about Reuel.'

'Did you call me?' Reuel looked up from his bed.

'Were you sleeping?'

'Yes sir, of course, sir.'

Parks stood in the middle of the room.

'Let me see your hands, both of you.'

They both put their hands over their covers. Both their hands and sleeves were clean.

'Stay in your room until notified.'

Parks went back to sick bay. Tanu was back in bed, asleep.

'How is he?' Parks asked.

'Shocked, but his arm will be fine,' Nefar said. 'I've sedated him to calm him down. Did you catch his attacker?'

'Everyone is accounted for and no sign of blood. You're going to have to test them all.'

'I was hoping that would not be necessary. I like my sleep.' Nefar sighed. 'Come, I will have to test for cleansers too.'

There was uproar among the crew when they were disturbed again and their hands tested. Parks supervised, but only told them Tanu had been attacked.

He couldn't tell them why, because he didn't know. When he caught the culprit, he would find out.

Unfortunately, there was no trace of blood or cleanser on anyone. He and Nefar reported to Darrow in his cabin. Darrow insisted Nefar test the three of them too.

'I hate to think one of our own did this,' Darrow said.

'It can't be anyone else,' Parks observed. 'There are only the crew and Tanu on board.'

'He must have worn gloves. Obviously the action was planned,' Nefar said. 'No use searching for the gloves, of course. Probably destroyed straight away.'

'I've always felt the Kestrel was a close ship - most of the crew get on well,' Darrow said softly. 'What does this mean? How can someone do this? Why didn't they come to me if they had a problem with Tanu?'

'You are not their father,' Nefar said. 'They are different species, with varying lengths of service, so there are bound to be clashes. You cannot know everything.' He looked up from his equipment. 'I have been impressed with how you run this ship, Captain, and am glad to serve with you all. Some things you just have to wait for them to work through in their own time.'

Nefar left, but Parks waited. He knew this would have affected his old friend.

'What is it with this Tanu?' Parks said. 'First the Bokans, then the Casparans, and now there's someone on board trying to kill him!'

Darrow ran his hand through his hair. 'Well, he'll have to be kept under guard until we get to the bottom of it. The problem is, who do I put to guard him? I could assign the very one who wants to kill him.'

'Well, I'm still on light duties,' Parks said, 'I'll do it. Move him into my cabin tomorrow, and I'll keep the door locked. For tonight, I'll sleep in sick bay, and we'll lock that too. We all need to get what sleep we can. That includes you too.' He got up to leave. 'I'll tell Hoy to unlock the cabin doors and tell everyone to settle down on my way.'

***

With the scalpel in his hands, Reuel had felt rage rise within him. How dare this man use him so! Befriend him, get rescued by him - twice! - bring him to safety aboard his ship. Now he had transport anywhere he wanted to go and a crew to do his bidding. He must be stopped. Reuel had felt like the hero from legend who had shielded his mind from the Rayt and blown them all up.

If only Tanu had not moved at the moment of the strike. *Curse him!* The adrenaline rush propelled Reuel out of sick bay and down the stairs to his cabin on the lower deck. He disposed of the gloves in the recycler and climbed quickly into bed. He tried to calm his breathing and his spines.

When Parks came in a second time, Reuel wasn't scared, he was annoyed. How dare he come and disturb them and enforce a scan of their hands! How could Reuel be suspect? He had rescued the man twice, why would he want to kill him? He forced himself to appear calm and confused, but he felt sick. *What was the matter with him?*

After Parks had left and the lights were out, Balitoth spoke softly in the darkness.

'I was not asleep, you know.'

Reuel gave a sharp intake of breath, but said nothing.

'What has changed you so suddenly? We have shared this cabin for a long time, and you have always been gentle. What has happened?'

'I do not know what you mean.'

'I saw you leave, and return in haste. And I saw the look on your face. What did you do?'

'It is none of your business. Kindly do not jump to conclusions before you have the facts.'

Balitoth frowned. 'What is the matter, my friend? You have never spoken so harshly before.'

Reuel took a deep breath and controlled himself. 'I am sorry. I was merely using the facilities when you saw me out of bed. It has been a stressful time and I think it has affected me. Let us try to go back to sleep.'

They laid down, but Reuel couldn't sleep. He had failed! As long as Tanu lived, no one would be safe, but killing him would be harder now. The crew were not allowed to carry weapons on board, since most of their missions were peaceful. The armoury was kept locked.

Reuel racked his brains for ways to get to Tanu and kill him. He had hoped to remain undiscovered, but he now faced the possibility that he would have to kill him in front of witnesses, ending his own career and liberty. Surely it was worth it to protect people against the Rayt?

Chapter 16

Tanu woke to find Parks sitting by the bed. Parks called Dr Nefar, who came over, smiling down at Tanu.

'How do you feel?' Nefar asked.

'Fine, I think.' Tanu shook his head. There was something wrong. 'Wait - what have you done to me?' He tried to move his arms and found they were restrained. Legs too. The movement pained his bandaged arm. 'What's this?'

I don't believe it, he thought. *These people helped me, rescued me, twice. I thought I was safe. Can I ever be safe away from home? They will always fear me.*

Nefar put his hand on Tanu's arm. 'It is just a mild sedative, and precautions until I am certain there is no brain damage. You have had some severe treatment and I want to be sure you are recovered.'

Tanu frowned. 'Sedation I understand, but restraints?' Tanu's face fell. 'You know.'

He lifted his head and felt a sudden rush of nausea and dizziness. When he looked up, his face was flushed with anger.

'You're afraid of me, aren't you?' He strained against the restraints. 'Everywhere I go people are afraid of me, and then they want to use me as a weapon.'

I was so naïve, he thought. *I really thought I could help people.*

'Now listen to me,' Parks said, getting to his feet. 'This ship and its crew have been through a lot for you, but we don't know you at all, and you've proved there's a lot you haven't told us. For all we know, you could be a megalomaniac and want to control us.'

Nefar interrupted. 'What we are doing, we are doing so we can meet on equal terms.'

Tanu sank back on the bed. 'Not really equal terms, Doctor. I am as much a prisoner here as I was before. No doubt your captain will deliver me to his government and they will want the same as the others did.'

'That is up to him to decide. He wants to talk to you, when you feel up to it.'

Tanu gave a bitter laugh. 'I'm not going anywhere, clearly. The captain can talk to me whenever he likes.'

Nefar paused, thinking. 'Can you remove these restraints yourself?' he asked.

'With my mind free I could, but your drug works, Doctor,' Tanu said.

'How do I know you are not faking?'

'You only have my word. How could I convince you?'

Nefar hesitated, then came to a decision. 'I will release you, but I am not stopping your medication.'

'Whoa,' Parks said, raising a hand, 'not so fast. We don't know yet if we can trust him.'

'I thought you were the one who objected to restraints used in first contact?

'I know, but we've never had a situation like this. The captain ordered him to be restrained. I think the captain should decide if the restraints can be removed.'

Tanu looked from one to the other as they discussed across the bed. He felt like an object to be fought over. He had had enough.

'Stop, please,' he said. 'Leave the restraints on, if it keeps the peace. I'm helpless anyway.'

Parks and Nefar looked shamefaced at him and each other. Nefar broke the awkward silence.

'We are going to move you into Mr Parks' cabin. I have brought you something to eat and then you must rest until you feel stronger. I will tell the captain he can visit you later.'

Moving Tanu was simple, since he was strapped to a stretcher lying on top of the bed. In Parks' cabin Nefar fed him and gave him water in a beaker. Once he finished eating, Nefar suggested he relax and in moments he was asleep. He dreamed of monsters with tentacles unravelling his brain.

***

Reuel awoke in the morning with a pain in his abdomen. *What is the matter? Is this just tension?* Then he had an idea: if he went to sick bay to ask Dr Nefar for pain relief, maybe he would have a chance to kill Tanu. He washed and dressed and went to sick bay. Tanu wasn't there. The pain gripped in Reuel's abdomen.

'Doctor, I need some pain relief please,' he said, clutching his abdomen. 'It must be the stress of the last few days.'

'I will decide that,' Nefar said firmly. 'Lie down and let me examine you.'

Reuel lay on the bed and Nefar pressed around his abdomen. Reuel cried out in pain. Nefar fetched a medscanner and studied the display.

'There are some changes in your abdomen, but it is not clear what is happening. I want to keep you under observation for a while. Return to your cabin and rest. I will see you are excused duties.'

He gave Reuel pain medication and dismissed him. This was the worst thing that could happen. Reuel was so tense, he wanted work to distract him. Worse was to come. When he returned to his cabin, Balitoth was up and dressed.

'I am afraid you must speak to me, my friend. I need a good reason not to go to the captain.'

'You would betray me?'

Balitoth recoiled. Reuel's mind whirled looking for a way out, but he could find none, and the rage clouded his thinking. His spines trembled and he stroked them to calm them down. There was a long silence, then Reuel looked at him once, and laid down on his bunk, as if it was easier to say without looking at him. He gave a sigh.

'This Tanu - he is Rayt. Many, many centuries ago, the Rayt came to our system. They were powerful in body and mind. They were violent and sadistic. We could not stand against them. They took what they wanted, including our minds. Many Altairian minds were destroyed - they forgot who they were, they even forgot how to eat. They had to be fed and dressed. They were used as slaves in the mines and the fields.' Reuel's voice broke. He coughed and continued.

'There could be no resistance, because they could read our minds. Our old gods deserted us, and we began to worship the Rayt as gods, because of their power. Then one man found a metal which shielded the mind from the Rayt, and he worked it into a helmet which he covered with a hood. He waited for a special occasion, when all the Rayt would be gathered in one place.

'The Rayt Emperor visited Altair and there was a great celebration. The man took a bomb into the palace and destroyed them all. The few Rayt who were not present, fled, and were never seen again. This story has passed into legend, but all our children are taught to beware of the beings with the horn, in case they ever return.'

Reuel sat up and looked Balitoth in the face.

'Tanu will surely enslave us all, and through us have access to PACT. I cannot allow this man to live. No one will be safe.'

'You must tell the captain.' Balitoth raised his hand to still Reuel's response. 'The senior staff have discussed Tanu, I know, but I do not think they know anything about him. Since he was rescued he has been weak, and may have hidden his powers. If this man is dangerous, for the safety of the ship, they must be told.'

'But the captain must punish me for trying to kill him.'

'Maybe not, when he understands why you did it. You must see that he needs to know.'

Reuel's shoulders sank, his head dropped. 'It is hard to talk of it, but you are right.'

'I will come with you,' Balitoth said.

***

Balitoth contacted Darrow and asked to see him privately on an urgent matter. Balitoth and Reuel met him in his office.

'What's this about?'

Reuel looked at Balitoth, who took a deep breath and explained what Reuel had told him.

'So, it was you.' Darrow said. 'Was it you who drew the symbol on the sick bay door?'

'Yes, Captain.' Reuel replied. 'You would call it superstition. I hoped the A-Rayt glyph and the incantation would take his powers, but then I had to make sure.'

'I understand why you acted as you did,' Darrow said. 'I just wish you'd come to me first. Your action is a court martial offence and would most likely see you out of the Fast-Response Fleet and sent to prison. But I will reserve my judgement until I've looked into your story.'

Darrow grasped Reuel's shoulder. 'Thank you for telling me now. I want both of you to say nothing of this to anyone else. The events you speak of were a long time ago, and Tanu is neither muscular nor violent as you describe. He does not even have the horn you described. He told us his people shield themselves from the outside world and are peaceful.'

Darrow stepped back. 'Dr Nefar has found a way to suppress his mental powers, so he is harmless at the moment. I will give him a chance to explain, and then make a decision. Promise me you will take no further action.'

Reuel nodded.

'That's not enough, Ensign. If anything further happens to Tanu, you will be the prime suspect, do you understand?'

Reuel looked away. 'May I be excused, sir? I am unwell and Dr Nefar ordered me to rest.'

Darrow dismissed them.

They both saluted and left. Balitoth laid a hand on Reuel's shoulder. 'That was not so bad was it? I will see you later.'

Reuel returned to his cabin and Balitoth went to his shift. Reuel paced restlessly back and forth for a while, then his abdominal pain subsided and his eyelids grew heavy. Despite his agitation, he found himself tired. He lay down for a nap.

When he awoke he was disoriented for a moment. Not just because he had been sleeping fully clothed when he should be on duty. Even when he remembered, he couldn't shake the strange feeling. His chest was hurting now, and he shivered. *What is the matter with me?* he thought. *I haven't felt like this since* -- His eyes went wide with the shock.

Chapter 17

The news of the attack was soon the subject of discussion among all the crew. Darrow was looking forward to reaching the moon so they could have the repairs to occupy their minds instead. Reuel remained in his cabin and Balitoth took him food.

They reached the moon of the gas giant mid-morning ship's time, and after a quick orbit, Chambers chose to land with the wings still folded against the sides of the ship. There was no atmosphere to give the wings lift and there would be less chance of damage if the ship keeled to one side.

The starboard thruster wasn't working at all and the port one was little use on its own, except for turning. He managed the landing with the VTOL engines and a touch of the port thruster to swing the ship round for the best position on the rocky ground. They landed not far from a crater, its rim a continuous pile of stones the height of a man.

In consultation with Blackwell, Darrow had assigned duties for repairs. By the time the engines stopped, Hoy was ready and suited up for a visual inspection of the ship's exterior, especially the scorching on the hull, and Stubbs and Tomos left with him to repair the port thruster. Balitoth and Reuel had been assigned to work on the starboard plasma cannon but Balitoth contacted Darrow.

'Excuse me, sir,' Balitoth said, 'since Ensign Reuel is excused duty, shall I work on the starboard plasma cannon alone?'

Darrow thought for a moment. 'Yes, for now.

Lieutenant-Commander Hoy is outside if you need any help.'

'Aye sir.'

Everyone went to work on the repairs, even Dr Nefar. He had no experience of engineering but was skilled at micro surgery and could follow instructions. He was assigned to work for a while with Blackwell on the internal repairs to systems which had shorted out.

Darrow planned to stay on the bridge with Chambers and work their way through every system to check they were all operational. Parks worked in his cabin, keeping an eye on Tanu while he documented everything. Everyone was on comms letting Parks know what they found and what was repaired.

***

When Tanu woke the second time, Parks called Darrow and as soon as he could, Darrow called Nefar to meet him outside Parks' cabin.

'Are you sure the drug is working?' Darrow asked Nefar.

'Without a doubt,' the doctor confirmed. 'To check whether he was faking, I tossed a swab towards him without warning. Anyone else would have ducked. Tanu instinctively tried to use his mind - and it hit him. I must say, he was most upset. I do not think he is faking, he has taken it hard.'

Darrow set his jaw. 'Well, we have to protect ourselves. Let's go. It's time for explanations.'

They went in and Darrow sat down beside Tanu's bed. Parks went back to his console.

'Captain, please do not talk for long,' Nefar held up his hand, 'Tanu is still weak and needs to rest.'

Darrow began bluntly. 'What happened to the pursuit ships and to my crew?'

Tanu flinched, drew a deep breath. 'I destroyed the ships with my mind, Captain.' He paused. 'I have never done anything that big before. I was not able to control the power tightly and you all got caught in the psychic fallout. There will be no lasting damage, I assure you.'

'I can confirm that, Captain,' said Nefar. 'Everyone checks out fine. Except Tanu, that is. He just about burned himself out.'

Darrow returned to his questions. 'You're telekinetic?'

Tanu nodded. He looked defeated. 'I am - I was, a mental adept. My people only do physical things for relaxation, we do everything by the power of the mind. But it requires concentration. What the Bokans didn't realise was that the pain they put me through...' he choked, his voice breaking. 'Pain made it all the more difficult to use my mental abilities. It became impossible for me to concentrate.'

Darrow glanced at Nefar who nodded at the confirmation of his theory.

'What else can you do?' Darrow said. 'Do you read minds?'

'Only with another adept. With others I can only pick up strong emotions. I'm an empath. Some of my people can teleport, but I never mastered it. I can also detect things I can't see, if I concentrate.'

Darrow took a few moments to digest all that.

'What about mind control?' Nefar asked in the silence.

A spasm crossed Tanu's face, and he shook his head.

Parks asked gently, 'Why did you go to Boka in the first place?'

Tanu took a deep breath and his explanation came out in a rush. 'My people keep away from everyone else, and our planet is shielded. Although we are taught there are other species in the galaxy, it is forbidden to leave the planet. Our space ships are only used to patrol and to maintain our shields. I resented the restrictions. I wanted to explore and meet new people. I thought we could share and learn from one another. I refused to listen when they tried to explain why we must remain hidden.'

His head dropped and he sighed.

'Eventually I stole a ship and went to meet the other species. I was a fool. As soon as people found out what I was they tried to use me. I've spent the whole time running away. My luck ran out when the Bokans caught me.'

Parks looked from Tanu to Darrow and back again. This was so fantastic, he clearly didn't know what to believe.

'So what do you want to do now?' asked Darrow. 'Do you want us to take you home?'

Tanu's voice was a whisper. 'That cannot be. You would then know where my planet is, or I might be followed and put my people in danger. The same applies to sending a message. Anyway, if I did go home I would be punished for stealing the ship and leaving the planet. But there is a bigger reason.'

He paused.

'My best friend tried to persuade me to stay, but when he saw I was determined to go he agreed to help me, on one condition. I allowed him to erase the memory of my world's location. I can never find my way home.' His voice broke and he turned his head away.

Darrow felt awkward but steeled himself to go on.

'How did people know who you were? Is it just the lump on your forehead?'

Tanu took another deep breath and collected himself to reply. 'Mostly, but I didn't hide my abilities in the beginning. Legend has it that we had a horn, but now it's only this lump. Still, it's very distinctive, for those that know about it.'

Nefar intervened, pointing to the vital signs monitor he had set up. 'That is enough Captain. Tanu needs to rest.'

'I have more questions,' Darrow said, 'urgent ones.'

'I'm sorry but I must insist.'

Darrow stood. 'Call me as soon as he wakes.' He turned to Parks. 'Watch him.'

As he left, Darrow thought about Reuel's assertion that Tanu was Rayt. How dangerous was he?

Chapter 18

'Good job the scanners found this moon,' said Tomos to Stubbs as they struggled to remove the piece of hull plating. 'It's always tricky working in space.'

Stubbs huffed. 'I know we've got some gravity and something to stand on, but I wish we didn't have to wear these suits. I'm always clumsy in a suit.'

'Everyone is, Roy, just take your time. Why do you always find something to moan about?'

Stubbs bristled. 'You just lay down and accept what you're given, do you? Some of us had to fight for everything, you know.'

'Now, don't go taking offense, Roy. Life on a cargo ship isn't a bed of roses. My parents did their best, but it wasn't easy. They taught us kids to always make the best of things, that's all. You should try it sometime.'

They worked in silence for a while, Tomos hoping Stubbs wasn't angry with him. Tomos had been assigned to help Stubbs with the thruster repairs because of his engineering experience. Hoy was also outside to supervise, but he was visually checking Kestrel's exterior. He had nothing to supervise until they got the plating off. Blackwell was seeing to the internal repairs - no getting that man in a spacesuit unless it was an absolute emergency.

'I wish I had your way with the girls,' Stubbs said with a sigh. 'Birsha and Emim were sweet, weren't they?'

'Yes. Great to meet some Casparans who actually wanted to know what was going on outside their own planet,' Tomos said. 'You need to relax and try to get to know a girl first, no strings attached.'

'We didn't learn any airs and graces where I come from,' said Stubbs. 'I can bluff it out with blokes, but I never know what to say to girls.'

'Hello is a good start,' Tomos laughed. 'Then ask them about themselves. Girls love to talk about themselves. They like being flattered too, but don't lay it on too thick. Unless they're Casparans of course. They love you to bow and scrape and flatter them.'

'Not my style,' Stubbs pulled a face.

They got the plating off and called Hoy to inspect the damage. Once he had decided what needed doing, and checked with Blackwell, Tomos volunteered to go back inside for the parts. He moved quite well in a suit, so didn't mind. When he got back, Stubbs had most of the couplings undone, and they got to work again.

'What was it like, growing up on a cargo ship?' Stubbs asked.

'Lots of room to play in, for a start,' Tomos said, 'but not many playmates. We only had two other crew, apart from Mum and Dad and my younger sister. Once you're loaded up and pointed in the right direction, there's not much to do on board, just maintenance. We had plenty of vid time with the crew, but it's not the same.'

He pulled a face. 'That's why I had so much schooling - Mum and Dad thought we should make the best use of the time. We learned regular subjects with the online school and then everything on the ship: navigation, scanners, weapons, engineering, hydroponics. I liked engineering and medicine best. They're kind of similar, fixing a ship or fixing a body.'

'You've got a point there, I never thought of it that way. I check all the diagnostic equipment in sick bay, and that's just engineering. So how come you're out here?'

'Dad hopes I'll take over the cargo business one day, but until then he encouraged me to spread my wings a bit. PACT Academy seemed a good start. There's a crew shortage at the moment, so I was able to get the medic post here.'

'Yes, our last medic left to get married and finish qualifying. He met his wife on our last major mission.'

The conversation paused while they worked on the tricky job of replacing the fused wiring and seating the new components.

Then Stubbs said, 'There was a girl on that mission I liked, Tabitha, but she wasn't interested.'

'Two women on the ship? That's unusual.'

'Not so unusual in the Fast-Response Fleet, but they were unusual in that neither of them were part of the crew. Anna was a mystery woman rescued from a ship crash. She's marrying Sam Ryan our ex-medic. The other, Tabitha Enns, was a trainee the captain co-opted because of the crew shortage. She was only eighteen, and I reckon she'd never had a boyfriend.'

'Wow, so you had to handle her carefully.'

Stubbs looked away. 'Well, I don't think I did.' He sighed. 'I don't think I know what to do with women really, not respectable women anyway.'

Tomos thumped him on the arm. 'Did you enjoy our time with those two girls on Caspar?'

Stubbs considered for a moment. 'Yes I did, actually. It was kinda nice not to be thinking of my next move all the time.'

Tomos laughed. 'Well, now you know how to start - with all women. Maybe you'll meet Tabitha again one day. What was she like?'

'All wide-eyed and eager in the beginning. She was

from Alpha, you know, short and sturdy from the high gravity, but very sweet. She helped me up once and lifted me right off my feet!'

'What happened to her?'

'Because of the crew shortage, I think the captain hoped to keep her on and finish her training with us. But she blotted her copy book by sneaking on board the shuttle for a first contact mission. Could have caused all sorts of trouble.

'As it turned out, the contact went sour and she helped them escape, but she still had to be disciplined. So she was sent back to the Academy under a cloud. I ought to look her up, find out what happened to her. She deserves to do well. Her record will be in the database.'

'Maybe you should look her up in person too,' Tomos suggested. 'Try out your new conversational skills.'

'You know, when the mission got dangerous, Tabitha was afraid, and I told her we wouldn't have to fight because we were junior members of the crew. But then I had to go in the rescue party and got shot. Then when we were attacked the other day, I broke my wrist. Now these space battles. It's not what I signed up for. I don't feel safe anymore. I'm leaving, first chance I get.'

'But what will you do? Don't you love it here?'

'Maybe I can transfer to a cargo vessel or something.'

Tomos shook his head. 'I don't recommend it. It was different for me, we were family, but it gets dull and lonely. Besides, there are always dangers in space.'

'There must be plenty of other opportunities for an engineer that don't involve violence or danger,' Stubbs said. 'Maybe I could work in the shipyards or maintenance. I'm going to spend my spare time researching.'

'I don't mean to be picky, but you're not an engineer yet, are you?'

'One exam away from Junior Engineer. So that's my goal.'

'Well good luck. Pass me the splicer, will you?'

Stubbs threw the tool towards him. It flew in a graceful arc and Tomos reached out and grabbed it.

'Be careful, in this lighter gravity you might lose it all together.'

'Not if you know what you're doing. I'd have thought you'd be good at this, being brought up in space and all. Didn't you play in zero gravity?'

'Yes, but this is different. It's hard to judge in different gravities.'

'You mean there's something I can do that you can't?'

'I didn't say I can't, I was just warning you.'

'Oh yes? Let's see you then.'

Tomos finished with the splicer and tossed it to Stubbs, but he did misjudge the gravity and it went over Stubbs' head. It landed a short distance behind him on the pile of rocks at the edge of the crater and clattered down the far side.

'I *am* better than you at something!' Stubbs cheered as he went to retrieve it.

He couldn't find a way around the rocks, they were a continuous ridge. He began to climb over when he suddenly swore and disappeared. Tomos called after him, afraid he had fallen.

'No Tomos, stay back!' Stubbs shouted.

'Don't be silly,' Tomos said as he jogged over to the rocks, 'I'm coming to --'

As Tomos' head came above the rocks he found

himself face to face with a blaster. Stubbs was on his back at the bottom of the slope, another man standing over him with a gun.

'Get back on board and see the captain, quickly,' Stubbs said.

The blaster waved him away and Tomos almost ran to the airlock, gasping out, 'Kestrel, mayday! They've got Stubbs.'

He was vaguely aware of a recall command going out to everyone outside, but he scrambled into the airlock and hit the button. It seemed to take a long time to cycle. When the inner door opened Parks was waiting for him. Tomos stood to attention and saluted, and Parks indicated he should remove his helmet.

'Did you see anything?' he asked as soon as Tomos lifted his helmet off.

'There's men with guns sir, they've got Stubbs - -'

'Confirmed, sir,' Parks spoke into the comm. He turned back to Tomos. 'We picked it up on the comm. Stand by in case you're needed.' He left before Tomos could answer.

Tomos sagged against the wall and tried to collect his thoughts. It had all happened so fast. Stubbs was white as a sheet and the men looked grim.

***

Darrow arrived at the airlock, fastening his spacesuit with one hand, his helmet in the other. He put on the helmet and entered the airlock without a word to Tomos. The airlock cycled and he stepped out. Hoy and Balitoth were waiting and he waved them into the airlock.

Darrow spoke into his communicator. 'Kestrel do

you copy?'

'Aye aye, sir.'

'Begin recording.'

Darrow headed for the crater. He wasn't scared, he was angry. How dare they touch his crew? A helmet bobbed above the rocks and the man climbed higher when he saw Darrow and the captain's patches on his arms. He waved a blaster, which Darrow deliberately ignored. He wasn't going to be intimidated.

'Where's my crewman?'

The blaster waved to him to climb up the rocks and retreated down the other side. Darrow climbed and Stubbs came into view, on the ground and held by another man.

'Stubbs, are you all right?'

Stubbs shook his head and the man thumped his arm.

'What have you done to him?' Darrow snapped.

'Nothing,' said a voice in his ear, 'he's just scared witless.'

'Who is this?'

A gruff voice replied, 'Names are not important, Captain. What is important is you landing your PACT ship on my moon.'

Darrow drew a calming breath. 'There's nothing in the database about this moon belonging to you, or anyone else for that matter, otherwise we would have asked permission,' Darrow said. 'You need to register the title deeds. We had no choice about landing, I'm afraid. Our ship was damaged in battle and needs repair.'

There was silence while the man thought about it. Darrow started to climb over the edge of the crater. The man waved the gun but Darrow ignored him. Down in the bottom of the crater he could see piles of crates whose colour was similar to the rocks. Other things were covered by rock-coloured tarpaulin, so it was all camouflaged. *Smugglers or pirates*, Darrow thought. His comm came on.

'How long to finish the repairs?'

'Twenty-four hours, minimum.'

'You will do no repairs until after we leave. That way your ship won't be spaceworthy to follow us.'

'How long?'

'Several days, at least. We have a lot of work to do. Thanks to you we have to move all our stores off this moon.'

'Contraband you mean.'

'Now you listen to me. We have your crewman. He won't be harmed if you and your crew behave. These are the rules: no long-range communications. Any attempt to report our location will be met with violence. No scanning and no exploration. We'll move our stores and you will not be allowed outside your ship until we finish. Anyone leaving the ship will be shot. We'll leave your crewman behind when we go.'

'Make sure you look after him, or - - '

'Don't make threats, Captain, just go.'

Darrow had no choice but to return to the ship.

Chapter 19

Darrow returned to the ship and immediately called a crew meeting in the mess hall. There were only seats for eight around two tables, but there were only eight crew plus the captain at the moment. Kestrel was on patrol with ten crew instead of eleven, and now Stubbs held hostage. Parks locked Tanu in his cabin and came to the meeting. He figured Tanu was safe because all the crew would be present.

Darrow entered and they all came to attention. He told them to sit and raised his voice.

'As most of you are aware,' he began, 'we are not alone on this moon. A band of smugglers use it to store their contraband. Everything is inside a crater and camouflaged, which is why we didn't detect it. Ensign Stubbs climbed over the crater's edge and stumbled on them and they are holding him hostage.'

'What do they want, sir?' Hoy said.

Darrow frowned at the interruption and continued. 'They want us out of the way while they move everything off the moon, and they won't let us do the external repairs until they've left, so we won't be able to follow them.'

They all spoke at once and Parks called for quiet. Tomos raised his hand.

'Sir, how is Stubbs?'

'Scared, but he seemed to be all right,' Darrow said. 'It's in the smugglers' interest to look after him.'

'So, what's the rescue plan?' Hoy said.

'There isn't one,' Parks said, 'because as soon as someone leaves the ship, the smugglers will shoot them, and then they'll probably shoot Stubbs.'

'But they won't see someone leave the ship if we use the starboard airlock, it's hidden from view by the ship.'

Parks turned on him. 'You need to think things through before you act, Lieutenant-Commander. How are you going to get from the starboard airlock to the crater without being seen, and what do you propose we do there?'

Hoy's face went red and he sank into his chair.

'Don't any of you do anything to endanger that boy's life,' Blackwell said.

The room fell silent.

Darrow scanned the room and held every eye. Reuel had his head down and had to be nudged by Balitoth. 'There will be no rescue attempt, or communication attempt. Is that clear?' He waited until everyone had nodded, then turned to Blackwell. 'Can we use short range sensors to monitor activity outside without being detected?'

Blackwell shook his head. 'I wouldn't recommend it, Captain.'

Darrow turned back to the crew. 'Well, whoever's on the bridge when the smugglers leave, do a full sensor sweep and try to determine which way they're headed.'

'It may not do any good, sir,' Parks said, 'they're bound to change course once they're out of sensor range.'

'Do it anyway. All the data we can get.' Darrow turned to Blackwell again. 'I need new schedules for completing the internal repairs asap, and any way you can think of to reach some of the external damage from inside.'

Blackwell nodded and stood. 'If you were already working inside, get back to it. Anyone working outside, stay here and wait for your new assignment.'

He sat down and looked to Darrow, who said, 'It's getting late, so once you have your assignments, get some sleep and start tomorrow. Commander Parks with me, everyone else, dismissed.'

Outside the mess hall Darrow said, 'We need to speak to Tanu again,' and headed for Parks' cabin.

***

As soon as Darrow and Parks left the room, conversation started.

'Why weren't the smugglers detected on the scan before we landed? Tomos asked. 'Who was on duty?'

'I was,' Chambers said. 'There was nothing registered on the scanners, I swear. You heard the captain: all their stuff is camouflaged.'

'But there's got to be a ship out there somewhere, otherwise how did they get here?'

'Maybe it is cloaked,' Balitoth said.

'Oh, come on,' Hoy said, 'you know cloaking technology is a myth. It can't be done.' He paused. 'Trouble is, I can never tell when you're joking.'

Blackwell interrupted. 'I don't think this is an appropriate time for joking, with Stubbs out there in danger.'

There was a chorus of 'Sorry sir' and Nefar, Reuel and Chambers left hurriedly. Balitoth, Tomos and Hoy gathered round Blackwell to be given their new assignments.

***

Darrow had been thinking about Reuel's tale, but the events of the day had prevented him doing anything about it until now. He really didn't need all these complications when he had to deal with the smugglers. His first instinct was to dismiss it as folklore, but put together with Dr Nefar's theory, it became more plausible.

Although Altarians could be aggressive, Darrow had never known Reuel to be violent or even bad tempered. This behaviour was out of character, so extreme, it was clear Reuel was convinced Tanu was a threat. He had attempted to murder Tanu, which was a court martial offence and would mean prison and disgrace. But Reuel was trying to protect his crewmates, in which case he understood how Reuel would consider himself a hero.

If Reuel's claim was false, Darrow would have to deal not only with his behaviour, but also his state of mind. If Reuel's claim was true, it gave rise to a bigger problem: just how dangerous was Tanu? It was imperative Tanu's identity be established.

Darrow and Parks went to Parks' cabin. Tanu was still restrained.

'Has he had the suppressant this morning?' Darrow asked Parks.

'Aye sir.'

Darrow turned to Tanu and said bluntly, 'What is Rayt?'

Tanu jumped as if he'd been shot, and went white. 'How do you know that word?'

'Never mind that, what does it mean?'

Tanu was trembling. 'The Rayt are long gone, Captain. Please believe me, I am nothing like them.'

'But they were your people, weren't they?'

'Yes.' Tanu's reply was a whisper. 'There must be an Altairian on board.'

Parks was looking from one to the other in

confusion. Darrow gestured to him not to interrupt.

'What happened? I want to hear it all, if I'm to trust you.' Darrow sat beside Tanu's bed, his face grim.

Tanu took a deep breath. 'The Cerebrans have always had a variety of mental talents. Thousands of years ago, there were those who could control the minds of others. They were arrogant, and used their powers for their own ends, instead of to benefit others. They called themselves the Rayt.'

He sighed. 'There were a few people who were immune, but too few. The Rayt could not be stopped, and soon came to dominate our society. Eventually they grew even more ambitious and set out into space to conquer other planets. Altair was the first and the last.'

His voice failed. He cleared his throat and pressed on.

'I don't know exactly what they did on Altair, but it was brutal. There is no defence against that sort of power. Somehow, the Altairians managed to set off an explosive, which killed most of the Rayt, including their leader. There is no record of how they did it.

'The remaining Rayt fled back to Cerebra, where the people were ready for them. They were immediately executed. The whole population was horrified at what they had done, and terrified the Altairians would retaliate. It was decreed such power would never be allowed again. Children who manifested such power, were… mentally adjusted, before it developed any further.

'After many generations, it died out, but children are still checked to this day. All Cerebrans renounced violence and deliberately avoided physical activity as much as possible from then on. We made sure such a thing as the appalling Altairian conquest could never happen again.' He closed his eyes and took another deep breath.

'You're all safe from me, I assure you.' He opened his eyes, which were wet with tears. 'I'm not a violent man, I've never done anything like that before. In fact, part of the reason for my collapse was the shock of all those deaths. I wanted to save you all, as you saved me. Violence is unethical. My society is very strict about other people's rights. I wouldn't dream of doing anything that affected anyone else without their permission.'

Darrow studied his face with care and then turned to Nefar. 'Release the restraints.'

Nefar released Tanu, who rubbed his wrists. Nefar helped him to sit up, and propped some pillows behind him as he swayed.

'I'm a little light-headed,' he said. 'I have to concentrate before I move because I'm used to using my mind to support myself, as well as in manipulating things.'

Darrow thought about what Reuel had said. So it was true, but who should he believe? And how should he discipline Reuel? The silence allowed Parks to say something. The trouble was, he clearly didn't know where to start. He glanced from one to the other.

'So you are … He is … I mean … Did you say Altairian? It was Reuel?'

Darrow nodded. 'Yes, and now you mention it,' he turned back to Tanu, 'there is someone else you need to convince.'

Tanu looked from Darrow to Parks and back again. He looked exhausted. 'The one who tried to kill me? You want me to speak to him?'

'Do you want to spend your whole time on the

Kestrel under guard, with your powers suppressed?' Darrow said. 'And if you can't convince one man, what will you do with the rest of the galaxy?'

Chapter 20

The next day Reuel and Balitoth were summoned to Darrow's office.

'Stand easy, please sit,' Darrow said and waited for them to sit down. 'I have spoken to Tanu, and he claims that, even with his powers, he's not dangerous. For now, he will continue to have his powers suppressed, while I decide how to proceed. But,' he paused and looked closely at Reuel, 'I want him to speak to you, and for you to make up your own mind. Are you well enough? You look different somehow.'

Reuel's heart leaped into his throat, but Darrow just shook his head to refocus. 'You can have Balitoth with you if you want, and Commander Parks and I will listen in to the conversation.'

Reuel could only nod. He was stunned. He didn't know what to think. Speak to the man he was so afraid of? How could he? Shouldn't there be some revenge for his people?

Darrow continued. 'I appreciate that you were trying to protect the crew, and I can't confine you to quarters because we need all hands on deck to work on the repairs. But you must not take any further action until you have listened to what Tanu has to say. Report to me when you come off duty.'

Darrow dismissed them. Outside the office Balitoth grasped Reuel by the shoulders.

'I can guess how you feel, but it will be all right, my friend. I must go on duty, you will feel better when you have time to think about it.'

***

When Reuel and Balitoth reported to Darrow that evening they were taken to Parks' cabin and then Darrow took Parks back to his office. Reuel and Tanu were alone, with Balitoth unobtrusively in the corner.

Reuel and Tanu stood awkwardly in the middle of the room.

Reuel dropped his voice, 'Do you think the captain is listening?'

Balitoth nodded.

Reuel continued, 'Then we had better not make any noise,' and grabbed Tanu by the throat. He moved so fast, Balitoth didn't react at first. Without his powers, Tanu was unable to resist, physically he was no match for Reuel. Tanu's face was getting redder and he gasped for air as he clawed at Reuel's hands. Balitoth sprang forward and grabbed Reuel's wrists, trying to prise his hands apart.

'Shom, no,' Balitoth hissed, 'give him a chance to explain.'

'It may be the only chance to save everyone,' Reuel said. 'Don't.'

But Balitoth was too strong for him. Tanu was released and collapsed on the floor.

Darrow's voce came over the comm. 'Is everything all right in there?'

'Yes sir,' Balitoth called. 'No problem.' He helped Tanu to a seat and waved Reuel to the other.

Reuel took a deep breath and asked Tanu, 'Are… are you… Rayt?'

Tanu shook his head and cleared his throat. 'There have been no Rayt since they fled from Altair back to Cerebra. They were all executed, and any children manifesting such powers had them suppressed, until they died out.'

'You killed your own people?' Reuel hadn't expected that.

'They were no longer our people. They had betrayed everything we stood for. Our leaders were afraid there would be reprisals from Altair and they needed to take drastic action to show that the Rayt were not part of Cerebra anymore.'

'How can I be sure?'

'You rescued me from Boka,' Tanu said with a half smile. 'Do you think I would have been in that state if I was Rayt?'

Reuel collapsed backwards in his chair.

'All these years - all these centuries - we have feared the Rayt would return.'

'There will be no return. No one has left my planet for hundreds of years, and after my escape I expect security to be even tighter. My planet is skilfully shielded and will not be discovered. Trust me.'

Reuel put his head in his hands. His emotions whirled, such a change from how he had felt the night before. His spines writhed and his stomach rolled so much he thought he might be sick. He looked up when he heard Tanu move, to find him kneeling before him, tears falling down his face. He noticed Balitoth had moved nearer.

Tanu bowed his head to the floor and said in Altairian, 'I beg your forgiveness on behalf of my people.'

Reuel sat in stunned silence, lost for words.

'Please believe me.' Tanu continued in Altairian. 'The past is gone, and I am not Rayt.' When Reuel remained silent, Tanu got up from his knees and said, 'I ask you one thing. Please do not betray me. I ran away from

Cerebra and can never go back. I am alone.'

Reuel turned to Balitoth for agreement, but Balitoth was puzzled.

'What did he say? I didn't follow.'

Tanu turned to Balitoth and spoke in Zoan. Balitoth was amazed at the language switch but stuck to the matter at hand. He said to Reuel, 'I think we should keep his secret, at least for now.'

Reuel nodded. 'Your secret is safe, but only because the captain has commanded it. I need time to think about this.'

Tanu nodded. After a few awkward seconds Balitoth raised his voice. 'Captain, the conversation is over.'

Darrow and Parks arrived and dismissed them.

Outside in the corridor Reuel turned to Balitoth.

'How could you betray me? The whole crew is in danger, and after that, the whole civilised galaxy. I thought you were my friend.'

'I am your friend, which is why I stopped you.' Balitoth grasped his shoulder and rushed him down the stairs into their cabin. 'We have no proof of his identity, you would have been tried for murder, and you would have had no defence.'

'He admitted he is Rayt, we have the proof out of his own mouth.'

'No, he admitted he is Cerebran. He said the Rayt are long gone.'

'He would say that to protect himself. We cannot trust him.'

'Well, you had better prepare to explain yourself when he reports you to the captain,' Balitoth said, and left.

Reuel's head was in a whirl. The monster Rayt had begged his forgiveness. The man he had felt such sympathy for, had rescued twice, then turned out to be a monster. Now the monster claimed not to be a threat after all and begged forgiveness. If you could believe him.

Doctor Nefar insisted Tanu's powers were suppressed. How could Reuel be sure? How could any of them? Maybe Tanu was fooling them all and pretending not to have his powers. Maybe he was controlling their minds to think whatever he wanted them to think. But what about the Bokans? Why would he let them torture him if he could stop them? He seemed so upset, Reuel's heart went out to him. But away from his presence, Reuel couldn't be sure.

Oh, if only he could think straight! How was he going to hide the changes in his body? What if he burst into tears in front of someone? His emotions were in a turmoil and there was no place of safety.

***

Listening to the conversation over the comm, Darrow and Parks both had a sharp intake of breath when Tanu spoke to Reuel in Altairian, and again when he switched to Zoan.

'Wait!' Parks said. 'We didn't think anything of it when he spoke Standard on Boka, because most people do. But then we assumed he was human. What language do Cerebrans speak anyway?'

'How did the Bokans interrogate him?' Darrow added. 'He must have spoken Bokan. And on Caspar he must have spoken Casparan. I thought he couldn't read minds?'

Every conclusion he had come to about Tanu was up in the air again.

When Balitoth called them in Darrow marched back to Parks' cabin and dismissed Balitoth and Reuel. He rounded on Tanu as soon as the door shut.

'How come you speak so many languages?' Darrow demanded. 'And why didn't you tell us before?'

Tanu looked bewildered. 'Languages? But I can't…'

'You told us your powers were only telekinesis and empathy. If your planet is isolated as you say, then how come you know all these languages?'

'Why would we learn languages when we never meet anyone else?' Tanu said. 'I only know my own language -' He stopped, puzzled. 'How do you speak Cerebran? I never thought of it before.'

Parks interrupted. 'You have always spoken Standard to us, but you just spoke to Reuel in Altairian and Balitoth in Zoan.'

'Did I? I didn't realise… I don't know…'

Darrow shook him by the shoulders. 'How do you expect us to trust you if you hide things from us?'

'Captain,' Parks said, 'may I try something?'

Darrow nodded and moved away. Parks pulled over a chair and sat in front of Tanu.

'Concentrate on me,' Parks said. 'Tell me it's a lovely day.'

Darrow started to protest, but Parks held up his hand.

'Tala till mig,' he said, looking intently at Tanu.

With no hesitation, Tanu said, 'Det är en underbar dag.'

'What was that?' Darrow asked.

Parks turned to Darrow with a smile. 'I said "speak to me" and he said "it's a lovely day" - in Swedish!'

Darrow and Tanu were equally surprised.

Parks explained. 'I'm no expert, but I think it's an

offshoot of Tanu's empathy. He can pick up the language of anyone he talks to.'

Darrow's face darkened. 'But his powers are suppressed, he's not supposed to be able to do anything.'

'It obviously comes from a different part of his brain,' Parks said, 'because he could do it when we met him on Boka, when he was being tortured.' Parks got up from his seat and went to Darrow. 'I think it's added proof he's being honest with us, because he would have hidden it.'

Behind him, Tanu had his head in his hands. 'I didn't know, I don't understand.'

'Don't worry,' Parks said to him, 'it's a very useful skill to have. We still believe in you, don't we Captain?'

Darrow nodded, but said nothing.

Parks became serious. 'Captain, don't you think Tanu could be allowed out of this room now? I think he has answered all our questions and with the suppressant drug he is no danger to the crew or the ship.'

'Would it be painful for you to cover up the lump on your forehead?' Darrow asked. 'It seems to me without that everyone would assume you were human. Not all crew members know about you. Perhaps the Doctor can help you fashion a headband, and you can mingle with the rest of the crew without any suspicion.' He frowned. 'Whether that's a long-term answer, I don't know.'

'Mingle with the crew as long as I'm tame, eh Captain?' Tanu gave a sarcastic laugh.

Darrow raised his hand. 'Give us a chance, will you? I just don't know what to do with you. After all, we've rescued you twice, at considerable risk. I don't want you to be afraid of us here on Kestrel, no one will misuse you, but you've put me in a very difficult position.'

Tanu sighed. 'I'm sorry, Captain. I want to thank you for everything you've done for me. If I can be of any help to you, please say.'

Chapter 21

Tanu appeared in the mess hall for breakfast, looking pale and nervous and wearing a padded headband made from green surgical cloth. Parks showed him the way, helped him choose a meal and reconstitute it, then left him alone to eat. He looked a bit lost, and Hoy, who was off duty, called out to him.

'Hey Tanu! Come and sit with me. How are you feeling?'

Reuel raised his head, saw Tanu, and left, leaving his meal half eaten.

Tanu sat down with a grateful smile. 'Much better thank you. You're Hoy aren't you? I owe you a lot.'

Hoy was embarrassed. 'That's OK, and call me Dan. Is all right if I call you Tanu? Do you have another name?'

'My family name is Pe'Rod, but ... I feel I forfeited that when I ran away.' He bowed his head.

'Hey, don't get upset. We'll just call you Tanu. Balitoth only has one name.'

Tanu waved his knife and fork and gave him an embarrassed look. 'Can you help me with these? I'm not used to them.'

'No problem,' Hoy laughed, and they spent the next ten minutes on cutlery lessons. Encouraged by the interaction, Hoy asked the burning question. He dropped his voice to a whisper.

'So Tanu, what's it like, having all these mental powers? Is everyone the same on your planet?'

For a moment, Tanu's face softened. 'Oh, it's amazing, you can't imagine. Right from when we are children...' He stopped. His face clouded. 'But that's all lost to me now. I threw it all away when I left.'

There was an awkward silence. Hoy coughed. 'Hey, I'm sorry. I didn't mean to upset you. It's just that no other species we've discovered has any powers like this, and our imaginations run away with us. Has the Doc really suppressed it all?'

'Yes. He's a very clever man, Dr Nefar. He saved my life after you rescued me from the Bokans, but I find it hard to thank him for this.'

'Look, we need to keep everyone safe, do you understand?'

Tanu nodded. 'Is it because of me that Captain Darrow is so worried?'

Hoy started up from his chair. 'How do you know ...'

For a second Tanu didn't understand, then he realised what he had said. 'No, oh no.' He reached for Hoy's arm and pulled him back into his seat. 'I have eyes, I can see something has changed, that's all. There's a tension in everyone I meet, but the Captain most of all. I'm sorry if I've caused him even more worry.'

Hoy relaxed. 'You spooked me there.'

'I'm sorry. The suppressant drug does work.'

Hoy sighed. 'The tension is because one of the crew has been taken hostage by smugglers. Stubbs, the assistant engineer. We're all concerned.'

***

Now Tanu was well and free to move about the ship, Parks gave him a tour.

'There isn't much to see, really, because lots of the rooms are cabins, and the crew won't appreciate you walking in there.' Parks laughed.

'So, what about the other rooms?' Tanu asked. 'I've only seen sick bay, the mess hall and your cabin.'

'Well, let's start forward.' Parks took him out into the corridor. 'That's the bridge - off limits of course. To port, the left of the bridge, is the Captain's office and then the Captain's cabin, the mess hall and the Engineer's cabin at the end. On the other side of the corridor is the Second Officer's cabin - that's Hoy, who you know. Then sick bay, the Doctor's cabin and my cabin as First Officer - our cabin at the moment. The designers felt it best to have the Captain and First Officer at opposite ends of the ship, to increase the chances of a senior officer surviving a battle or a crash. Except when I'm on duty of course.'

They walked slowly down the main corridor as Parks explained. There were rails inset into the wall on either side, and everything was pale green, with a darker green floor. At the end of the corridor was another corridor. Parks stopped and pointed.

'Aft is a crosswise corridor with access to Engineering on both decks. One end of the corridor is a small stores, behind the Engineer's cabin, and the other end is hydroponics, so we get some fresh food. At either end of the main corridor are staircases down to the lower deck, where there are three double cabins, the cargo bay and the shuttle bays. Any questions?'

Tanu thought for a moment. 'So you're saying I've seen all the places I'm allowed to go?'

"Fraid so,' Parks said. 'But you do need to know the way out. There's an airlock either side of the cargo bay, with suits hanging in a cupboard. We do have spare, so you'll be all right if there's an emergency. Come and see the way.'

Parks took him down the stairs and into the main

corridor back towards the bow. The cargo bay was actually on either side of the corridor, allowing access to the shuttle bays at the end. Parks showed him how to check the air pressure before opening the door. They went into the starboard cargo bay. There were a few containers along one wall, about two metres on each side, but it was largely empty. Parks turned to Tanu.

'Would you like to try on a suit? We can't go outside because the smugglers are watching, but I can take you into the airlock and depressurise it. The gravity will reduce too. How are you in low gravity?'

'I've no idea, I've never experienced it, though the gravity back home is less than here. Can we really do that?'

'We should get permission first, but since I'm the First Officer, I give us permission.' Parks smiled. 'I'd better let the bridge know, we don't want to panic them when the airlock depressurises.' He pressed a button on the wall. 'Commander Parks to bridge. In a short while, Tanu and I are going into the airlock, which will cycle, but we will not be opening the outer door. Is that clear?'

'Aye, sir. Clear.'

Parks turned back to Tanu to find him very pale.

'Are you all right?'

'I'm not very brave, you know,' Tanu said.

'You don't have to do it, it was just an offer. Maybe it's too soon.'

That galvanised Tanu. 'No, no, I might not get another chance. Go ahead.'

It took some time, but they got into suits and Parks showed Tanu the controls for his air and communication. He could hardly walk in the suit without the use of his mental powers, but Parks helped him into the airlock and shut the door. He nodded at

Tanu, and when Tanu nodded back, he pushed the button to depressurise. For a while Tanu didn't feel any different. Maybe the suit wasn't quite so heavy now.

'The airlock gravity is the same as outside,' Parks said, 'which is minimal, but will keep you upright and on the ground. I'm going to reduce gravity to zero.'

Parks operated some controls and then reached for Tanu's arm. With barely a twitch, he lifted Tanu off the floor and let go. As Tanu floated, Parks gave a tiny push and rose to join him. Tanu's face lit up.

'It's like when I'm using my telekinesis,' he said, raising his arms. The action made him spin slowly in the air, and his attempts to stop it made him tumble head over heels. 'Only then I have control,' he laughed.

Parks rescued Tanu and brought him down to the floor. He watched Tanu's face. It was good to see him laugh. He had been through a lot, and wasn't out of the woods yet.

Chapter 22

The next day Balitoth entered the cabin he shared with Reuel to find it in chaos. Reuel was throwing things about in a rage.

'Stop, stop!' Balitoth said, grabbing Reuel's arm and retrieving the tablet he was about to throw. 'That is mine. What is going on?'

'Do not interfere!' Reuel said and spat some Altairian words Balitoth didn't understand. 'I am looking for my tablet. I cannot work without it, and I am most careful about where I put it. I am beginning to think someone has taken it.'

Balitoth reached up to the top of the lockers. 'I think you will find you put it up here last night when you were getting something out of your locker.'

Balitoth held the tablet out to Reuel, who looked from it to Balitoth and crumpled into tears, sinking to the bed sobbing uncontrollably. Dumbstruck Balitoth dare not move, staring at his friend's aberrant behaviour and still holding out the tablet. Tears, mess, this wasn't Reuel, what was going on? With a great gulp of air, Reuel finally got control of his tears, Balitoth slipped the tablet onto the nearest surface as Reuel wiped his face with a cloth.

'Forgive me, I am not… myself at the moment.'

'Indeed you are not. I am concerned. Is it this Tanu business? Will you talk to me?'

'That is part of the problem,' Reuel said. 'I must not speak of it.' His shoulders slumped, his spines hung limp.

Balitoth began picking things up and putting them

away. Then he remembered something.

'I have a message for you. Dr Nefar wants to see you to follow up on your stomach pains.'

Reuel jumped as if he had hit him. 'No! That is not possible, I cannot allow it.'

'You have no choice my friend, we are all under the Doctor's jurisdiction. Why would you not permit him to treat you if you are unwell?'

'Because I am not unwell.' Reuel stood and began to pace. There wasn't much room, with Balitoth standing and the mess strewn all over the floor. Balitoth moved a couple of things out of his way and then gave up and grasped Reuel by the shoulders.

'Enough!' Balitoth said. 'Are we not friends as well as crewmates? Is it because of Tanu, because I stopped you killing him?'

Reuel shook his head.

Balitoth continued, 'I will do everything in my power to help you, but you must tell me what is wrong. You can trust me to keep it secret, if that is what you want.'

Reuel studied him for a long moment while Balitoth's mind whirled with speculation about what could have upset Reuel so much.

'It *is* a secret,' Reuel said at last. 'A huge secret across the whole galaxy. A secret every Altairian promises not to reveal.'

Balitoth waited, resisting the urge to speak. *An Altairian secret? Not a Reuel-only problem,* he thought.

Reuel gave a deep sigh. 'I cannot do this alone, and would rather turn to you than to anyone else. But you must swear not to speak of it, ever, not even to hint that you know it.'

'Of course, I swear. I will do nothing without

consulting you first. What is it my friend?'

Reuel sat on his bed, Balitoth took the chair and leaned forward, elbows on knees.

'Have you met many Altairians?' Reuel began.

'Quite a few.'

'Have you ever seen a female?'

'No.' *Where is this going?*

'That is because there are none. All Altairians are male, but not all the time. Every few years, at different times, each adult Altairian will turn into a female. We call it the "ripening". No non-Altairian has ever witnessed it.

'There are signs when the ripening is approaching, and if we are off-planet, arrangements are made to return home. There we mate with someone who is still male, and have a child. The child is breastfed for a short while, to ensure its good health, and handed to the family to raise. Once breastfeeding ceases, we revert to being male.'

Balitoth interrupted. 'Is that what is happening to you? Are you... ripening?'

Reuel nodded and wrung his hands. 'There were no signs, no warning, and it is only a year since my previous ripening. I believe this was brought on by the shock of the Rayt.'

'Is there any way to stop it?'

'A drug has been developed for those who cannot get home - deep space explorers, for instance. But it must be taken at the first sign, and I did not have any signs.' He shrugged. 'I also do not have the drug and the ripening is upon me. It is too late to stop.'

Balitoth thought for a moment. It was a big surprise. 'I had no idea,' he said. 'Why do Altairians keep it so secret? Other species have different mating practices.

PACT guarantees non-judgement.'

'It just is. In spite of PACT guarantees, there are prejudiced people. Creating new life is sacred, and not to be mocked. Very rarely, one of us doesn't revert after the ripening, but stays female. These are called Taira and are revered. They form a priesthood and serve God. Every Altairian makes a solemn vow when they reach adulthood that they will never reveal it to anyone. I have just broken my vow.' His voice caught in his throat and he dropped his head.

Balitoth rushed to reassure him.

'I am deeply honoured that you trust me with this secret,' Balitoth said, laying his hand over his heart and bowing his head, 'but surely you must tell the captain, or the Doctor.'

Reuel's head shot up. 'No! No one else must know.'

'But we could ask the captain to find an Altairian ship. They could help you.'

'The captain would not divert without a good reason, and we cannot give him that reason. An Altairian ship would not help either. Do you know what would happen if they found out I had betrayed the trust of my people? I would be in disgrace, maybe I could never go home again.'

Tears began to fall once more.

'But worse than that,' he continued, 'I do not know what they would do to any non-Altairian who knows the secret. We can be violent in defending our own, you know.'

Balitoth's mind whirled. He must help his friend.

'Then we have to work out how to divert attention. Tell me, does the ripening incapacitate you? How do you change?'

'Um, ah,' Reuel tugged at the neck of his tunic.

'There are mild pains as the ... womb grows, and later the ... breasts, and there are emotional changes,' Reuel waved his hand at the mess, 'as you can see. Pregnancy, of course, is tiring, but I have never heard of anyone ripening and not mating. I am ignorant of what that will be like.'

'It is possible then you will be able to continue your duties, and not raise suspicion. Among my people, the breasts do not enlarge until later pregnancy, in preparation for breast feeding, so perhaps...' Balitoth stopped and shook his head, as if to clear it. 'I cannot quite come to terms with you and I discussing breastfeeding.' He laughed, a sound rarely heard.

Reuel smiled for the first time in days. 'I am glad I confided in you. I feel a great weight lifting, even if the future is going to be difficult.'

***

Balitoth first went to see Dr Nefar. He had to be persuaded not to see Reuel. Balitoth had a plan, now he would see if it worked. He breathed deeply as the sick bay door opened.

'Excuse me Doctor, are you busy?'

'Nothing I cannot put down,' Nefar looked up from his screen with a smile. 'How is Ensign Reuel?'

Balitoth came into sick bay and closed the door. 'He is well, that is what I came to see you about. I delivered your message, but there is no need for you to see him again.'

'Please allow me to be the judge of that, Lieutenant. Pain is a warning that must be heeded.'

'The pain is gone, I assure you he is all right. He is fit for duty.'

But Nefar wasn't going to be put off so easily. 'My records must be complete.' He waved at the screen. 'I recorded a problem, I must record the return to health.'

Balitoth drew another deep breath and moved on to phase two of his plan. 'Doctor, do you believe in patient confidentiality?'

'Of course. I would never disclose any information about a patient, except to the captain if it affected his ability to do his duty.'

'Well, what if there was information so confidential, it could not be revealed even to you?'

'What? I have never heard such a thing!'

'Now you have. Ensign Reuel is well and will report to you in a few days. It is vital you keep this confidential. Thank you Doctor.' Balitoth made a hasty exit and hoped the Doctor would be convinced.

***

Reuel examined herself in the mirror. Someone else would say they saw Reuel, just a little changed. Reuel saw a stranger. She had changed so much in just a few days. She didn't remember the changes being so alarming before. Her face was softer, fuller, and especially her lips. They looked like they needed to be kissed. *I can't think that about my own reflection!* she thought, shaken.

She looked again. Her breasts were small, but, along with the slight bulge of her stomach, they gave her figure the soft curves of a female. She shook her head. This time, she couldn't enjoy it. *I can't be a female,* she thought, *I must be the male they all expect.*

Her eyes filled with tears, another female reaction. Her emotions were all over the place. She wiped her eyes with the back of her hand and turned away from the mirror to get dressed.

It was so hard not to think of the last time - her first time. She had been jealous of friends who had their first ripening before her. Her youthful angst was increased with the thought that she might not ripen at all. In fact, when it came, she was glad to have seen others, because it gave her an idea of what to expect. Her friends from the Academy on Altair went from enjoying the rough and tumble of youths messing about together to batting their eyelids and swinging their hips.

As soon as the ripening signs appeared, an older person - usually the parent, but not always - came to support and guide them. Her parent had supported her, but her best friend Arvad was the most important one.

Arvad had ripened a whole year before and had completed the post-ripening transition and returned to being male. They became close in a new way while Arvad was female. Relationships between male and female were subtly different to those between males. Once the places were switched, Reuel had been glad Arvad had gone first, because he was there for her when her turn came. She couldn't think of anyone who she would rather have as the father of her baby.

This time there would be no baby. Reuel felt her eyes grow moist again and her throat constrict. *Stop it!* She punched her pillow. Better to be angry than soft. Better to be fierce and determined and defiant. But it was so hard.

How long would it take until it was over? A normal ripening took about ten months. The change to female took a few days, the baby was conceived, born eight months later, and breastfed for about four weeks. Then he was handed over and the change back to male took a few days more. Reuel knew she was ready, but the baby was not going to happen, so at what point would the body decide to change back? How long would she have to pretend to be male?

Chapter 23

Reuel told Balitoth she feared she would have to hide as her face started to soften and she was still short tempered. That would be hard to explain. On a small ship, everyone was needed, she couldn't stay on the sick, especially as that would require a report from the MO. Balitoth managed to get the two of them assigned to the starboard plasma cannon repairs.

Because the cannons were in the shuttle bay, it could be depressurised, so they would be in space suits and not working near any of the other crew. Reuel was an expert in low gravity, so it wasn't hard to fix. The rest of the time she kept her head down. When her breasts started to show, Balitoth helped her to bind her chest to keep them flatter.

Balitoth watched Reuel work. Was it his imagination that Reuel's movements were more delicate now she was female? No point speculating, it helped no one. What was beyond doubt was the spasms of pain he could see Reuel experiencing.

'I see you are having pains,' Balitoth said, switching to a private comm channel. 'Do you need to rest?'

'I cannot take the chance someone will arrive and ask why I am not working,' said Reuel. 'I will continue here, so I appear to be working. I am grateful for your help.' She smiled at Balitoth, who was sure she batted her eyelids. Balitoth had to turn away.

***

As they worked in silence, Reuel thought about her situation. On Boka she knew an unexpected fear, of being tortured. Now, she feared an unexpected event, her ripening. The shock from encountering a Rayt, the emotional turmoil of having a living myth before her, must have caused hormone changes and they in turn must have triggered the change because females are better able to deal with emotions. She prayed for forgiveness for telling Balitoth and for strength for the coming days.

Her last time was a time of joy. Everyone rejoiced that her maturity had come, and a new life was coming. She was glad too, because no one was allowed to leave Altair until they had had one child, a replacement for themselves. Once you had your replacement you were free to go wherever you wanted.

The mating too was a wonderful event, made special because she was able to mate with her best friend. She hoped she would be around for one of her friend's ripenings, so she could return the favour. Her eyes grew moist thinking about it. The memory gave her some comfort.

This time was so different. No one ever spoke about ripening without mating, it was unheard of. Now she thought about it, surely she wasn't the first? She didn't know, and that was the fear - the unknown. Ripening was such a precious time, but not this time. Now she must wait to see how her body reacted without the mating.

Now also it was overshadowed by Tanu, whatever he was. His telekinetic power was clear, what other powers did he have that he had not told them? How could they be sure the suppressant drug worked? That added to her fear, was another twist in her gut.

***

When their shift was finished, Balitoth and Reuel repressurised the shuttle bay and changed out of their spacesuits in the cargo bay. Reuel decided to tidy their toolkit, as it had got messy while they worked. It slowed work down a lot if you couldn't find the tool you wanted.

'You go ahead,' Reuel said. 'I will not be long.'

'Thank you,' said Balitoth and left. Reuel put the toolkit straight and stowed it under the seat. She was leaving the cargo bay when she almost bumped into the captain.

'Oh, sorry sir,' she came to attention, but kept her head down. *What is he doing down here?* she thought.

'As you were, Ensign.' Darrow smiled, and then looked at her closer and frowned. 'Are you all right? You look different somehow.'

This was the moment Reuel had been dreading. She wanted to scream, 'leave me alone' but this was the captain.

'Is something wrong?' The Captain reached out to grasp her arm.

Reuel instinctively moved away and realised that made everything even worse. As the panic rose she forced herself to smile and shrugged. 'It is all right sir, but I need a shower after being in a suit all shift.'

Darrow smiled. 'I know what you mean. It must be the lighting in here. Carry on.'

Darrow went on his way and Reuel sagged against the wall. Her heart was beating fast. *How much longer?* she thought. *Taira intercede for me.*

Luckily for Reuel, she didn't have to mix with the crew again. In the mid-afternoon, ship's time, Commander Blackwell declared the internal repairs completed and Captain Darrow gave the crew free time until the smugglers left. That left Reuel free to stay in her cabin and not risk discovery.

***

Balitoth returned from the mess hall to find Reuel doubled up in pain on her bunk. She had removed her chest binding and her figure showed her new, generous curves. With the softening and rounding of facial features, Reuel looked, and indeed now was, very feminine. Beads of sweat stood out on her brow. Balitoth had rarely seen anyone in so much pain. Had he not taken an oath to keep Reuel's secret, he would have called the doctor. He dropped to his knees beside the bed.

'What is the matter? What can I do for you?'

'I am in great pain, and... need.' Reuel flushed red against the bright pink of her skin, and turned away.

Balitoth held back the idea, he wasn't sure of the protocols in this situation, but Reuel had become his close friend and it hurt to see him - her! - in such pain. He decided if he offended now, he was sure they would work it out later. 'You need to mate?'

Reuel nodded.

Balitoth looked at his friend. Neither of them knew what would happen to a ripened Altairian who didn't mate. And it wasn't as if, with the new curves and all that she wasn't attractive. And she was still Reuel, someone Balitoth cared a great deal for.

'Could I...?

'No, my friend, but thank you for the offer.' Reuel smiled. 'I will pray for relief and try to sleep.'

'I will sit with you.'

Balitoth pulled up the chair and sat by the bed, but after a while decided, oath or not, he couldn't see her suffer any longer. He slipped out and went to sick bay. Nefar was using a handheld regenerator on Hoy's right forearm.

'Hi Balitoth,' Hoy said, 'trust me to get too close to a plasma duct, right after the Captain said we had free time.'

Balitoth nodded to Hoy, but concentrated on Dr Nefar.

'Doctor, may I speak with you privately?'

'Certainly,' Nefar said, 'give me one minute.'

By the time Nefar finished work and Hoy left, Balitoth was agitated.

'What is it Lieutenant? It is not like you to show agitation, I am concerned.'

Even now, Balitoth hesitated. 'You are sworn to confidentiality, is that not so?'

'Absolutely, but what is wrong with you?'

'Not with me, with Reuel. What do you know about Altairian sexuality?'

'Reuel?' Nefar frowned at the change of patient, then light dawned. 'Oh no, is he ripening?'

Now it was Balitoth's turn to be surprised. 'You know about the ripening?'

Nefar smiled. 'It may be the Altairians' greatest secret, but Reuel is not the first one to be caught away from home.' He started to bustle about the synthesiser, making drugs. 'How long has this been going on?'

Balitoth thought. 'She told me two days ago, but about a week, I think.'

'She? Oh, it is coming to a head then. Come, there is no time to waste.'

Nefar grabbed his bag and put two phials in it. They

left sick bay and headed for the cabin, where Reuel was in the same condition as when Balitoth left - doubled up with abdominal pain. When she saw Nefar, she recoiled, but Nefar took her arm and pulled her back towards him.

'Don't worry, Ensign,' Nefar said, 'I have dealt with this before. I wish you had come to me sooner. This secrecy is nonsensical.'

While Nefar prepared the hypospray, Reuel turned to Balitoth.

'I thought you were my friend. How could you betray my confidence? You traitor!'

'I could not see you suffer any longer,' Balitoth said, but Reuel turned away from him.

Nefar gave her two shots, one for the pain and the other to correct the hormonal imbalance. 'That should end the ripening,' he said to Balitoth. 'Keep an eye on him, her, and let me know immediately if it worsens. You did the right thing.'

Nefar left and Balitoth sat by the bed. Reuel turned her back on him.

'I will be here for you,' Balitoth said, 'as your friend, whatever you think. Sometimes the presence of a friend is a comfort.'

Balitoth sat with her for several hours, until her agitation and fever subsided. Only then did he move up to his own bunk and try to catch some sleep.

When Balitoth awoke the next morning and climbed down he found Reuel pale and still in bed. He touched her arm, Reuel's eyes opened and she glared.

'It is over, and so is our friendship.'

'Thank the gods,' said Balitoth, ignoring the friendship comment. 'How are you?'

'I do not wish to speak with you,' Reuel snapped.

'You betrayed me.'

Balitoth stepped back. 'Dr Nefar knew about the ripening already. He had dealt with it before, and was able to help you. I could not see you suffer. Now please, how are you?'

'Weak, but I felt it pass some hours ago, and my strength is starting to return. In a day or two I will be back to normal.'

Balitoth tilted his head to the side. 'Surely you were always normal. It is normal for Altairians to swap sex, is it not?'

Reuel frowned. 'Yes, but do not ever say that aloud again.'

Chapter 24

The comm came to life at midday ship time.

'Captain, you will find your crewman where you left him.'

Darrow, on the bridge, called Parks and headed for the airlock. Within ten minutes he was suited up.

Parks went to the bridge and scanned the area. He confirmed the trail of a ship leaving the moon.

'Full scans,' Darrow said.

He left the airlock and made his way to the crater's edge in loping strides. He climbed the rocks and as his head rose above the top he could see Stubbs on the ground. Stubbs gave a feeble wave and rose up on his elbows as Darrow jumped down.

'Thank God,' Darrow said. 'Are you all right?'

'Hurt my leg,' Stubbs said, 'and I'm starving.'

Darrow bent down, grabbed him by the shoulders and looked in his face. It was a sickly shade of blue-grey. 'Did they mistreat you?'

'Not really, sir. They locked me in a shuttle to save my air supply, and gave me water, but nothing else.'

'How did you hurt your leg?'

Stubbs took a few shallow breaths before he replied. 'When I climbed over the rocks to fetch the splicer, the guy pushed me down and kicked me. I think it's broken.'

Darrow checked Stubbs' air gauge, but there was plenty. Why did he look like his air was running out?

Stubbs continued. 'They didn't care, wouldn't even look at it. Geller said it was my own fault.' He gasped and shook his head.

Darrow spoke over the comm link. 'Tell Dr Nefar to suit up, come to the airlock and bring a stretcher.' He said to Stubbs, 'Dr Nefar will look at it, I want him to give you a complete physical anyway. Let's get you back on board, I'll debrief you later.'

They were silent for a few minutes, just the sound of Stubbs' laboured breathing.

'Who's Geller?' Darrow asked as they waited for Nefar.

'He's their leader. Nasty piece of... work.' Stubbs swayed and Darrow grabbed him. 'Sorry, sir, feel a bit woozy.'

'Where's Nefar?' Darrow asked over the comm.

'I am leaving the ship now,' Nefar replied and expertly made his way to them in great strides, towing a hover stretcher.

'He thinks his leg is broken and his breathing isn't right,' Darrow said.

Nefar looked concerned. 'There is nothing I can do for him in this suit. We must get him on board as quickly as we can.'

They lifted Stubbs between them and laid him awkwardly on the stretcher. The bulky equipment on his back got in the way. Darrow let Nefar lead as they returned to the airlock.

'Sorry to have caused so much trouble, sir.' Stubbs said once they were in the airlock, waiting for it to cycle.

'It wasn't your fault, you're not in any trouble, Ensign. We've been pulling the scanners apart trying to find out why we didn't detect the smugglers when we arrived.'

The display finally signalled green and the inner door opened. Tomos was there and so was Parks, who started unfastening Stubbs' suit. Tomos moved to help.

'Be careful,' Darrow said, working on his own suit, 'his leg is injured.'

It took the three of them to remove Stubbs' suit and lay him back on the hover stretcher. There was a lot of blood on his leg. They were moving off when Stubbs gave a cry and a low, rattling moan. Nefar bent over him as Tomos cried out.

'Sir, the monitor readings! He's dead!'

***

Nefar banned Darrow from sick bay so he paced up and down the corridor outside. Nefar had quickly established that Stubbs couldn't be saved and he and Tomos were now doing an autopsy. Darrow was confused. Stubbs had a broken leg and hadn't eaten properly for days. How could he die? It didn't make sense.

Darrow was dimly aware of the other activity about the Kestrel. Parks had ordered the external repairs to begin immediately and marshalled everyone into suits and outside. Blackwell hated space suits and considered his seniority gave him exemption, so he wouldn't go. He was checking systems on board as the repairs were done. No one knew about Stubbs, so the mood was upbeat and eager to be back to work.

So no one saw Darrow pacing. No one saw the grief on his face.

The sick bay door opened and Tomos slipped out, his head down. Nefar beckoned Darrow in. He looked around.

'Where is he?'

'In his casket,' Nefar said. 'I have not had time to

check his preferences. Tomos is excused duties for the next few hours. He is not dealing with it well, but this is something he will have to learn to deal with if he continues as a medic.'

'Yes yes, of course,' Darrow said impatiently. 'What about Stubbs?'

Nefar sighed. 'It was a pulmonary embolism. A large blood clot formed at the site of his broken leg because it wasn't treated, and he was left immobile. It was carried in his bloodstream to his lungs. I am so sorry, Captain.'

Darrow was silent, stunned. Eventually he whispered, 'A blood clot?'

Nefar nodded.

'Bastards!' Darrow made Nefar jump. 'They killed him by neglecting him, just as surely as if they'd shot him. I won't let this rest.'

There was an awkward pause. Nefar broke the silence.

'What now, Captain?'

Darrow's shoulders slumped. 'I have to break it to the crew.'

'Captain, may I suggest you wait until this evening? The repairs must take priority. As far as I know, the majority of the repairs will be done by then. Also, Tomos needs some time to recover. It is only fair for him to attend.'

Darrow ran his fingers through his hair. 'I guess I could use some time too.'

Darrow shut himself away in his quarters. He had to do something. He couldn't help feeling responsible. His mind pored over every detail of Stubbs' hostage taking. What could he have done differently? He went to his console and called up the scans from Kestrel's approach to the moon. They had orbited to check it was uninhabited and the scans showed nothing. How did they miss the smugglers' ship? He checked the scans again. They *must* have missed something. But there really was nothing.

A cloaking device? The Prin had cloaked ships, but their technology was far advanced and they were out beyond the galaxy rim. Darrow knew none of the species involved in PACT were even close to cloaking technology. This was strong grounds for an investigation. He would suggest it in his report. Still, it wouldn't bring Stubbs back.

Darrow looked up Stubbs' personnel file. No next of kin listed, no preferences over burial. It seemed like Stubbs had no family but the crew. He had been on board for two years and during that time had grown from a scrap of a kid into a young man finding his place. If, no when, he passed his engineer exam, Darrow was planning to recommend him for promotion. What a waste!

***

That evening they all gathered in the mess hall, eager for news. Darrow tasted bile as he thought of what he had to say. The crew were all cheerful: the repairs were nearly done and Stubbs was back safely. Only he wasn't. Darrow raised his voice to get their attention.

'I have some bad news. When we retrieved Roy Stubbs from the smugglers he had a broken leg, which had been left untended for days. Dr Nefar tells me a blood clot developed at the break and when he was moved it went to his lungs. It was a pulmonary embolism. I'm afraid Stubbs is dead.'

He waited for the hubbub to die down. 'It's a tragedy, no mistake, and I won't miss any opportunity to hunt those smugglers down. But right now they've gone and we can't track them. The sooner we finish the repairs, the sooner we can look for them.'

'What about Stubbs' funeral, sir?' Tomos asked. His face was tear-streaked.

'He left no instructions, so his casket will be sent into the sun once we leave this moon. You will all have a chance to say something when we send him off.'

The crew were silent.

Parks spoke up. 'We'll finish the repairs tomorrow. Get some rest tonight. If anyone wants to talk, I'll be in my cabin.'

Darrow nodded. 'Dismissed.'

***

When Balitoth and Reuel returned to their cabin, Reuel was visibly upset. Balitoth showed no emotion as usual, but Reuel guessed he was also upset. Reuel sat on the bottom bunk and Balitoth took the chair. Reuel's cranial spines were rigid with shock, but started to soften and gently writhe as she let her emotion out.

'It is such a shock,' Reuel said, wiping her eyes with the back of her hands. 'Poor Stubbs, how awful.'

'It is indeed unfortunate,' Balitoth said, 'and so unnecessary. I do not suppose the smugglers even know about his death.'

Reuel's eyes blazed. 'Are you sympathising with the smugglers? It was their direct action that caused Stubbs to break his leg, and their inaction to leave it untreated. The blood is on their hands.'

Balitoth raised a hand as if to ward off the attack. 'I

was not sympathising with the smugglers, merely saying they don't know the outcome of the way they treated Stubbs. I agree with you, they are guilty, whether they know it or not.'

'Speaking of guilty, what has been happening with Tanu?'

'His mental powers are still suppressed, his horn is hidden with a headband as you saw in the meeting, and he is mingling with the crew.'

Reuel scowled. 'He could still sabotage the ship, with all the repairs going on, he does not need powers to do that. I still believe he is dangerous.'

'What could he do to convince you he is harmless? He is pleasant and helpful and the crew suspect nothing. He is not allowed near any critical systems. He spends most of the time in Commander Parks' cabin, reading.'

'So he has won you over already. Our friendship counts for nothing, as you showed when you betrayed my trust with Dr Nefar.'

'I believe I may have saved your life,' Balitoth said curtly, 'or at least saved you from a lot more suffering. As for Tanu, I have watched him when I can, aware of your concerns. Remember what the Captain said about any further attacks on him.'

There was a knock on the door. Reuel jumped.

'Ensign Reuel, it is Dr Nefar, come to see how you are.'

Balitoth let Nefar in.

'I see the crisis has passed,' Nefar said after performing a quick scan. 'You should revert quite quickly now, after this.' He administered a hypospray that made Reuel wince.

'Thank you Doctor,' Reuel said, his spines writhing.

'I am sorry you were brought in.'

'Now, there is no need for that, Ensign, the Lieutenant did the right thing. Unconsummated ripening can be fatal, you know. Do you think you are the first Altairian to ever be caught away from home? This secrecy is nonsense! These days there is no prejudice about sexual matters. Secrecy always causes problems. Did you know the first egg a Kohathi lays is non-viable? How devastating would that be if the youngling didn't know?'

Balitoth and Reuel looked at each other in surprise. They didn't know the doctor's people laid eggs. Nefar bustled off, oblivious.

***

The following morning the atmosphere was subdued, but lifted slightly with the announcement from Commander Blackwell that the repairs were complete. Darrow called for a standard calibration check as each system was brought back online. He had all the stations manned on the bridge: Chambers on helm, Hoy on navigation, Reuel on scanners, Parks on weapons, and Balitoth on comms. The bridge was so crowded Darrow had to stand. Tomos was with Blackwell in Engineering. The engines powered up, the VTOL thrusters kicked in and on Darrow's command the Kestrel lifted off the moon, a perfect takeoff.

Darrow spoke to Reuel. 'Full long-range scan, Ensign, check for engine emissions, anything that will indicate the direction of the smugglers' ship.' He turned to Chambers. 'Slow orbit round the moon, Lieutenant.' Darrow thumbed the comm. 'Engineering, how are the engines looking?'

'Everything looks fine, Captain,' Blackwell said.

'We're doing a couple of orbits and then we'll head off. Let me know if there's any cause for concern.'

'Aye aye, sir.'

A few minutes later Darrow confirmed with everyone that all systems were working. Before leaving orbit he asked Reuel about the long range scans.

'Anything, Ensign?'

Reuel shook his head. 'Sorry sir, there is too much local traffic to identify one particular ship.'

Darrow dropped his head and muttered, 'One day, one day.' He looked up. 'Set course for this system's sun. Let's give Stubbs a good send-off.'

***

The Kestrel was in orbit just outside the gravity well of the Casparan system's sun. The whole crew were gathered in Engineering for Stubbs' funeral. Bridge controls had been transferred to Engineering and Hoy had volunteered to man the console during the service, so he could be present and monitor the ship at the same time. Engineering was where the casket capsule could be launched towards the sun, but it was an appropriate place for Stubbs, as this was where he had worked.

The crew stood around the capsule as Darrow began.

'We are gathered on this solemn occasion to say farewell to our crewman Ensign Roy Stubbs. He was taken from us much too soon and is a sad loss to this crew. He has no family, so we shall be his family and always remember him. Those who want to speak may do so now.'

There was a short silence and then Blackwell cleared his throat and spoke. 'Roy came from a rough background, and everything he achieved, he did on his own. His life could have gone the same way as most of his childhood friends, but he wanted more. Ironically, when his parents were killed in a house fire, he was sent away to foster care, and this was the break that enabled him to get a better education. He was a fighter and though a bit rough around the edges, was always ready to learn. He had ambitions that will now never be realised. I will miss him.'

Tomos spoke softly in the silence that followed. 'We were becoming good friends and I admired him. He told me he wanted to transfer to a base because being out in space was too dangerous -' He choked and couldn't continue.

The silence stretched out this time, and Darrow decided no one else was willing or able to speak.

'Ensign Stubbs listed no religion or burial rites on his records, so I will use the old words: Ashes to ashes, dust to dust. Goodbye Roy, thank you for your service. I promise that if those smugglers and their leader Geller ever cross my path again, I will get justice for your death.'

Darrow nodded to Blackwell, who put his hands on the capsule to push it into the launching tube. The other crew members each put a hand on to join him. Then Blackwell closed the door and pushed the launch button. With a soft hiss, the Kestrel released the precious cargo and Hoy watched on the sensor screen as it was drawn into the sun's gravity.

Chapter 25

The following day Captain Darrow got an urgent call to meet Blackwell in Engineering.

'We have an emergency, Captain. We've been sabotaged.'

'What?' Darrow had been hoping for a quiet time, to give the crew time to get over Stubbs' death. 'How serious is it? Do we know who did it?'

'I'm pretty certain it was the Casparans, when they did the repairs.' Blackwell rubbed his hand over his face. Darrow thought how stressed he looked. 'Once they found out about Tanu,' Blackwell continued, 'they wanted to be sure we never got back with the information about him.'

'But they sent pursuit ships!'

'To stop the Bokans getting their hands on him. And don't forget, we rescued him. They hadn't expected that. They still wanted him for themselves.'

'How serious is it?'

Blackwell picked up a scanning screen and walked Darrow over to a panel near the engines. He switched it on and the schematics of what was behind the panel showed on the screen.

'There is a time-delay device designed to go off after we were away from Caspar, to rupture the fuel line and ignite it where it enters the engines. We wouldn't have stood a chance if it had gone off, thankfully it was damaged in the attack. As it is, it could go off at any moment. We found it just now by accident.'

'Can you remove it or make it safe?'

'Not easily, I'm afraid. Once the engines started on

Caspar the area was irradiated. We may not have time to shut the engines down and wait for it to clear, and the radiation will spread if the panel is removed sooner. So we would have to seal the whole of Engineering and send someone in with a radiation suit to remove it. Then we need to flush the atmosphere and purify the radiation before anyone can get back into Engineering.'

'How long?'

'Forty-eight hours at least. And we dare not restart the engines without someone in Engineering, so we would be adrift for the whole time. Ideally we ought to get everyone into the shuttles in case it goes off.'

Parks arrived and caught the end of the conversation. He gave a snap salute and dived right in.

'What's this about being adrift? And the shuttles? I was just about to report all the reports are done. Commander Blackwell was the last one to check with.'

'We've been sabotaged by the Casparans,' Darrow said, 'and we can't remove it without irradiating the whole of Engineering.'

Parks whistled, then clicked his fingers. 'There is one solution, Captain, but you're not going to like it. I'll bet Tanu could do it without even opening the panel.'

Darrow drew a quick breath as if he was going to say something, and sighed. 'I said we couldn't keep him drugged forever, but I didn't expect to have to make that decision so soon.' He turned to Blackwell. 'Is there no other way?'

Blackwell shook his head. 'We don't know when it will explode, we've no time. But I'm not happy about restoring Tanu's powers Captain, what else might he do?'

Parks opened his hands and shrugged. 'But it's that

or die, not much of a choice. He seems like a nice guy, you know. How else are we going to find out, except by letting him loose?'

Darrow made his decision. 'Parks, go and fetch Tanu, bring him to sick bay.'

Parks saluted and left. Darrow went straight to sick bay. Dr Nefar was startled when he burst in.

'Doctor, how quickly can you reverse the effects of the suppressants you've been giving Tanu?'

'Within minutes, but I don't know how long it will take him to regain full control. Why would you do this?'

Tanu arrived with Parks and Darrow took him by the shoulders.

'You say you're no threat to us, and want to help. I need to know I can trust you.' He scrutinised Tanu's expression looking for any sign of treachery, but the man met his gaze steadily.

'What can I say Captain? I have no desire to hurt anyone or take over the ship. I owe you my life. I want to help in any way I can.'

Darrow stepped back and looked at Tanu and Nefar. 'The Casparans sabotaged us, and we can't remove the device without irradiating the whole of Engineering and being adrift for two days with no engines. We need you to disconnect the device without opening the panel. Can you do that?'

'I'll need to see schematics so I can visualise what I need to do. It's much harder when I don't know exactly what I'm doing. An active scan would be even better.'

'I'll arrange it. Doctor, reverse the drugs and get him fit as soon as possible.' Darrow turned to go. 'Parks, when he's ready, fetch him to Engineering.'

Within seconds an alarm went off throughout the

ship, and the captain's voice came over the comm system. 'All hands are to make their way to the shuttles and leave the Kestrel. Please do so calmly and quickly. This is not a drill.'

Everyone began hurrying to the shuttle bay. In Engineering, Parks and Tanu did not appear. Instead, Parks was on the comm.

'Captain, you need to come back to sick bay.'

Darrow arrived to find Tanu sitting on a bed with his head in his hands. 'What's the matter? Is he OK?' he asked Parks.

'He's an empath,' said Parks. 'His powers started to come back, but he's picking up the emotions from everyone. He's overwhelmed.'

Tanu looked up and swayed. He had removed his headband and his 'horn' was turning red. 'I feel people's emotions, strong emotions,' he gasped. 'Fear, rage, desperation. This is awful. Someone is in despair, I can't think straight.'

'I'm sorry,' Darrow said, 'the rage is mine.'

'And mine,' Blackwell chipped in. 'I will try to calm down, for everyone's sake.'

Darrow took a deep breath. 'Look, you have to control it. We need you to think calmly to destroy this bomb, or we'll all be in more than despair.'

'I haven't felt this for some time, Captain. I didn't expect it. Fear from those who know about the bomb, yes, but this is different.' He groaned.

Parks lifted Tanu's arm over his shoulder and helped him off the bed. Darrow supported him on the other side. They almost dragged him towards Engineering. A thought occurred to Parks.

'Do you detect emotions less strongly with greater distance? As the shuttles take the crew to a safe distance, will you feel it less?'

'Yes!' Tanu gasped.

There was a slight bump as a shuttle took off, and Tanu found his feet.

'That's better,' he said. 'Whoever is so desperate is on that shuttle. I can think now.'

As they entered Engineering, Tanu asked, 'Am I to be left alone with it?'

'No,' Darrow assured him, 'Commander Blackwell and I will be there to guide you and operate the scanner. Everyone else is going to a safe distance. They are holding the last shuttle for Parks.'

***

Blackwell was waiting in front of an innocuous panel in the wall. Parks wished Tanu luck and left. Tanu shook his head and stood on his own. A scanner screen had been rigged on the wall to the right of the panel. Blackwell was operating the controls to show an image of the tubes, circuits and wires inside. Blackwell went over it with Tanu calmly, slowly, as if there were no hurry.

'It's important you know exactly what to do. This rectangle here is the device. See how it's inserted into the fuel feed? It's powered by connections here, and here. You need to cut the power and remove the device, but that will open up the fuel line, so you need to reconnect it as fast as possible. If any fuel leaks towards this area here, and it will ignite, and explode.'

Blackwell looked at Tanu to be sure he understood. Tanu nodded.

'However,' Blackwell continued, 'there is a possibility the device has a sensor which may set it off if it's moved. Can you prevent the sensor registering as you move it?'

Tanu blinked and shook his head to clear it. 'I will be honest with you. Normally, this would not be a problem. I don't know how fine my control is right now. I will do my best.'

'Thank you,' said Darrow. 'Go ahead.'

Tanu paused. 'Captain, there is no need to risk your lives as well as mine. Please get to safety, both of you.'

'This is my ship, I stay.' Darrow turned to Blackwell. 'I'm capable of directing a scanner too, so you --'

'It may be your ship,' Blackwell interrupted, 'but these are my engines. No one takes care of my baby like I do. Let's get on with this.'

The next few minutes were tense as Tanu's "horn" began to glow as he stared at the panel. The scanner showed the components moving slowly, disconnecting themselves. As the fuel line came apart, the fuel began to flow through the gap and stopped as if meeting a barrier. The device moved out of the way and the fuel flowed back into the line as the two ends met and sealed. Tanu sagged and turned.

'It's done, Captain. Do you want the device left there as evidence? I would prefer to destroy it to make sure it's safe.'

Darrow let out the breath he was holding. 'Destroy it, if you can, and if it's safe to do so. We've no proof it was the Caspar, and we wouldn't get far trying.'

Tanu turned back to the panel and concentrated. As they watched on the scanner the device disintegrated to tiny pieces, which settled on the bottom of the compartment.

Blackwell slapped Tanu on the back. 'Well done, lad!

I wouldn't have believed it if I hadn't seen it with my own eyes. You've saved us all!'

Tanu almost fell over and raised his arm to protect himself. Darrow reached out to steady him and gave him a smile.

'Sorry about the enthusiasm. The Commander was just congratulating you. Do you need to rest now?'

Tanu looked up and a smile lit up his face. 'Oh no, Captain. I feel wonderful.' His face clouded. 'Will you be putting me back on the suppressant again now?'

'Is that what you want? Are the emotions of others too much to bear?'

'It's something I must get used to if I'm to function. But are you going to stop me?'

Darrow only paused for few seconds.

'I don't think so, after this. Anyway, I rather think you could prevent us if you wanted to, eh?'

'I told you, Captain, I am not a man of violence --'

'It's all right, I believe you. Come on, let's give everyone the all clear and get them back on board. You're going to be a hero.'

Chapter 26

Darrow had to speak to the crew about Tanu. Up to now the knowledge of Tanu's abilities had been restricted to the senior crew, but after the evacuation and Tanu destroying the bomb, there was no way to keep it quiet, especially if he was to have his mental abilities back.

He decided not to call a meeting, but see everyone individually, to gauge their reactions. As Captain, he could lay down the law, but Darrow didn't work that way unless he had to.

Balitoth and Reuel were going to be the hardest to convince, and he wasn't sure how Reuel would cope. Darrow couldn't shake the feeling there was something odd about Reuel lately. They were both off duty so Darrow visited their cabin first.

'So, you see I'm afraid Tanu's secret is out, and he will have his powers. How do you feel about that?'

'Captain, it is too dangerous,' Reuel said, looking up for a moment. Then he remembered his changed features and dropped his head. 'He could be deceiving us all.'

Darrow took a deep breath. 'The senior crew have decided he is genuine and not a threat. I take responsibility for that decision. I won't have you being disruptive, is that clear?'

'I will act just like the rest of crew, Captain,' Reuel said with a sigh, 'and pretend I didn't know. I think it is best, to avoid questions.' He kept his head down, so Darrow couldn't judge by his expression, but his spines were agitated.

There was a long pause. Then Balitoth spoke. 'You

must understand, sir, it is hard for Reuel. After so much fear...'

'I will never trust him, Captain, and will watch him closely,' Reuel said. 'But, I will obey you, and cause no trouble.'

Darrow left feeling that was all he could hope for at this stage.

Blackwell was perfectly happy to accept the man who had saved his ship, and Nefar was relieved to stop suppressing Tanu's powers. Parks and Hoy were more cautious, but willing to accept Darrow's decision. Parks raised the question of the emotions Tanu picked up when his suppressant was reversed.

'Someone in despair is a worry. Who do you think it can be?'

Darrow shrugged. 'Whoever they are, there's been no sign of anyone not doing their duty. So, for now at least, I'm prepared to carry on as if we knew nothing of the situation. Because in truth, without Tanu we wouldn't have known anyway. If they come forward because they can't cope, then we'll deal with it. I suggest you look into Alliance policies regarding such a mental health issue, the last thing I want is anyone making things worse for the sufferer. Let's get back on patrol.'

Tomos was off duty, in his cabin. He was surprised, but at least it gave him something else to think about, other than Stubbs.

'Aren't you afraid, sir, he will control our minds?' Tomos said when Darrow told him.

'No fear of that.' said Darrow quickly. 'He can't do that. His abilities are telekinesis and empathy. He picks up strong emotions, so if you have strong feelings about him, you had best say now.'

'No, no, Captain. If you think he's safe, that's good enough for me.'

Chambers was on duty on the bridge. He was not at all happy.

'Excuse me, sir, but how do you know he's not faking it, just to gain your trust?'

'He risked his life to save the ship, and I have seen enough of him to be convinced he's genuine. Dr Nefar thinks so too. Before you ask, he can't control minds, so we haven't been forced to think this way. I'm asking you to trust me now, you can make your own judgement when you get to know him.'

'Well, you made a judgement about me after the accident when I couldn't get a posting, and I'm very grateful, so I'll trust you now.'

Darrow went back to his office, thinking about his crew, who were now only nine instead of the regulation eleven.

***

When Tanu arrived in the mess hall a short while later, everyone knew what he had done and a cheer went up when he appeared. His embarrassment at this did not diminish the light in his eyes and the joy in his step at the recognition.

His physical appearance was different too. Instead of his long dark hair being loosely tied back, it was intricately braided. When Hoy commented, Parks described how he had watched as the hair braided itself, under Tanu's mental command.

'It was amazing to watch. He has such fine control, and to be able to do so many braids at once, as well. He's like a kid with a new toy, playing with everything, just because he can.'

'What's going to happen to him?'

'The captain's not decided yet, but none of us want him to be handed over to be experimented on. The senior staff have all been asked to come up with proposals. There's a meeting at 1600 hours tomorrow.'

As Reuel came into the mess hall and collected food, Tanu wanted to thank him, but as he moved towards him, he could feel the despair. *So this is where it comes from.* He steeled himself and spoke.

'I have been hoping to see you, Reuel. It was you who insisted they rescue me from the Bokans, and you came for me again on Caspar. I owe you my life. Thank you so much.'

Reuel dropped his head and muttered, 'There is no need. Please leave me alone.'

***

Tanu's empathy was causing him problems. On Cerebra everyone was a telepath or an empath, so thoughts and feelings were more guarded. Here, the crew were used to their emotions being private.

They could, for example, be angry but not show it. On such a small ship people had to get along. But inside they might be raging, and Tanu got the full force of it. He tried to hide it, because people felt it was an invasion of their privacy. Most of the time the crew's emotions were on an even keel and he was okay.

Except for one.

Reuel was suffering. He was hiding it well, because it seemed no one knew. Tanu so completely understood the feeling after his recent experiences that his heart went out to the sufferer, but he didn't know what to do.

He eventually went and stood outside the door of Balitoth and Reuel's cabin when he knew Balitoth wasn't there, and that confirmed it. There was something very wrong with Reuel. He was not just in distress, he was afraid.

Tanu stood outside the cabin in indecision. *What should I do? Should I report it? Why hasn't Reuel asked for help, spoken to the captain or gone to sick bay? I know, somehow, he hasn't. It's more than fear of the Rayt. Maybe he is afraid of being discovered. So I shouldn't report it.*

Maybe the fear is of something happening to him. What's that? Surely Balitoth knows? This has been going on for a while. He would have reported it if Reuel wanted him to. Should I speak to Reuel? He still doesn't trust me.

Maybe this will show him I am concerned for him.

Maybe he will think it's an intrusion.

Tanu turned away, hesitated, and turned back. He knocked.

'Who is it?' Reuel's voice came from inside.

'It is Tanu. Please may I speak to you?'

'Go away. I am not speaking to anyone, least of all to you.'

Tanu took a deep breath, and switched to Altairian. 'I know you are afraid, upset about something, confused perhaps?'

The cabin door opened. Tanu barely had time to focus on Reuel before he was dragged forward by a handful of his shirt and propelled into the room. He heard the door shut and he was reeling in a new direction. His spine hit the door and Reuel had him pushed up against it, snarling down at him.

Tanu was buffeted by emotions, his own and Reuel's,

and each as strong and violent in their way as Reuel's actions. Tanu was lost for words, he had no experience of anything like this.

'What do you know?' Reuel demanded.

'Only what you're feeling.' Tanu lifted his hands as if to ward off the emotional onslaught. 'I can't read minds, I keep telling you. I just pick up strong emotions. I was concerned for you.'

'Well, keep your concerns to yourself, or you will see how violent I can get. Leave me alone!'

Tanu closed his eyes and recoiled at the rush of aggression. Reuel held him while he opened the door and thrust him out. Tanu staggered down the corridor, up the stairs and back to his cabin, glad it was near the top of the stairs. Luckily Parks was out. He collapsed on a chair.

This was not the Reuel who had taken pity on him and rescued him. This was not the Reuel who had tried to kill him to protect others from a monster. This was something very different.

Someone very different.

***

Reuel's emotional condition made dealing with Tanu's presence hard. Tanu unfettered made it harder still. Tanu had been in a hopeless situation on Boka, until they rescued him. He was rescued again on Caspar. Of course, he was extremely grateful to the Kestrel crew.

Destroying the bomb was a great way for Tanu to show he cared for their safety. But he was saving himself too. Not everyone was completely won over, but the general consensus was that Tanu was a great guy, a hero.

There was no evidence of him tampering with anyone's mind, Reuel thought as he paced in the small area of his cabin, *but would it show? Subtle influencing of feelings and thoughts might not be noticed by anyone, not even the person themselves.*

The captain had offered to keep him on board for a while. Reuel wondered if Tanu had a hand in that decision. He assumed that eventually Tanu would be taken to PACT headquarters, or even to the Earth government, and handed over. Tanu couldn't want that. No one could guarantee how he would be treated or what he might be expected to do. Dropping him off anywhere else would mean a life on the run. Not a pleasant prospect.

But, Reuel worried, *if Tanu had his own ship and people to serve him and cover for him, life could be much sweeter. Why wouldn't he do all he could to win them over? It would be Rayt all over again, just a more benign dictatorship.*

And yet, Tanu seemed to be a gentle soul, filled with wonder, seeing what he ran away from home to see. He seemed innocent, he didn't know the way life worked, he had been sheltered. It was easy to respond, to take him under your wing, to feel the excitement of introducing him to the wonders of the universe. But was that what he wanted everyone to see?

Reuel realised his thoughts were as circular as his pacing back and forth. One thing he was certain of: Now Tanu had his powers it was vital to find a way to prove he was dangerous.

Chapter 27

Darrow met with Tanu and the senior staff in the mess hall: Parks, Hoy, Blackwell and Dr Nefar. Tanu looked worried.

Darrow began the discussion.

'I know this is difficult, so let's take it one thing at a time. Tanu has these unique abilities of empathy, telekinesis and languages, and wherever he goes people will seek to take advantage of him. He's not strong enough to defend himself and has no desire to live a life in hiding. The first question is, are we going to hand him over to the Planetary Alliance?'

Everyone looked at Tanu, and they all tried to speak at once. The gist of it was they were unanimous - Tanu was to be free. The relief on Tanu's face was obvious. In fact, he slumped back in his chair as if he was going to faint. Then he looked at the captain, who had not ratified the decision. Darrow smiled.

'Well, much as it goes against the grain of everything I've ever done, I agree with you. Handing over a weapon is one thing, but not when it's a sentient being. The next question then is what do we tell them about our mission?'

'We were sent to find the Bokan weapon,' said Hoy. 'How can we explain coming back without it?'

'No we weren't, actually,' said Parks, the depth of his thinking clear in the way his left index finger rubbed a diagonal across his chin.

'We were sent to investigate the rumours that the Bokans were developing a new weapon. What we found on Boka was a new and incredibly painful torture tool in that pain-giver thing that they used on Tanu and I.' He wagged his finger.

'We can report that and tell them the truth, that while on Boka, we found no evidence of any other substantiable rumour of weaponry.'

'In my experience,' said Nefar, 'it is always best to tell as much of the truth as possible. One of your Earth writers once said, "If you never tell a lie, you never have to remember anything." There is much has happened that we can tell exactly as it was. I suggest we omit reporting the Casparan sabotage unless we can convincingly report we fixed it ourselves.' He turned to Blackwell. 'Do you want to be a hero, Commander?'

Blackwell shook his head. 'Not me!'

'I can't believe we're sitting here making up lies to tell the authorities.' Hoy said.

Darrow ran his fingers through his hair. 'Technically,' he said, 'we're discussing telling them the truth, and the omission of certain facts that don't necessarily need to be revealed. Nefar is right, if we can tell as much of the truth as possible it makes it easier. It also has to fit in with what we've reported so far, after Boka and after Caspar.'

Tanu sat forward in his seat and Darrow nodded for him to speak.

'Captain, while I was a prisoner of the Bokans, I heard they were interrogating all strangers, and one actually died. There was an argument between some of the guards as to who would be blamed for his death. This could explain why your away team were captured, and myself.'

Parks nodded. 'What if we tell the truth that they were trying to use someone with psychic powers as a weapon, but make him the one who died? Everyone knows no one has been found with psychic powers of any substance. If they tried to force someone, it would likely have killed him. So the Bokans didn't have a weapon, and it appears they no longer have what they thought was a weapon, so they're no longer a threat.'

Now it was Hoy's turn to run with the story. 'The Bokans chased after us because they didn't want the information getting out. The Casparans had also heard about the Bokan weapon and thought we had it, which explains why they turned nasty. When we escaped, they detected the Bokans on our tail and came after us to stop them getting their weapon back. We didn't have it, so they were wrong.' He raised his hands. 'We're in the clear.'

Darrow let them enjoy themselves for a minute. 'OK, it sounds like we have a plan. I'll fine-tune it, and check with each of you if there are any loopholes. We will have to make sure all the crew are word-perfect. The last thing to consider is what to do with Tanu.' He turned to him. 'What do you want to do?'

Tanu's face clouded. 'I don't know, Captain. Everywhere I go my mental abilities betray me.' He looked towards the doctor. 'And I can't live without my talents. I'm not familiar with the other species - that's why I came out to meet them. If you know of anywhere safe, I would be grateful.'

There was an awkward silence, broken only by the rumble of the engines.

'Can Tanu stay on board for the time being?' Parks asked. 'I'm happy to share my cabin for a while and it would give us all time to get used to things. I'm sure we can think of something, but it doesn't have to be right now.'

'Very well,' Darrow said. 'Fast-Response Command

already know we rescued someone from Boka, so we just haven't dropped him off anywhere yet. Report to me if you have any ideas. Now, the repairs are finished, so let's get back on patrol. Dismissed.'

***

Tanu found staying in Parks' cabin the nearest thing to normal living he had experienced for a long time. He couldn't be sure how long it was since he left home, but home felt like a distant memory. He hadn't had much time to enjoy his freedom, what with the Bokans and the Casparans, and then the Rayt question and the bomb, but at last he felt whole again.

Now the past was settled, and the present at least was secured, he decided to enjoy it and worry about the future when it arrived. Now he was in a situation where he didn't have to hide who he was, and there was little fear of being abused. It felt very good indeed.

Cerebra was hidden from the outside universe, and he had learned almost nothing about anywhere else. Being here amongst these different species was something he hadn't experienced, and every day bought some nuance to the fore, like the non-human crew members not using contractions when they spoke.

He knew a bit about Altairians because of the shame of the Rayt episode of his own people's history, but meeting an Altairian made it so much more real. Back home the history of the Rayt was taught as a warning to watch out for anyone developing mind control abilities. But the stories concentrated on the Rayt and gave little detail about the Altairians.

It was a shame the Altairian on board wouldn't talk to him. His encounters with the Bokans and the

Casparans had taught him all the things he didn't want to learn. He suspected that without their fear and potential use of him, it might have been a different experience. Then there were the humans, who rescued him and helped him to recover. But he didn't know anything about them either.

When Parks came off duty, Tanu asked him question after question. He discovered Parks was a good person to ask, because of his years in security dealing with all the different species. Parks was also a great storyteller. Tanu felt like a little child, full of wonder and insatiable curiosity.

'Wait a minute,' Parks said one day, as they sat in their cabin, 'I think we're going about this all wrong. You're asking me whatever comes into your head, and trying to piece it together later. I think it would be much better if I gave you a basic introduction and showed you how to use the console to do your own research. I'm sure the captain will give permission for limited access, but it will be enough for what you need.'

'That sounds great,' Tanu said, 'but I don't know if I can operate the computer mentally. I've watched you, and I think I'll need to use the keys and the touch screen.'

'And learning to do that would be a bonus.' Parks pointed his finger. 'If you're going to hide what you are, you're going to have to get much better at doing things manually. You can't stay hidden forever, and you can't use your mental capabilities in public. You have to look and act like the rest of us.'

'I hadn't thought of that.' Tanu's shoulders slumped.

'Don't be defeatist, look on it as a challenge, a new skill to learn. Think of it, you'll be the only Cerebran with manual dexterity.'

'Not that they'll ever know.'

'Oh sorry, I shouldn't have mentioned it,' Parks said. 'The crew are bound to ask you questions, though, it's only natural. You mustn't let it upset you.'

Tanu sighed. 'You're right. I have a lot to learn. So, where do we start?'

'With PACT, I think,' Parks said, standing up and touching his chin to help him marshal his thoughts.

Tanu laughed.

'What?'

'You look like a schoolteacher in front of a class. Perhaps we should get you a sash.'

'Do Cerebran schoolteachers wear sashes? Our's wear robes.' Parks shook his head. 'We're getting off the subject already. PACT stands for the Planetary Alliance for Cooperation and Trade. It's a peaceful alliance between the various species with warp capability.

'At the moment the members are Earth, Altair, Zoa, Kohath, Caspar, Ochra and Anak. Most of the crew, including me, are from Earth. Reuel is Altairian, Balitoth is Zoan and Dr Nefar is Kohathi. PACT also includes their colony planets. When Boka discovered warp power they were invited to join, but they're a suspicious lot and we're still negotiating. You can look up each species on the console.' Parks stopped for a breath.

'The Kestrel is part of the PACT Fast-Response Fleet. We deal with incidents outside local space and sort out jurisdiction later. We also help with emergencies, transport of dignitaries, and do anything that will smooth relations between member states. We normally have eleven crew, nine at the moment, so you haven't met them all yet.

'When we're not busy we study, either for promotion

or other qualifications, or just subjects of interest. I think you ought to meet the crew and learn from them. Even the humans on board aren't all from Earth - young Tomos was born and raised on a cargo ship. He grew up in space, and has been to more places than any of us.'

Parks paused at Tanu's wide-eyed look.

'There's just so much to take in!'

'Well, you don't have to learn it all overnight. Take your time, get to know how people work.'

'But first,' Tanu said, moving to the console, 'I have to figure out how to use this computer.'

***

Later Tanu went to see the captain, who was working on the bridge.

'Captain, I want to help.'

'Help with what?'

Tanu shrugged and lifted his hands. 'Anything, something. I'm learning manual dexterity and I need to practice. Or I can use my mental powers. The ship needs maintenance or cargo shifting. There must be something I can do.'

Darrow thought for a moment. 'Come with me.'

Darrow led him out into the main corridor and all the way aft, to Engineering. Tanu hadn't paid much attention when he was in here before and he wasn't familiar with any kind of engine or ship's systems. He looked around in amazement.

The Engineering section stretched the full width of the rear of the ship, which, since the Kestrel was triangular, was the widest part. It also took up both decks. The upper deck, which they were on, was a wide gantry around three sides, making room for the engines in the centre and the rear. There were switches, dials and lights everywhere and several computer terminals. And it was noisy, with the constant hum of the engines much louder here.

'Commander Blackwell?' Darrow called.

'In here,' came a muffled voice, and a burly red-faced man climbed out of a service hatch. He didn't stand to attention, but he did offer a half-hearted salute. 'Captain.'

'Tanu here wants to make himself useful.'

'I'm practicing manual dexterity, sir,' Tanu said, trying to counter the wave of scepticism coming from the older man.

'You'll need that, if you're going to help me,' Blackwell said. 'Mind you, maybe your mental dexterity might come in useful. Come over here. See those loose wires inside this panel? They need connecting to those pins. I'm not so good at the fine stuff these days.'

'Like this?' Tanu said, as the wires neatly attached themselves.

Blackwell grinned. 'You can leave him with me, Captain, we'll get along fine.'

Chapter 28

Darrow received a call from Chambers, on duty on the bridge.

'Sir, we've a new mission - earthquake relief, but you're not going to like it.'

'I'll be right there,' Darrow replied, and stepped out of his office and onto the bridge. 'Why won't I like it, Lieutenant?'

'It's the Casparans, sir.'

Darrow's heart sank.

'Oh, that's rich. Shall I ask them where to send the bill? Change course, best speed.'

'Aye aye.' Chambers set the course change while he continued talking. 'There's been an earthquake on a Casparan colony planet, and there are no ships to take aid or supplies. I've forwarded the full message to your console. We're conveniently near, so to PACT we're the logical ones to send.'

'Yes, I see. PACT received my report on recent events, but they don't seem to consider that Caspar has a problem with us.' He opened the comm. 'Commander Parks and Lieutenant-Commander Hoy to my office.'

'Notify me at once if any more details come through.'

Darrow turned and left.

When Parks and Hoy reached his office, they sat around his desk.

'We have a new mission, which is going to present our first challenge regarding Tanu's presence. There's been a severe earthquake on Sabteca, a Casparan colony planet, and we are called upon to collect aid and supplies from Caspar and transport them to Sabteca. I had hoped to avoid this area of space for a while to let things blow over, but we're being sent back into the thick of it. Suggestions?'

'We'll have to keep Tanu hidden from the Casparans, sir,' Hoy said. 'We don't want them trying to take him again.'

'Why don't we tell them he died in the attack?' Parks suggested. 'They must know we took damage in the battle.'

'Both good ideas,' Darrow said, 'and it occurs to me we could claim we never found out about his powers. That way they'll think they're safe from repercussions and the secret is only with them.'

Parks chipped in again. 'The Casparans can't make a big fuss because they were holding Tanu against his will.' He leaned back in his chair and folded his arms. 'Tanu was with us, we took him to Caspar for help, and he should have been returned to us. They won't want his powers to be revealed, and they won't want anyone else to have the use of them. If we can convince them he died, they'll have to let the matter drop.'

Hoy said, 'Wait! They told us he had died and been cremated, so how could we have stolen him or indeed caused them any insult, incident or upset?'

'You're right,' said Darrow. 'Tanu will have to be confined to quarters while we're on Caspar. We don't want to risk anyone seeing him, and the away parties will have to be briefed not to mention his name.'

'Now,' said Parks, rubbing his hands together, 'what about this mission?'

Darrow gave them the details.

'It's basically transport they need,' Darrow said. 'Relief supplies, temporary housing, digging and lifting equipment. They haven't said how much, so we had better make as much room as we can. Parks, you check crew rotas and availability. I want as many crewmen as possible loading to reduce our time on Caspar, and all hands on deck once we reach Sabteca, but they still need to sleep.'

He checked his notes.

'Hoy, check the cargo bay and anywhere else we can store things. Parks will tell you who's available to help rearrange the cargo bay - it'll be safe to use Tanu for the preparation, he wants to be useful. Also check with Commander Blackwell about the maximum weight we can carry - it's not just a question of space but lifting capability.'

'Humans are bigger and stronger than the Casparans,' Hoy said with a smile, 'so that should speed up loading and unloading.'

'Yes.' Darrow checked his screen again. 'I think that's everything. Dismissed.'

When Parks and Hoy left, Darrow turned his mind to the question of Tanu. They were making trouble for themselves by sheltering him, but Darrow still didn't see anywhere else Tanu would be safe from exploitation. He would have to be hidden on Caspar, but perhaps he could help on Sabteca. No one would know him there, and with his horn covered, they wouldn't look at him twice. It would be a good experience for him, even if his physique wasn't up to any heavy duties.

***

The Kestrel soon approached Caspar and was hailed by their space traffic control.

Darrow was on the bridge to respond to the hail. 'PACT Fast-Response ship Kestrel reporting as earthquake relief for Sabteca colony. Captain Joseph Darrow here.'

'One moment please Captain.' The screen went to a holding pattern, green of course, with the symbol of an orange tree. Darrow recognised it as the Casparan flag.

During the pause Darrow said to Chambers with a smile, 'I'll bet there's a flag against us and now they don't know what to do.'

A new face appeared on the screen - the senior controller. He was an older man with a sour look on his face. 'You are not welcome here, Captain.'

'I can't imagine why, we did nothing wrong last time we were here,' Darrow said with a straight face. Then he shrugged. 'Of course, if you wish to deal with the earthquake on Sabteca as an internal affair, that's your choice. I will notify PACT that help is not required after all. They called us because we were the closest vessel. They seemed to think it was an emergency, clearly not. I apologise for the misunderstanding, we'll get out of your airspace. Kestrel out.'

'Wait! Please hold.'

The green and orange holding pattern filled the screen again and there was another pause during which Darrow amused himself imagining the discussion. They would rather have anyone else answer the emergency call, but here he was.

The death of the Prime Minister's son on board the Kestrel, added to his getting in to see the Prime Minister against their wishes was bad enough, but taking Tanu was so much worse. *The security authorities can't reveal we stole Tanu*, he thought, *because they shouldn't have kept him in the first place.*

He had to wipe the grin off his face when communication resumed. The senior controller looked even more waspish, as though the words tasted bitter.

'We thank you for your assistance, Captain. Do not land at the spaceport, proceed to the coordinates I am sending you where the aid is assembled. They are expecting you.'

'Roger that, Kestrel out.'

Tanu was perfectly happy to be locked in the cabin. He picked up on the strained reception and wanted to keep as far away from the Casparans as possible. Darrow had authorised him to have access to some basic training modules on the console. He may as well learn how the universe he now found himself in worked, and it would stave off any boredom. Darrow reminded himself to see he got fed while he couldn't go to the mess hall.

Unaware of the Kestrel's previous visit and the authorities' dim view of the crew, the staff at the supply depot were friendly and grateful that PACT was sending assistance. The man in charge met Darrow, Parks and Hoy as they disembarked.

'Welcome,' the man said, when Darrow introduced them. 'My name is Javan Rifath. We have gathered as much aid for Sabteca as we can, we need to see if it will all fit in your ship. We had hoped for a larger one, but time is short.'

He led them into an office in the depot. Before they could say anything, there was the sound of ground vehicles driven at speed and shouts from some of the workers.

Darrow made for the window where he saw armed security men spilling out of three vehicles and heading for the Kestrel. He threw open the door and ran towards his ship, Parks and Hoy right behind him.

'What's the meaning of this?' Darrow shouted. 'This is a PACT ship on an aid mission.'

A man dressed in black, with the green sash of officialdom across his chest, came striding towards Darrow.

'I require an interview with you, Captain,' he said.

'And I want some explanation for this.' Darrow waved his arms at the men who were now positioned around the Kestrel.

Rifath introduced them. 'This is Ser Togarma, our Head of Security. This is -'

'I know Captain Darrow,' Togarma said. 'I investigated when Desmar Barok, the Prime Minister's son, died on the Captain's ship.' He turned towards the Kestrel. 'This very ship. And now it is in more trouble.'

'I think you'll find that Ser Barok's death held no secrets,' Darrow said. 'Perhaps you should speak to his father, whom I visited only days ago.'

Togarma scowled and Rifath found something else to do and hurried away.

'Now, how can I help you, Ser Togarma?' Darrow asked through gritted teeth.

'There are some matters which need resolving.'

Darrow stared at him and tried not to smile. *I'll bet it was you that ordered Tanu's detention,* he thought, *and you're in trouble for losing him. This is your chance to get him back again and redeem your reputation.*

Since Darrow hadn't moved, Togarma said, 'I need to meet with you, Captain.'

'I thought that's what we were doing.'

'No, on your ship.'

'Why? Anything my ship did, it did under my command. You need to speak to me.'

'Captain, I must insist.'

'Ser Togarma,' Darrow said with exaggerated patience, 'I am going to lose my temper in a minute. You have no jurisdiction over my ship, unless you've been in touch with PACT and have a warrant.' He held out his hand for the warrant. It did not appear.

Togarma was getting red in the face. 'I can have it taken apart and searched.'

Darrow turned and walked away, looking around for Rifath, and shouted, 'Ser Rifath, please inform the government that the emergency rescue is being delayed by Ser Togarma.'

Darrow decided to get it over with so he returned to Togarma and put on a polite face. 'Perhaps we should go to my office. This way.' They started walking across the orange grass towards the Kestrel. Darrow motioned to Parks and Hoy to wait. 'While we speak, can we start loading the aid? This is an emergency you know.'

'That would not be wise, Captain, in case we ground your ship.'

'What?' Darrow stopped dead and turned to Togarma. 'You cannot ground a PACT fleet ship unilaterally. We came here to help, not to be treated like the enemy. If you do not want our help, then we will leave now.' He turned to Parks. 'Close the cargo bay doors and prepare for take-off.'

'Please stay calm, Captain,' Togarma said, 'it all depends on this interview. Shall we proceed?'

As they turned towards the ship, Darrow nodded to Parks, who spoke into his communicator. The cargo bay doors began to close.

***

Two security men fell into step behind Darrow and Togarma as they entered the Kestrel. They walked through the cargo hold on the lower deck, along the corridor past the cabins, and up the stairs. All the way Togarma was craning his neck to look into every nook and cranny. Darrow decided to take the bull by the horns. He stopped at the top of the stairs.

'You seem to be very interested in my ship,' Darrow said. 'Would you like a tour?'

'That would be good,' Togarma said, 'thank you.'

'As you see, the lower deck contains the cargo hold, shuttle bay, and 3 double cabins. I can show you the shuttle bay on the way out, since it's at the bow. Would you like to see a cabin? They're pretty much all the same, so you'll be able to get an idea of what they're like.'

Darrow bustled him downstairs again past the two men and knocked on a cabin door. Balitoth opened the door.

'Oh Captain, sir!' He looked at the people outside his door and snapped to attention, which startled Togarma. Balitoth was tall and stocky and his lizard-like appearance could be daunting, especially since Togarma was only one and a half metres tall.

'As you were, Lieutenant,' Darrow said. 'Mr Togarma is Head of Security on Caspar. I'm giving him a tour of the ship. He is *most* interested.' Darrow gave him a wink Togarma couldn't see. 'May he look at your cabin?'

Balitoth snapped to attention again. 'Yes sir!'

Togarma jumped again. He edged past Balitoth and peered at the bunks, the lockers, the desk, and the console.

'Would you like to see the head?' Balitoth asked,

crossing the cabin and opening the door.

Togarma withdrew in disgust. 'That will not be necessary, thank you. Shall we continue, Captain?'

'Thank you, Lieutenant,' Darrow said, trying not to smile. Balitoth didn't show emotion, but he still appreciated a joke.

'Sir!'

Togarma scowled and hurried up the stairs. Darrow caught up with him, followed by the men, and continued the tour.

'Aft is Engineering, of course, across both decks. Then there's hydroponics, more cabins, sick bay, the mess hall and the bridge. Would you like to look at all the common areas?'

Togarma pulled himself up to his full height. 'I would be obliged, Captain.'

So they trailed into every room that wasn't a cabin, and Togarma looked around. Darrow knew what he was looking for, or rather who, but Tanu would not be found. Eventually they came to the captain's office and sat down. Darrow made a point of pushing a button on his console to record their conversation. Togarma told the two men to wait outside. Darrow reminded himself to stay calm.

'Now,' said Darrow, 'what did you *require* to see me about?'

'Concerning your last visit --'

'When Casper was so good as to repair this ship,' Darrow interrupted, with a smile. 'It's good to have the opportunity to help Caspar in return, even in such unfortunate circumstances.' He watched Togarma to see his reactions.

'There was another matter,' Togarma replied, 'we gave medical assistance to a member of your crew.'

'Oh, Tanu, you mean. He wasn't a member of my crew. He was just a poor man we had aboard. Much good it did him, since the hospital informed us he died. It was a shame he was cremated though. I didn't think you Casparans believed in cremation.'

Togarma blinked, coughed, and continued. 'Then there was the incident at the sanatorium.'

Darrow thought, *Incident, is that what you're calling it? Having a ship on your back lawn in the middle of a gun fight is hardly an incident.*

Darrow leaned forward over the desk. 'Incident at a sanatorium? What incident would that be? Why would I or any of my men go near a sanatorium when our guest had, according to *your* records, died while in *your* care, and *your* men disposed of the body, according to *your* records and against *your* customs, by cremation? I can imagine my men trying to pay their respects to the man at the crematorium, but they would have no need to go to a sanatorium. Unless there is a problem with Casparan record keeping. I'd be happy to report to PACT central command and send them a copy of the recording of this meeting.' He pointed to his console. 'I'm sure they would be more than willing to come to Caspar with their computer experts and auditors and run some *very thorough* checks against your record keeping.' He leaned back. 'What do you think, Mr Togarma?'

Togarma got up from his chair. 'That will be all Captain,' he said. 'I should like to leave now.'

Got you! Darrow thought.

'Would you like to finish your tour?' Darrow said. 'You haven't seen the shuttle bay yet.'

'That will not be necessary.' Togara bowed. 'Good day to you Captain.'

Darrow stopped the recording, and opened communication to Parks. 'Open the cargo bay doors, Commander, and begin loading.'

***

Togarma took his men with him and Darrow rejoined Parks, Hoy and Rifath in the depot office.

'Sorry about that,' Darrow said, 'a simple misunderstanding. It's all sorted now.'

There was a collective sigh of relief.

'Time is critical, Captain,' Rifath said, 'we cannot afford any more delays.'

'The delays were not on our side.'

Parks put a hand on Rifath's arm and spoke to Darrow. 'Don't worry Captain, we continued in your absence. Between us, we've worked out what the Kestrel can take. We were just waiting for the go-ahead, so loading has started.'

'What about personnel?' Darrow asked.

'To make the best use of the space,' Rifath said, 'we have decided not to send any personnel. Once you have unloaded at the main town, we need you to transport people from another region of Sabteca to the disaster site. That way there will be more room for cargo.'

Since it was all agreed, the loading proceeded quickly. They filled the cargo hold and other available spaces: the shuttle bay for the digging and lifting equipment, sick bay for the medical supplies, foodstuffs in the mess hall, and various boxes even in the cabins. Blackwell insisted that as much as possible was tied down.

'Health and safety, you know,' he said. 'You can't be too careful. What if things get rough or the artificial gravity goes?'

Chapter 29

It took most of the day to stow everything. When evening came they were ready to leave. Rifath shook Darrow's hand and gave the Casparan bow of respect, arms wide and palms up.

'Every hour counts, Captain, make best speed.'

'We will.' Darrow bowed in return and boarded the ship.

On the bridge he opened the comm. 'All hands, take-off in ten seconds.' He closed the comm. 'Helm, best speed for Sabteca. Navigation, have you received the coordinates for the earthquake site and for the pickup site for the rescue personnel?'

Chambers on helm and Hoy on navigation confirmed both the order and the request.

Darrow left them to it and went to his office, assuming they would have a clear run to Sabteca. They had barely left Casparan space when a Bokan ship appeared. Hoy contacted Darrow as soon as the ship registered on scanners, so he was ready on the bridge, a stone in the pit of his stomach, when the ship hailed them.

'This is Captain Dodan of the Bokan gunship Put. Stop engines and prepare to be boarded,' the lizard-like figure said.

What? Darrow thought. 'This is Captain Darrow of the PACT Fast-Response ship Kestrel. We're on a humanitarian mission to Sabteca, we don't have time for this.'

'We believe you are carrying a fugitive wanted on Boka. Hand him over or we will board and find him for ourselves.' The last word ended in a hiss.

Darrow kept his face blank. 'I don't know what you mean, Captain. We've had nothing to do with Boka.'

'Our sensors show you were in orbit only a few days ago.'

'Correct, we dropped off a team of sociologists who were going to study your culture. We haven't heard from them since. Is there some problem? We are on an emergency aid mission.'

'We will see for ourselves. Prepare to be boarded.'

'This is unacceptable. You have no right to board my ship.' Darrow's hands were clenched tight and so was his jaw.

Hoy spoke up. 'Captain, they're powering up weapons and locking on target.'

'Shields up, weapons lock. Prepare for evasive manoeuvres.'

'Captain, their weapons outclass us. With respect, sir, we won't win a fight.'

Darrow paused to consider Hoy's words. He was right, although it pained him to give in without a fight. Kestrel had been in too many fights recently. The Bokan plasma cannon fired across their bow, close enough to leave a burn mark. Darrow raised his hand to tell Hoy not to return fire. The Bokan captain ran out of patience. He hailed them again.

'Captain Darrow, you have two of your Earth minutes to yield before we open fire.'

'This is ridiculous, Captain Dodan,' Darrow said. 'We have no fugitive aboard. There is no need for any of it, and we are on a mercy mission for the Casparans. If it will satisfy you and allow us to move on all the sooner, then so be it. Remember there are lives at stake here. We will prepare to receive your party, but be aware it's a tight squeeze with all the humanitarian aid we're carrying. Darrow out.'

As soon as the comm channel was cut, Darrow gave the command to stop engines and contact PACT.

'Send a mayday Lieutenant-Commander. Tell them we're being boarded by Bokans.'

Darrow took a deep breath and opened the internal comm.

'Attention all hands! We have been intercepted by a Bokan ship, and they will be boarding us. They are searching for a *fugitive*. Do not offer the Bokans any resistance, don't speak to them, don't answer any questions. Darrow out.'

Darrow left the bridge and headed down the corridor to Parks and Tanu's cabin at the end. Tanu was at the door.

'Come with me,' Darrow said.

Parks arrived at a run. 'What are they doing?'

'God knows, but Command might construe this as an act of war. I hope it doesn't provoke anything.'

Darrow led Tanu to Engineering, to Blackwell.

'Commander, hide him?'

Blackwell nodded. 'This way.'

***

Darrow went to meet Dodan, the Bokan captain, and his boarding party of six as they came through the airlock after their ship docked with the Kestrel. When the door opened the Bokans were surprised by the amount of cargo in the cargo bay. Boxes, bales and crates were stacked floor to ceiling, secured by straps, with just a narrow passage from the airlock.

'I told you, we're on a mercy mission,' Darrow said.

'We're carrying aid for an earthquake on Sabteca, a Casparan colony. Damage anything and you'll have the Casparans to answer to. Remember they have a veto on whether you can join PACT.'

Dodan signalled to four men, who attempted to fight their way in between the tightly packed boxes and canisters, crates and bales. They didn't get far, and one man got stuck and had to be extricated by the others. Darrow watched their faces in amusement. They didn't speak so he held his tongue too and led the seven of them forward to the shuttle bay.

The two shuttles could hardly be seen for the equipment and boxes everywhere. Dodan signalled to the same four men to search and they squeezed between things as best they could. It was clear they weren't going to be able to do a thorough job. All the time, Dodan watched in silence, as his face grew darker and his breathing more rapid.

Darrow was cheered by every setback. He led them to the three cabins on the lower deck and Dodan split his men into three pairs. Once again, they were met with boxes, but not so many this time. After all, the crew had to be able to wash, dress and sleep.

Tomos was alone in his cabin. He stood to attention when he saw Darrow, and Darrow kept him there to minimise the risk of him losing his temper.

The Bokans stopped short of violence but were rough with the crew's possessions. It was hard for the crew to keep their tempers when their things, like mementos from home, were being flung about.

'Captain, tell your men to have more respect for the crew's possessions,' Darrow snapped, 'or I shall be advising the Council the Bokans are too uncivilised to be allowed to join PACT.'

He thought for a moment he had pushed Dodan too far as the man went for his weapon, but he mastered himself and hissed a few words to his men, who were more careful from then on.

In Balitoth and Reuel's cabin, Dodan was surprised to find another reptilian species. Darrow could almost see him cataloguing the differences, the greater height, the shorter jaw of the Zoans, smaller scales, Balitoth's padded jacket. Boka is less warm than Zoa, meaning Bokans are used to a lower temperature, and have no need for thick clothing, as Zoans did.

The two reptilians looked at each other until Balitoth growled. Dodan decided not to take it any further. Reuel, in shadow lying on the bottom bunk, never moved, though his spines did.

Darrow led the boarding party to Engineering, where Blackwell stood to attention.

'There are no fugitives in here,' Blackwell said, 'and if you damage anything I shall see to it personally that your government gets the bill.'

'If you show us where Tanu is,' Dodan said, 'there will be no need for all this.'

Blackwell squared up to him. 'I don't know what you're talking about,' he said, 'and if I did I wouldn't tell you anyway.'

Without warning Dodan punched Blackwell in the stomach. He doubled over and stumbled back to his chair. Darrow instinctively reacted, but Dodan's weapon was in his hand in the blink of an eye. Blackwell raised a hand and shook his head at Darrow. The Bokans finished searching Engineering and Blackwell's cabin, which led off it, and moved on.

They made a mess of sick bay too, but Nefar stayed silent and didn't retaliate. It was the same story in the senior staff's cabins, the mess hall and hydroponics. Then they came to the bridge. Dodan signed to his men to wait outside and entered with Darrow.

Dodan looked around hungrily. Darrow remembered the Bokans had only recently discovered warp drive. Some of the Kestrel's technology was very advanced in comparison. Darrow stepped in front of him, blocking his view.

Dodan stormed off the bridge, back to his men. 'Gather all the crew in the mess hall, now!'

***

Tanu huddled in the tiny crawl space. It was carrying pipes and cables, but there was just enough room to one side for his slim frame. It also meant anyone opening the hatch and looking in, wouldn't immediately spot him.

There was a small grating above him which let in some light but there was nothing to see but pipes and cables. It did mean he wasn't in total darkness, for which he was grateful. If anyone passed he would hear them, but his most useful sense was his empathy.

He was starting to recognise the emotional tone of the different members of the crew. Right now they were all very tense, understandably. Parks, Hoy and Reuel were no doubt remembering their experiences on Boka, he felt the undercurrent of fear in them. Parks and Hoy had their's buttoned down but Reuel was agitated. Tanu wondered again what was the matter with Reuel, because his emotions were quite extreme. Blackwell wouldn't stand for any nonsense, and the captain was angry. Theirs were the strongest emotions he could sense.

He knew when the Bokans boarded, because he felt a wave of new emotion. He was getting used to the crew's emotions but these were strange to him. The one he assumed was the leader was furious. Maybe he was personally involved in Tanu's interrogation and in big trouble for losing him.

Tanu couldn't recognise his emotional signature because on Boka he had been afraid and in pain and unable to use his powers. He shuddered at the memory and told himself to stay strong in case he had to defend himself. *Defend himself?* He hadn't a clue how to do that.

His physical health was improving but he was still coming to terms with the trauma. When Blackwell confronted the Bokan captain, Tanu was terrified. His perception wasn't strong enough to locate everyone, but since it faded with distance he could tell how near people were. Since Engineering was at the back of the ship, most people were scattered away from his location. Blackwell, however, was working at a console nearby and muttering to himself for Tanu's benefit.

'Don't you worry now. The electromagnetic field down there should confuse any scanners they might bring with them. Just keep still and you won't be seen in the shadows.'

A few minutes later:

'The captain is being polite and helpful and getting in the way as much as possible.' Blackwell chuckled. 'They tried to fight their way through the cargo to search the hold, but the captain told them they would have Caspar to deal with if anything was damaged, so they gave up.'

The comm chirped.

'Uh-oh. They've decided they want the crew rounded

up. We'll be in the mess hall. Sit tight and you'll be fine.'

Blackwell left and Tanu was alone with his empathy.

The Bokans had worked their way through the ship and at one point passed right over him. But they sensed nothing and went straight on. After a while, he picked up a change in the emotions, first fear and then rage. As far as he could work out, first the crew were being threatened, and then Darrow was having an argument with the Bokan captain.

Chapter 30

The crew were gathered in the mess hall with the Bokans. They were made to sit on the floor, so Captain Dodan was looming over them in the small space. All except for Blackwell, who complained about arthritic knees and declared there was no way he could reach the floor. He sat on a bench and they left him there. A tiny victory, but it heartened the crew to see someone defy the Bokans.

Darrow, being first there, sat at the back in the corner, where he could watch his crew. Dodan couldn't see everyone at once, because the two tables and benches obscured his eyeline. He paced back and forth so everyone got a glimpse, and he saw everyone.

'You will all listen to me,' he growled. 'We know you have the fugitive, Tanu. If someone tells me where he is, there is no need for anyone to get hurt.'

'You did send that message, Lieutenant?' Darrow said loudly to Chambers.

'Yes sir!'

There was a pause.

'What message?' Dodan demanded.

Chambers dropped his head to hide a smile.

'When threatened with being boarded by a clearly hostile race it is PACT standard procedure to put out a mayday with details and position,' Darrow said calmly. 'PACT will have received it by now. No doubt there is help on the way already. There will be serious repercussions.'

Dodan waved a hand dismissively, but his tongue flicked out and back again. 'That is not my concern. My superiors have charged me with retrieving the fugitive.

The repercussions [*hiss*] are their problem.'

'Oh, but it should be your concern. It should be every Bokan's concern.' Darrow shrugged, and prayed help really was on the way. 'You may out-gun us, but as you've searched this ship, you've doubtless realised PACT technology is more advanced than current Bokan technology. When a planetary system belongs to PACT, amongst other things we share our technology. Which means you won't be getting anywhere near it.'

Dodan's head snapped round. 'Why not?'

'Because you're violating so many of our rules PACT will never let you in. Well done for ruining the best chance of progress your whole planet will ever have.'

'Not my problem.'

But the tongue flicked out again and Darrow thought he detected a hint of fear in Dodan's eyes.

Dodan reached forward and grabbed Tomos by the hair and dragged him to the front. Tomos yelled and kicked until Dodan backhanded him across the mouth. With a roar the crew had never heard before, Reuel leaped to his feet and lunged at Dodan. His claws raked Dodan's face before he became aware of the weapons drawn by the two boarding party members inside the mess hall.

'As you were!' Darrow shouted and Reuel sat back down. Tomos subsided and nursed his cut lip. The weapons stayed drawn. Dodan pulled a cloth from his pocket to dab at his face.

Darrow watched the tension amongst the crew jump, his mind racing. *Where had that come from?*

'This one seems to be the youngest and most puny,' Dodan said, indicating Tomos. 'I wonder how loyal you are to each other? I have found in my experience that men can withstand their own pain much better than seeing it administered to someone else.' He kicked Tomos in the ribs, who cried out and doubled over. Reuel growled and Parks laid a warning hand on Reuel's shoulder. 'Now which one of you is going to take pity on him and tell me what I want to know?'

The crew shifted uncomfortably. Darrow wondered if Tanu could pick up their emotions from here. He hoped not, for his sake.

'Captain Dodan,' Darrow said, 'can I have a word with you in private?'

'You can speak here.'

'I don't think you will want your men to hear what I have to say. The fewer people involved, the better.' Darrow got to his feet and stepped over legs towards the door. The nearest guard moved to intercept him.

'Wait!' Dodan said. He turned to Darrow, 'Lead the way.'

Darrow and Dodan went to Darrow's office, leaving the other Bokans to guard the crew in the mess hall. They did not sit down, but stood toe to toe. Darrow stepped back to appear less aggressive.

'I repeat Captain, we are on an emergency aid mission for earthquake relief for the Casparan colony on Sabteca. Lives may be lost while you hold us here.'

'Your men escaped from Boka with another man. We insist you return him to us or reveal his whereabouts.'

Darrow decided to take a risk. 'You have seen my crew. Which ones do you think were on Boka?'

The Dodan snarled. 'The idiots in security failed to take pictures when they captured them. But we have descriptions.' He pulled a small tablet out of his jacket. 'Two were tall, one was shorter. One had blond hair, one dark and the third wore a hat. That one was very pink.'

Darrow was glad Reuel was looking paler than usual. 'Is that all you have? Are you going to arrest someone for being blond, or tall? We both know you have no case. Why were you holding this other man? What was he charged with?'

'I am not at liberty to say. It is a matter of national security.' Dodan folded his arms.

Darrow considered his next words carefully. 'If Boka joins PACT, you would have all the help you need with security. All the other species would be looking out for you.'

'All the other species would be spying on us, you mean.'

'I don't believe you have anything worth taking,' said Darrow with a scowl. 'After your behaviour here, PACT won't want you. Think of all that lovely technology we were going to share with you.' Darrow dismissed the idea with a shrug. 'It sounds to me like you were holding this man against his will. I wonder what my superiors will make of that when they read my report?'

'Report?'

'Of course. Every mission has its report, and we are on a mission, as I keep telling you. I will have to give a full report to PACT, and an explanation to Caspar on why we were delayed getting aid supplies to Sabteca.

'There is now also the matter of your ships attacking mine - twice. And you have no provable cause as to why you were attacking us, because you can't find this phantom fugitive you claim the sociologists rescued. You can't even prove any of my crew were on Boka, we were only in orbit to drop off the sociologists, something which is a matter of public record and agreement with your government.'

Darrow put his arm around the Bokan captain's

shoulder and dropped his voice. 'Perhaps you would rather I forget to report the attacks, and this boarding was a misunderstanding?'

Dodan stepped away from Darrow. They looked at one another for a long moment. Darrow held his breath. *First one to speak, loses,* he thought.

'I think that will be all, Captain.' Dodan said. 'You may proceed with your mission.'

He strode to the mess hall, barked a command at his men and they all made their way off the ship, passing right over Tanu's hiding place.

***

Tanu thought he was safe, because he felt the satisfaction and relief from Darrow as he followed the Bokans to the airlock. A minute or two later there was a vibration as the airlock disengaged and then the grating was lifted by Blackwell.

'Out you come,' Blackwell reached down a burly hand to help Tanu out. 'You're all free and clear. They won't come looking for you again.'

Darrow arrived as Tanu got to his feet. 'Are you all right? Did you pick up much down there?'

'Not clearly, Captain,' Tanu said. 'I thought it best not to try.'

'Good.' He looked from Tanu to Blackwell. 'Emergency meeting for everyone in the mess hall now.'

The mess hall was crowded, but at least they could stand up now and move around. There were nine in the crew and with Tanu that made ten people. No, he looked around - Reuel was missing. Tanu's heart sank. He didn't know how to convince Reuel he wasn't a threat.

Darrow saw his look and said, 'Reuel volunteered to man the bridge. I thought it best to agree. He still doesn't trust you, I'm afraid.' He raised his voice, 'Thank you all for your behaviour, and for not giving Tanu away. Special commendation to Ensign Tomos. How are you?'

'Cut lip, bruises and a cracked rib, sir,' Tomos gave a rueful smile and laid a hand on the padding he wore. He was a hero.

Nefar said, 'Nothing my regenerator can't fix, Captain. Straight after this meeting.'

Darrow continued. 'With a bit of luck we have now got both the Casparans and the Bokans off our backs.' There was a muted cheer. 'Lieutenant Chambers, cancel the mayday call when you return to duty. Say it was a misunderstanding. There is one other thing we need. Tanu's name is known, and may give him away, especially when we make our reports. He needs a new name. Any ideas?'

He looked at Tanu, who shook his head.

Hoy spoke up. 'Sir, we're already being careful not to mention Tanu's abilities, but it will be easy to slip and use his real name. The new one needs to sound like his old one, to make things easier. What about Tanner?'

There was a murmur of agreement.

'He needs two names, like other humans,' said Tomos. 'Well, he looks human, as long as he keeps the headband on.'

'Pick something ordinary and boring,' said Chambers, 'like John.' He looked at Blackwell, whose name was John, and everyone laughed. Blackwell shrugged.

Darrow turned to Tanu. 'John Tanner. What do you think?'

Tanu grinned. 'I think it will do well.'

Darrow turned to Parks. 'See to it that his name is *corrected* in all the records, Commander. And see if you can get him some identity documents, there must be lots of people who lose their documents. I'm sure with your experience in security you know who to contact.'

'Yes sir.'

'Right, full speed to Sabteca. Dismissed.'

***

'What was that?' Balitoth asked when he and Reuel got back to their cabin.

Reuel shrugged his shoulders. 'I just reacted to the ill use of Tomos.'

'Over-reacted, some may say. You startled us all. It is lucky the Bokans did not shoot you.'

Reuel thought for a moment. 'You know, I have realised life is too precious to spend it worrying. I let my reaction to Commander Parks' torture and the ripening make me fearful. But Stubbs' death made me think again. I have reconsidered what seemed to be your betrayals too.'

Balitoth tensed. 'In each case I was acting to help you. Friends need to look out for one another.'

Reuel smiled and his spines relaxed. 'Yes, I see that now. Thank you. You have been a true friend. I am not going to think about torture or secrets, or worry about Tanu. I am still going to watch him closely, but I am going to get on with my life.'

Balitoth gave a rare smile. 'My people have a saying: You cannot live yesterday again, and you cannot live tomorrow today. So live today and live it well.'

Chapter 31

The newly-renamed Tanner came to see Darrow.

'Captain, I want to help on Sabteca, but I'm not strong. I'm still learning to do things manually, but it's hard. I want to help, but I don't think I can dig.'

'Would you prefer to help in the hospital?' Darrow asked.

'No, because I think the emotions will be strongest there. I would like to help with digging for survivors. Really help, I mean.'

Darrow took a deep breath, but Tanner interrupted. 'I have my headband, which covers the glow, and I don't propose to move things by myself. I think I can assist those who are digging and lifting, to take some of the weight.'

'Are you sure? It could be dangerous.'

'You rescued me, Captain. I might be able to detect people still alive under the rubble, but I imagine it can take a long time to move it. I can speed it up a little. Please?'

'Very well, but I want you to work with Lieutenant-Commander Hoy. He will warn you if your help is too obvious. So, stick close to Hoy.'

'Yes Captain, and thank you.'

But when Darrow gave out the crew assignments, Reuel was unhappy.

'Captain, I must protest,' he said. 'It is one thing to have Tanu - Tanner - using his mind powers here, but surely you can't unleash him on a whole colony.'

'Ensign Reuel, I am not "unleashing" him anywhere. We have agreed to accept him and hide his identity for the time being, and he wants to help. He will work with Lieutenant-Commander Hoy and will be using his telekinesis to assist a little in the lifting and digging.'

'But if anything should happen…'

'Ensign, I have made the decision. I hope you can accept that and will serve with the rest of the crew, but if not, we won't be able to continue working together.' Darrow paused for the full implication to sink in. 'I have decided Tanner is trustworthy, and if you find it hard to trust him, then trust me.'

Reuel saluted. 'Yes sir.'

***

The rest of the flight was uneventful. They arrived at Sabteca to find the colony was spread over a large central continent, sited mostly in the northern hemisphere. The centre of the continent was mountainous, the small settlements were dotted around the coast.

The main settlement lay nestled in a wide valley below the mountains by a wide, sweeping bay on the western coast. It was a beautiful location, but this was where the earthquake had hit. South of the town was a rudimentary spaceport, little more than a landing pad, and some kind of processing plant, both badly damaged. Luckily the Kestrel didn't need a landing pad due to its VTOL engines. As they flew nearer the plant they could see the channel dug out to sea - a desalination plant.

The houses were built of grey stone quarried from the mountains, except for a series of linked beige plastic hexagonal buildings to the north that looked like habitat modules. Apart from those, it seemed no building was left intact. In addition, the earthquake caused a tsunami which flooded the whole settlement, and the nearest settlements to the south along the western coast.

The planet was more like Earth than Caspar, with green vegetation and a single sun, though the gravity was lighter and the atmosphere less oxygen rich, making it ideal for Casparans. They had even planted Casparan native plants with orange foliage around the town, all of which were now flattened and covered in mud, sand and debris. The sun was rising as the Kestrel came in to land on a raised open area of grassland east of the town.

They had contacted the leaders of the colony as they approached, and there was a group of people waiting for them, all Casparan - short and green. Darrow and Parks went to the airlock to disembark and Dr Nefar and Tomos joined them.

The four of them went to meet the colonists.

'Thank you for coming to our aid, you are most welcome.' The leader gave the traditional Casparan bow.

They bowed in return.

Darrow replied, 'I am Captain Joseph Darrow, and this is my First Officer Nathaniel Parks. This is our doctor, Dr Sebu Nefar, and Medic James Tomos. We have a small, but fully-equipped sick bay. The medical staff would like to start work immediately. My crew are at your service, and here is a manifest of everything we've brought.' He handed over a tablet.

The leader passed the tablet to another man. 'I am Calah Resen, the Governor here, and this is Anami Ludim, mayor of this town, Westtown.' He waved another man forward. 'Take these two to the hospital.'

As Nefar and Tomos left he indicated a group of men standing to one side. 'These other men are ready to unload what you have brought, while we talk details. There is no time to lose.'

Darrow raised his arm as a signal, and the cargo bay doors opened. Hoy stepped down to meet the approaching men. Governor Resen led Mayor Ludim, Darrow and Parks to some chairs set to one side. Luckily the weather was mild.

'I am sorry I have no office to invite you to, and cannot offer you refreshments,' Resen said with a bow. 'Let us begin.'

'When did the quake happen?' Darrow asked.

'Two days ago, at night, with about thirty aftershocks since. The tsunami came a few hours later and finished what the earthquake started. Most people were caught in their beds, which increased the numbers buried.' There was a catch in his voice and he paused to collect himself.

'We cannot use any buildings because they may come down in an aftershock, so the survivors are sleeping in the open. At the moment the weather is fair, though it gets cold at night. This is our autumn, so we lost our crops, and winter is coming. We were using some of the original habitat modules as storerooms and workshops and they withstood the earthquake quite well, so we emptied them to create a makeshift hospital.'

Ludim took up the story. 'Anyone with medical experience is treating the injured. Everyone else is digging.' His voice caught in his throat.

Resen put his hand on Ludim's arm. 'His wife died and we have not found his daughter.'

Parks said, 'My condolences. The Kestrel crew also

have skills and equipment. We have diggers and lifters and five other crew, including an engineer. What can we do?'

'The help of your engineer would be most welcome at the desalination plant, which was badly damaged. In the mean time, people are ferrying water from the mountains. We have had offers of help from the Eastside settlements,' Ludim said, 'but limited transport. If you can put all hands to helping with the unloading, then fly over to the Eastside to fetch more help; that would be wonderful.'

'We have two shuttles as well,' Darrow said. 'They are not as fast, but they can leave as soon as the shuttle bay is cleared.'

'The other settlements have offered to take in some of the survivors,' Resen said, 'to ease the burden on providing food and shelter. I think it would be good to get some people ready and transport them to Eastside when you go to collect the workers.'

'Why don't you send someone with the shuttles who can liaise with the Eastside and make arrangements?'

'I will go myself,' said Resen. 'I think I can be of more use there than here.'

'Then we have a plan,' said Darrow. 'Let's get the ship unloaded and the shuttles launched.'

Parks asked, 'Do you have people who can operate the diggers and lifters or do you need our crew?'

'Probably a bit of both,' said Ludim. 'I will introduce you to Gaptu, who is in charge of the digging.'

***

Tomos was glad the gravity here was lighter as he was lugging the medical kit, though he could see it wouldn't be enough. He had never seen devastation like it. Nefar warned him to steel himself.

'We must deal with the problem in front of us,' he said. 'The patient must always come first. Do not forget, we must be unshockable, for the sake of the patients. Keep your emotions out of the way.'

'Yes, Doctor.' Tomos swallowed hard as they reached the makeshift hospital, set on another grassy mound.

The habitat modules were hexagonal domes made of honeycombed plastic. There were about a dozen linked together in what seemed a haphazard way.

The first thing that hit them was the noise: crying, moaning, calling out. People were lying everywhere with barely space between for them to step. Some patients further in were bandaged and some had intravenous drips in their arms, but the newer arrivals were untreated, bleeding and covered in dust.

The man leading Nefar and Tomos took them to some cabinets covered in computer tablets where a grey-haired man stood.

'Dr Zemar, this is the Kestrel's Doctor and medic, Nefar and Tomos.' He introduced them and left.

Dr Zemar looked up and Tomos realised he wasn't old, his hair was full of dust. 'Thank the gods!' he exclaimed. 'We are exhausted.' He shook their hands. 'We have been unable to keep up with the casualties. It is slowing down now. Most of the finds now are dead.'

He waved his hands across the room.

'We gave up trying to keep records, so just dive in. The ones with red ribbon on them have internal injuries, as far as we can determine. Otherwise it is just what you see. There is little water, so don't waste it washing people, just clean the actual wounds. I have run out of antiseptic.'

Tomos was horrified and didn't know where to start. He turned to Nefar, who picked up a pile of the tablets and dumped them on the floor. 'Put the kit on here,' he said to Tomos. 'You do triage - do you speak any Casparan?'

'It is not a problem Doctor,' Zemar said, 'we all speak Standard, it was a prerequisite of being a colonist.'

Nefar nodded. 'Go first to those who have not been treated. Check them out and shout when you find one that cannot wait. Once we get the urgent cases dealt with, we can go back and set breaks and bandage wounds. Our regenerators are going to be working non-stop.'

Tomos nodded.

'Go!' Nefar said.

***

Reuel was glad to be himself again. This experience of being female was wonderful in supportive circumstances, but out here it was decidedly unpleasant. He vowed never again to be without the pills that prevented the ripening. His body was almost back to normal and it was great to go out on the surface of a planet and stretch himself. He felt like he wanted to run and run, but lifting and carrying would do fine.

The gravity on Sabteca was a little more than at home, but he could cope without his back brace. He had met some annoying, pompous Casparans, but he had met many more warm and friendly Casparans, and these colonists seemed to be the latter, so he was happy to lend a hand.

The Kestrel had landed on a rise behind the town. From there you could see the ravages of the earthquake and tsunami. Reuel had never seen anything like it. Rubble was everywhere, with just a few walls and corners still standing, but the flotsam and jetsam from the flood was scattered everywhere too. It looked as though the tsunami had flowed around the rise and all the way to the foot of the mountains.

Although it was now two days later, people were still wandering around in rags looking dazed. His heart went out to them, but the orders were to unload first.

He saw Tanner carrying some light packages and part of him was glad the man wanted to help, but part of him wanted to scream and warn everyone to stay away from the Rayt. Tanner was wearing his headband to cover his 'horn' and appeared to be lifting things manually. Reuel turned away to hide the hatred on his face and got on with the business of unloading the aid.

Chapter 32

As soon as they unloaded enough cargo to make space in the shuttle bay, Reuel saw Parks and Chambers pilot the shuttles, taking Governor Resen with them. Once they were gone, the rest of the aid and equipment could be unloaded. Hoy took the lead, with Balitoth, Reuel and Tanner helping. Reuel was initially horrified that he was being forced to work with Tanner, though he quickly realised this gave him the best possible opportunity to watch the Rayt and find out if all that domination was just hiding for now. Tanner seemed harmless, but that could be an act.

Tanner could carry things by using his telekinesis as well as his arms. On board, out of sight of the colonists, he was able to shunt the boxes from the cabins along to the cargo bay, moving far more at a time than he could physically hold. Reuel was still not comfortable around Tanner and watched him like a hawk.

All the aid was labelled, and Reuel assumed different items were being taken to different places where they would be best used. But most of the aid was just being unloaded onto the grass by some of the men, while others were carrying stuff away. Hoy called over one of the men unloading onto the grass.

'Hey there. Why is this not being taken away like the other stuff?'

'What do you mean?' the man said. 'We were told the ship was in a hurry to leave to fetch help from Easttown. We can shift it all to the right places later.'

'But they're taking it away.' Hoy pointed.

The man he was pointing at saw him and broke into a run.

'Thieves!' shouted the man with Hoy, and instantly everyone put down what they were carrying and ran. The men who had been taking stuff away ran into the remains of the town and tried to disappear. The other colonists ran after them.

The shouts brought a group of five men with green sashes across their chests. They were carrying weapons and set out after the men.

Balitoth, Reuel and Tanner gathered around Hoy.

'Should we go after them, sir?' Reuel asked.

Hoy shook his head. 'Best leave them to sort out their own problems. We haven't been here long enough to know who's who. Did anyone see where they were taking stuff?'

'There's a pile in that building with the roof hanging off,' Tanner pointed. 'We could go and bring it back.'

He was obviously eager to help.

'Go on then,' Hoy said, 'you and Reuel, but be careful under that roof. We don't want to have to rescue you too.'

'I can support the roof while we're in there, sir.' Tanner said.

Hoy nodded. 'Bring the aid back here, and Balitoth and I will stay and move stuff to the front of the cargo bay.'

Tanner and Reuel ran down the slope into the edge of the town, where a building stood out because it hadn't quite collapsed. The buildings on either side were mostly rubble, and as they drew nearer they saw the personal possessions strewn in the rubble: clothes, cooking pots, pictures, toys. The larger building had only lost one wall and a corner, and the roof was sagging where it had no support. When they got closer they could see tiny desks and chairs and books.

Tanner stopped. 'It's a school,' he said. 'Do you think there will be any children in there?'

'We've no time to ask, so we'll have to see, won't we?' Reuel said. 'Just be careful where you step.'

Reuel stepped carefully over the rubble. Tanner looked up at the roof and it shifted and groaned. Then he followed. The aid was stacked at the back of the room, under the sagging roof so as to be partly hidden.

Reuel said, 'It will waste time if we both climb in and out. I shall make a path here and pass them to you. Is that acceptable? Once we get it out of the rubble, we can both carry it back.'

Tanner agreed and they began to pass the boxes out. Suddenly Reuel shouted 'Quiet! I can hear something.'

They stopped and strained their ears. There was a soft mewling sound. Reuel moved to one of the desks, turned it over gently and lifted the lid. It was a young animal, which jumped out and ran off. They breathed a sigh of relief.

'Maybe someone's pet,' Reuel said. 'I hope it finds its owner.'

As they turned to resume work, they saw a young woman carrying away one of the aid boxes.

'Hey!' Reuel ran after her.

She dropped the box and burst into tears. Reuel put his arm around her, without thinking of the rule about not touching women, but the young woman didn't object. She was wearing clothes of a thicker fabric than the others. Her tunic was shorter too, only reaching just above her knees. It was torn and dirty and her slim trousers were caked in mud. Her tears had made streaks in the grime on her face.

'There is no need to steal,' Reuel said. 'We have brought lots of supplies and we are going to the

Eastside to get more. Wait a little longer and we can share it out.'

'I am from near Strand,' the young woman said, pointing down the coast. 'It has taken me all day to walk here from our farm. We waited, but no help has come.'

She staggered and Reuel bent and picked her up. It was like carrying a child. He turned to Tanner. 'You carry on, I'm taking her to get help.' He headed to where he had seen the leaders meeting.

Darrow and Mayor Ludim looked up as he approached. Ludim looked as if he was going to object, but obviously thought better of it. Reuel put the woman down into a chair and saluted Darrow.

'Excuse me, sirs, but this woman has come from further down the coast, near Strand, she said. Their farm has had no help. She has walked all day, and needs medical attention.'

'At ease, Ensign,' Darrow said, and turned to Ludim.

'We haven't been able to sort out our own problems,' Ludim said with a frown, 'let alone go looking for others.'

'But surely you're in touch with all the other settlements?' Darrow asked. 'How else did you arrange for help from Eastside?'

Ludim looked frazzled. 'We are only in communication with the larger ones,' he said. 'We don't have enough communication devices for everyone. If people will go off on their own, they must live with the consequences.'

'Or die with the consequences.' The young woman spoke up, a catch in her voice. 'You are quick enough to buy our grain and vegetables, because it benefits you. Who is going to grow your crops now?'

Darrow intervened. 'I'll ask one of the shuttles to come back via the coast and survey the extent of the damage. Once we bring the Eastside aid and personnel, we'll take a team round to the other affected places. Do you have a map showing all the settlements?'

'I can get you one,' Ludim said.

'Sir, should I take this woman to the hospital?' Reuel asked.

Ludim looked at the woman. 'Are you injured? The hospital is only taking emergencies at the moment.'

The young woman shook her head. 'I am exhausted, hungry and thirsty, but not injured,' she said.

'There is a feeding station south of here, on the next rise,' Ludim said, pointing.

Darrow nodded to Reuel. 'Take her there, then return to your duties.'

'Yes sir,' Reuel said. He turned to the woman, 'Can you walk? Come, I can help you.' He bowed. 'May I carry you again?'

She nodded and he picked her up and set off across the top of the town.

'I am sorry I did not ask permission before,' Reuel said. 'I am not used to Casparan ways.'

The woman smiled. 'We are not so strict here. The women are on more of an equal footing with the men. Not so far as we would like, mind you.'

Her smile lit up her face. It was quite a pretty face, with her green hair caught into a bun at the nape of her neck. At least, it was a bun once, now it was coming undone.

'May I ask your name? I am Shom Reuel from the Kestrel.'

'My, you are forward, aren't you?'

'Well, I cannot keep calling you "this woman" can I?'

'My name is Hazarma Almodad. My father is a farmer and my mother and I sew clothes.'

'Now we are properly introduced,' Reuel said with a smile.

Reuel carried her down the slope and across a soggy, littered place where the tsunami had come in, and started up the slope on the other side. As the crest came into view, Reuel swore and immediately apologised.

'What is it?' Hazarma asked, craning round in his arms to see. He turned so she couldn't see.

'No, do not look. There is a dead man tied to a stake. What are they doing? It is barbaric!'

She tucked her head against his chest and he carried her past. At the top of the hill there were tables and chairs and crates of food. Reuel approached a woman serving food.

'Excuse me,' he said, 'this is Hazarma Almodad. She has walked from near Strand to get help for her family. She needs food and drink, and somewhere to rest.'

'Oh the poor thing!' the woman said. 'Sit her down over there and I will bring her something. You can leave her with me.'

Reuel sat Hazarma on a chair by a table and pulled up another chair to rest her feet on. 'There you are. Good luck.'

He turned away and went back to the serving woman, who was filling a bowl with some kind of stew. 'Excuse me, but why is that dead man tied to a stake?'

The woman scowled. 'Looter!' she said. 'The mayor made an example of the first one he caught, to discourage others.'

By the time Reuel returned, Hoy and Tanner had finished retrieving the stolen aid and were back unloading the Kestrel. Mayor Ludim and Captain

Darrow were talking nearby. Reuel was reporting to Hoy when the colonists returned with the thieves. They marched up to Ludim and one of the men with green sashes spoke to Ludim.

'Permission to discipline, sir?'

Ludim nodded and they gathered round an upright pole with a short crossbar about two metres above the ground. One of the thieves was made to strip off his jacket and shirt and his hands were tied to the crossbar over his head. One of the green sashed men produced a crude whip made of knotted rope.

'Wait!' Darrow said, turning to Ludim. 'Are you going to whip this man?'

'Not just this one,' Ludim said, 'all of them. Captain, we have no jail. What do you propose we do with them? This way, they pay for their crime, but can still be useful citizens.'

Darrow had no answer for him. He turned away and hurried to the Kestrel to speak to Hoy.

'Go and check on Tanner in the cargo bay. I don't know what his empathic range is - this may upset him.'

'Captain,' Reuel spoke up and saluted. 'There is a dead man tied to a stake at the feeding station. They say he was a looter, and they made an example of him.'

Darrow scowled. Reuel knew this was not, should not be, the way of any culture in PACT.

'Thank you Ensign, carry on,' Darrow said.

***

At the hospital the injuries were nearly all from the impact of collapsing walls and ceilings: fractures, cuts, bumps and bruises. Minor cuts and clean fractures Tomos left, to concentrate on the serious ones. Then he came across a young child coughing and unable to catch her breath with the dust in her lungs, and a man who had had a heart attack with the shock. He called Nefar over to treat them. The dust was everywhere, and he had an idea.

'Doctor, I know drinking water is in short supply, but can't we clean the patients up with seawater?'

'As long as you don't get salt in the wounds, use antiseptic for cleaning wounds. But you can wash their faces and hands. It should make them more comfortable.'

Nefar turned to one of the local nurses. 'Is the seawater here safe to use for washing?'

'Yes, sir.'

Nefar got on his communicator. 'Captain, once the unloading is finished, can you spare some men to collect seawater for cleaning and washing the patients? And do we have any large containers for it?'

'Good idea Doctor. I'll get Lieutenant-Commander Hoy on it.'

Every now and then the rescue workers brought in another victim dug out of the rubble. It wasn't just the injuries Tomos had to deal with, it was the shock on the faces. Some of them had thought they were going to die, many had lost loved ones. Some of the people were vacant, unable to process what had happened, some wept uncontrollably.

Tomos was out of his depth, his training had been practical, not emotional. He retreated into professionalism, dealing with the physical injuries and moving on. As the flow of injured eased, Tomos slipped out. Dr Nefar found him behind the hospital, in tears.

'Oh! Sorry Doctor, I'll come now.'

'No Tomos, be still,' Nefar laid his hand on Tomos'

shoulder. 'This is good. Some medical people become distant from their patients. They will say, "This is the broken leg, this is the inflamed appendix." *This* is a person, and their condition is affecting their life, their wellbeing. It is good that you feel for these people. Never lose that. Understand their pain - emotional and mental as well as physical. But learn to master your feelings; otherwise you cannot help them in their need.'

'Yes Doctor, thank you.'

'I think we have identified all the serious cases. Go up to the ship and bring the rest of the medical aid we stored in sick bay. Then go and get some rest until morning. You have done quite enough, it has been a long day. See if there is anyone else free to help you carry the supplies. I will decide who we should take to sick bay first.'

'Yes, Doctor.'

Tomos went to the Kestrel only to find everything had been unloaded, including the medical supplies, and Captain Darrow was preparing to take off.

'Excuse me sir,' Tomos saluted. 'Dr Nefar asked me to prepare sick bay to receive patients. Are we leaving?'

'Stand easy, Medic,' Darrow said. 'Kestrel is going to the other side of the continent to bring more aid and more people to help. Does the Doctor have emergencies that must be treated at once?'

Tomos pulled out him comm unit. 'I'll ask him.'

'Tell him we'll be back later tomorrow. If there is someone who can't wait, they'll have to come with us.'

Chapter 33

Parks and Chambers piloted the two shuttles over to Easttown. Governor Resen travelled with Parks. His brown tunic was grubby and his green sash of office was torn. He smoothed them down.

'I have no change of clothes until they dig out my wardrobe,' he said with a grimace, 'and that is obviously not a priority.'

'This trip's going to take a while,' Parks said, changing the subject. 'Why don't you tell me about the colony?'

'We came here ten years ago,' Resen said. 'Full of optimism and high ideals. And it has been good, mostly. But there was nothing in the survey report about earthquakes. Some of the colonists want to go home, and they're talking about compensation.'

Parks spirits fell. 'That's unfortunate. Still, the first priority is to deal with the emergency.'

After a while Parks asked about the settlements. 'When did the colony split into separate settlements? Was there a falling out?'

Resen squirmed. 'Not really, it was all part of the original plan, but not quite so soon. But it was just as well, when the earthquake hit, otherwise it would have hit all of us. Westtown was the first site, and is still the biggest. It used to be called Prime, but the other settlements wanted equality. We said Prime meant first, because it was the first place, but they said it sounded like first importance, so we changed it.'

'What are the other settlements called?'

'We're going to Easttown which is the largest on the

Eastside coast, but the others picked their own names, based on their location, or something from home. There are Valley, Promontory, Riverbank, and New Caspar, for instance. The northern shores are cold, the southern shores are hot, and the centre is mountainous, so at the moment, the settlements are east and west.'

'Are they very large? How many colonists are there?'

'We were ten thousand when we came, and in ten years there have been about two thousand babies, but quite a few deaths too. After the earthquake, I dread to think how many dead.' His voice broke. 'We have not had time to count.'

Parks waited a moment before he spoke. 'How many were there in Westtown before the quake?'

'About four thousand. We only started building in stone about seven years ago. The mountains are close on Westside, so the stone was available, and there are not many trees, so we built in stone. The very stone that killed so many in the quake. It is the other way around on Eastside - less stone, more trees - so their houses are wood.'

'So, what help have they offered you?'

Resen laughed nervously, 'That was not specified, which is why I needed to come.'

This whole place is a bit of a mess, Parks thought. *Why is nothing ever straightforward?*

***

By the time they reached Easttown it was late in the evening, but the town was brightly lit. As Easttown came into view it was very different to Westtown, even what Parks imagined Westtown had looked like before the earthquake. The land on this side of the continent was much flatter and heavily forested. The trees near the coast were cleared and used to build the houses. There were boats and a harbour and people about the town.

As the shuttles touched down on a flat area north of town, a wheeled vehicle with a solar panel on the roof came out to meet them. Three men got out and waited for Parks and Resen to disembark and Chambers to join them. The men were all carrying weapons, and spread out to encircle the group.

'What is the meaning of this?' Resen spluttered. 'I am the Governor. Where is Uzal Havilar, the Mayor?'

Two similar vehicles drove up behind them. More men with weapons got out. The first men moved together again on the side away from the newcomers. It was a standoff with Parks, Chambers and Resen in the middle. Parks looked at Resen, who was clearly out of his depth. Parks' mind flicked back to his previous mission on Boka. It was his fault that went wrong. He wasn't going to let this misson go wrong.

'Let's all keep calm, shall we?' he said with a smile. 'Why don't we all introduce ourselves? You may know each other but Chambers and I have no idea who's who. I'm Nathaniel Parks, First Officer on the Kestrel, which has brought aid for the earthquake victims. This is Andrew Chambers, our helmsman.'

There was an awkward silence, the men looking at each other for guidance. That was a good sign to Parks - no one was in charge.

Parks stepped towards the first arrivals. 'You got here first, how about you start the introductions?'

He motioned to one man to start. The man cleared his throat. 'I am Lasho, this is Gether and Lud.'

'And what can we do for you?' Parks asked.

Gether said, 'We were sent to bring you to Jobak. He is the leader of the Resistance.'

Resen got red in the face. 'The Resistance?' he said, 'How dare you -'

'Now, now,' Parks said, laying a hand on Resen's arm. 'Calm, remember?' He turned around to the other men. 'Your turn.'

A man stepped forward. 'Our names are not important. Mayor Havilar sent us to meet you.'

Parks stiffened at the man's demeanour. 'Tell me, why did the Mayor send an armed guard? We were coming to see him, we just needed someone to show us the way.'

The man waved his gun at the other group. 'That is why. We thought they might try something.'

Parks thought quickly. 'Look, we've come to make arrangements for the personnel and aid you agreed to send to Westtown. It's not our business to get involved in your politics.' He turned to Gether. 'Do you object to sending help to Westtown?'

'That is part of it, yes.' Gether said.

'Right, you seem to be the spokesman. Come with me. And Mr No-name from the Mayor. You too, Governor.' He started towards the shuttle. All weapons were instantly raised. Parks waved them down. 'We're just going to talk, like civilised beings, one from each side. Sorry, Lieutenant Chambers, you need to stay here. I'm sure our new friends will look after you.'

Parks headed for the shuttle, one hand on Resen's back, showing more confidence than he felt. After a moment the other two men followed. He glanced back as they boarded the shuttle and saw Chambers had walked away to sit on a tree stump. That left the others awkwardly facing each other, until the Resistance group went back to their vehicle. Once inside the shuttle Parks rounded on the three men.

'Now listen. We are here to bring aid, not sort out your business. Gether, you have five minutes to put your case to the Governor, without interruptions. Then No-name can say his piece. Governor, after that it's up to you.'

He sat down and folded his arms. He was tempted to leave them to it, he had no interest in their squabbles, but he decided he needed to know what was going on. Dwarfed by the chairs, they looked like squabbling children. Parks had to suppress a smile. Gether spoke, though Parks had to remind the other men not to interrupt. Resen asked some questions, then the No-name spoke and Resen asked more questions.

What it boiled down to was that many in Eastside wanted to build their own little empire and become independent, but Mayor Havilar still believed in unity. So, he had promised help and offered to take in some Westtown people, but the Resistance objected. Resen was alarmed to find his Governorship in such danger, but rose to the occasion and promised talks with all the colony leaders, including the Resistance.

Parks decided the discussion had gone on long enough, he interrupted. 'Now, wasn't that more productive than belligerence? There remains one question. On humanitarian grounds alone, are you going to help the earthquake victims or not? Because if you're not, we're leaving.'

They all looked at Gether, who said, 'I cannot make that decision. I need to speak to the leaders.'

Parks got to his feet and headed for the door. 'Right, go and talk to them. PACT is built on cooperation. I hope you have the maturity to help your fellow citizens in times of need. I didn't risk my life, my crewmates or our ship coming here to face internal squabbles. People are dying in Westtown. If you won't help, then we need to get back and do so. We leave in half an hour with or without you.'

He ushered them out the door and called Chambers. 'Lieutenant, come and wait in the shuttle while these people make up their minds.'

Chambers strolled to the shuttle while the two leaders spoke to their groups. The Resistance drove away and the Mayor's men went back to their vehicles. The three in the shuttle collapsed into seats in various states of discontent.

'Thanks for leaving me out there like a sitting duck, sir,' Chambers said.

'Sorry Lieutenant, it was a sign of good faith.'

'What's going on?'

'They're not all working from the same schematic, that's what. The Resistance have gone to talk about aid for Westtown. If they say no, we're leaving. I'm not sitting around here while they squabble. We can do more good back at Westtown.' He reached for the comm unit. 'I need to let the captain know.'

He contacted Darrow and explained the situation. 'I recommend you don't bring the Kestrel over here until we're sure it's worth coming.'

'Roger that,' Darrow said. 'On your return journey, come via the west coast and check out the other settlements. It looks like they've had no help at all. Find out what's needed and report back.'

'Aye aye, sir. I'll let you know what happens here, and when we're leaving.'

Resen had his head in his hands. 'I had no idea this was going on,' he said. 'We must keep it secret from

Caspar. This is the first Casparan colony you know,' he looked up. 'We are the model for future colonies.'

Parks lost his patience. 'Well, why didn't you know? Why haven't you got to grips with it?'

There was an uncomfortable pause.

'Because I spend all my time in Westtown,' Resen whispered.

The half hour was almost up when the Resistance vehicle returned, this time with only Gether in. The Mayor's men were immediately on alert, so Parks took Resen and went out to talk to Gether at his vehicle. He told Chambers to stay put and keep the shuttle locked.

'We are happy for Easttown to provide aid for Westtown, because it is a disaster,' he said. 'But we want confirmation that talks will begin within two weeks, and there will be no hunting of the Resistance beforehand.'

'Thank you for being reasonable,' Resen said. 'This will go in your favour when the talks convene. I promise I will call talks as soon as the emergency is over.'

'That could be any time,' Gether snapped. 'We insist the talks are within two weeks.'

'Yes, yes,' Resen said, raising his hands to ward off the venom. 'Two weeks, of course.'

Gether drove away and Parks and Resen went to the Mayor's men.

Parks smiled to himself, having just spotted the opportunity to do something he'd wanted to do for as long as he could remember. He looked at No-name and said, 'Take me to your leader.'

***

Before he left, Parks told Chambers the plan. 'Tell the captain he can prepare to bring the Kestrel over. I'll contact you as soon as we agree the details. I suggest you get some sleep, I can't see much happening overnight, but you never know.'

Determined to stay on top, Parks refused to be separated from the Governor, insisting one of the men change vehicle so there were two seats together. They were driven into the town to the Mayor's office, where they were made to wait outside while No-name reported to the Mayor. Governor Resen was not impressed, having expected some deference to his position. The Mayor came out in person to welcome them into his office, so Resen was a little pacified.

Mayor Havilar was rather plump for a Casparan, with pale green hair worn long, below his collar and tied back with a leather thong. His orange tunic and trousers were topped with a green sash across his chest. He fingered it as he came to greet them, and bowed.

'Welcome, welcome!' he said. 'Such an awful time you have had, you must come and take a drink with me, Casparan Liqueur saved for a special occasion.'

They were ushered into his office, a simple wooden room but filled with cushions. They sat on cushions, leaned on cushions and had to drink the sickly-sweet liqueur. Parks was losing patience, squeezed into a small couch full of cushions while the two men exchanged pleasantries. Eventually they got around to talking aid.

'I could provide some large logs and tarpaulins to make shelters,' Havilar said, 'and some blankets. It must be getting cold at night, the same as here.'

'We need food too,' Resen said, 'and skilled people to help search for survivors and rebuild once the aftershocks stop.'

Havilar sat up in his seat. 'Aftershocks? You mean more earthquakes?'

'Of course!' Resen said with a dismissive wave of his hand. 'There are always aftershocks after an earthquake. Anyway, they may be over by now. We were talking about skilled people.'

Havilar shook his head. 'I wouldn't be happy sending my people into an active earthquake zone. I might be sending them to their deaths.'

'By the gods!' Resen shouted. 'There is nothing left to fall down, the town is flat!'

Parks thought, *We're always told not to talk down to Casparans just because they're small. Yet these two are behaving just like children.*

'Excuse me,' Parks said. 'The situation is urgent and the hour is late, so why don't you collect the aid together and ask for volunteers? I'll contact my captain and the Kestrel can set off, so you can be ready by the time she arrives.' Parks got to his feet in an attempt to close the meeting, but Resen didn't follow his lead.

'Thank you Commander Parks,' Resen said. 'You go and load what aid you can carry,' he turned to Havilar. 'You have assembled some aid already surely?'

Havilar looked embarrassed, but quickly recovered. 'In the morning my men will take you to the hospital to collect whatever spare blankets they have.' He wrote on a small sheet of paper and signed it. 'Here is your authorisation.'

'Very good,' said Resen. 'Go back to the shuttle and I will see you tomorrow.'

Parks decided to salute, to keep them sweet, and then went to find No-name to take him back.

***

Early the next morning No-name arrived to take Parks to the hospital. There, the atmosphere was very different.

'I am so glad you came, Commander Parks,' said the Matron. 'Those poor things! We have two piles of blankets and some medical supplies, and one of our nurses has volunteered to go.'

'Thank you, Matron. We'll take the blankets and supplies but tell the nurse to report with the other volunteers, since I'm detouring to survey the other affected settlements on the way back. The Mayor is shortly to make an announcement that he is looking for aid and volunteers which our ship, the Kestrel, will take back to Westtown more directly. The second shuttle has room for some supplies, but not additional passengers. I trust your nurse will report when the announcement is made.'

When they got back to the shuttles, Gether was waiting to speak to Parks.

'Some of us want to volunteer, and we have collected a box of food,' Gether said.

Parks told him the same as he told the Matron. He left and turned to No-name. 'Tell the Mayor there are people who want to volunteer, and I've told them to listen for the announcement of where to report, so he had better do it quick. The Kestrel is about to leave Westtown, so it'll be here in a few hours.'

Chambers saw Parks and left the shuttle, he overheard Parks' last remark.

'Captain Darrow is ready to leave, but waiting for your update, sir.'

'Right, I'll contact him now. Oh, Lieutenant, he asked me to go back via the coast to check the status of the other settlements. How do you feel about taking all the aid and Governor Resen straight to Westtown, rather than delay us both?'

'I'm fine with that.' Chambers looked at the aid Parks had brought. 'Is this it, sir?'

'Yes, I'm afraid it is. I think it will all fit in one shuttle, and leave room for you two. If it's too much, put any surplus in mine. I'll go and report to the captain. Don't leave until I tell you.'

Parks boarded his shuttle and contacted Darrow.

'Captain, are you alone?'

'Yes, I'm on the bridge, there's no one else here - they're all asleep. Sounds like you've run into trouble.'

'Yes and no, sir. There's been no "trouble" as such, but there is a Resistance group over here that wants the whole of Eastside to have independence from Westside, and Mayor Havilar is struggling. He's using armed men to keep order.'

'It's not much better over here. They've executed a looter and whipped several thieves. But you know the rules, no interference without authorisation. We're just here to bring aid.'

'Well I did put my foot down to get them to talk to each other, or we'd never have got a decision about what aid they're prepared to give. Captain, you asked me to survey the other settlements. From the air, or do you want me to talk to people?'

'Aerial only for now. We can review the scans when you get back here, see where the damage is, then we can plan to take aid where it's needed. Get back here as soon as you can.'

'Aye aye, sir. Lieutenant Chambers is heading straight to Westtown; bringing blankets, medical supplies, and some food, along with Governor Resen.

I'll come back the long way round. We're leaving now.'

'Roger that. Tell Easttown the Kestrel is leaving now, and urge them to be ready for a quick turnaround.'

Chapter 34

First thing the next day, at Westtown, Reuel gathered with the others to Hoy's call. As Balitoth had left with Darrow on the Kestrel, that meant there was Hoy, Reuel and Tanner.

'Now listen,' Hoy said. 'Tanner here wants to help take the strain with the digging and lifting. His headband will cover his horn, so it will remain secret, but it would be a lot easier if he mostly helped us. Tanner, make sure you don't... "telekenetic" anything that isn't being lifted by us. So, if something suddenly gets lighter, no one is to look surprised. OK?' He waited on their agreement. 'Let's go.'

They walked down from the rise into the devastated town. It was heartbreaking to see, literally for Tanner. Tears began to run down his face, and before they reached the main work gang, he halted.

'Wait!' he gasped. 'I have to stop. The grief, the shock and the fear, it's coming off these people in waves. It's too much to bear. I thought it would be worst at the hospital, but at least the people there have been rescued.'

Hoy said, 'Maybe it would be best if you went back to the rise where the aid is stacked. Help to sort it out to make it easier to distribute.'

'Lieutenant-Commander Hoy, the captain said I must stay with you. That would mean another pair of hands not helping. Just give me a moment.' He turned to the two of them. 'Your positive emotions are a great help. I know you are shocked and sorrowful, but you're determined to help all you can. I can feed on that strength to help me cope.'

Are my feelings about him adding to his struggle? wondered Reuel. *But how can I not distrust him?* His mind whirled, looking for an answer. He settled on trying to suppress all feelings. *At least I won't be making it worse.*

Tanner took some deep breaths and they went on. These were the lightest members of the Kestrel's crew. But they were all stronger than the Casparans, and they were three extra pairs of hands, so they were welcomed.

Most of the houses were single storey, but the Governor's residence had been two storeys, with offices below and living accommodation above. A large part of the building had come down on top of the neighbouring house, and that was where they were told to dig.

It was difficult to work out what part of the house they were looking at, with all the parts on top of one another. The only way to move the rubble was by hand. A digging machine could only be used once they established no one was underneath. Tanner assisted them to carry the stones so they could lift greater weights and didn't tire so quickly. Once they got the hang of working together it went well.

Reuel didn't want to work with Tanner, but he wasn't strong enough to manage the bigger slabs without him. He tried to work only on the smaller debris. The work was very dusty and they were grateful when a woman brought drinking water.

They were still trying to shift the rubble from the Governor's residence when Tanner motioned to them to stop a moment.

'Wait!' he hissed. 'I can feel something, someone.' He started to pick his way across the mound of rubble. He stopped and looked to see if anyone was looking their way, then pointed. 'Over here, there's someone over here.'

They scrambled over to him and started pulling things out of the way. Tanner assisted and kept indicating where to dig. Reuel, despite himself, was fascinated.

They revealed a corner of a bed, and as they dug down, a hand came out from underneath. The shout from the Kestrel crew drew the attention of the nearby diggers, who came to help. The sign of someone found alive lifted everyone's spirits and Reuel watched the stress drain from Tanner's face.

Tanner stepped back a little and stopped digging in order to concentrate. Rocks, beams and dust flowed away from the bed, and as more was uncovered, Tanner whispered, 'Lift the bed.'

Hoy heard him and repeated it with a shout. Three men braced themselves and gripped the bed. When the command came to lift, the men strained and then had looks of surprise as the bed lifted up. Someone dived underneath and dragged out a woman. A cheer went up and the bed crashed back down.

Wasting no time, Tanner scrambled across the rubble, "listening" for more survivors. As soon as he found someone he signalled to Hoy, and they started digging. Again, Tanner assisted with the work. They found a second survivor, and then a third.

Hoy soon had to speak to Tanner, to calm down and not be too obvious. He was so excited, and Reuel had to smile, despite his suspicion. There was no doubt in this case, that Tanner was genuinely delighted to help.

***

Reuel saw Tanner move away from where they were digging to rest for a moment after Hoy warned him to calm down. Reuel watched him all the time, he couldn't help himself. At the moment he was quite a sight, they all were. Everyone was covered in dust, and many had cuts and grazes where the rubble had scraped them as they cleared it.

Either this man was controlling everyone's mind, which seemed increasingly unlikely, or he was genuine. The only mental talents he showed were empathy and telekinesis, and he was only using them to help people.

Reuel turned away at the sound of rumbling. A digging machine was being brought in to move some of the rubble they had already worked through, to give better access further in. No, that wasn't all the rumbling. The ground started to tremble and dust rose in a cloud.

'Aftershock!' The cry went up. Reuel couldn't see who had shouted.

The searchers scrambled off the rubble to open ground. A woman screamed. A child cried. Men shouted warnings. The shaking increased. Walls, already damaged, cracked and fell. There was a roar and a whole pile of rubble caved in. It became impossible to stand, and those who hadn't fallen sat on the ground. And then it stopped.

The silence was so sudden everyone froze. Men hugged each other, went to check on friends and relatives. Reuel looked around for his crewmates. Hoy was on the move, checking on everyone. Tanner... Where was Tanner? He had been sitting up on top of the rubble. The rubble that caved in!

Reuel scrambled up to the edge of the cave-in and peered into the hole through the still-settling dust.

There was no sign of him. Reuel looked around again. Maybe Tanner had moved before the cave-in. Then why wasn't he in sight?

If he is under here, Reuel thought, *why does he not use his telekinesis to move the stones? He must be unconscious. No one else is looking up here, no one knows where he is. This is my chance to get rid of him.* Reuel was shocked at the thought, sickened by the implication and his own reaction against the idea. *I do believe I actually like the man! Somehow I have learned to trust him.*

Reuel shouted, 'Up here! Tanner is under the cave-in.'

Hoy bounded up the pile. Reuel slithered down into the depression and started lifting stones from the bottom and passing them up to Hoy and one of the colonists. The rubble began to shift and stones rolled into the depression. One hit Reuel on the ankle and he cried out.

'Come out of there Reuel,' Hoy said, 'I'll take your place.'

While Hoy was scrambling into the depression, Reuel lifted a slab and saw an arm. He grabbed the arm and cleared some smaller stones, and there was Tanner's face. Reuel reached down to push his headband back into place over his horn, so no one would see it. Tanner felt the touch and opened his eyes.

'Reuel, you're rescuing me again,' he said with a weak smile.

'Yes,' Reuel said, 'only this time I know who you are. John Tanner.'

***

259

Balitoth brought the Kestrel in to land at Easttown on the same grassy area where the shuttles had been. It was early afternoon, and this time the Mayor was there to welcome them, though with a large contingent of his armed guards. The cargo bay doors opened and Darrow stepped out. A group of about twenty men and women stood to one side, near a pile of various items: tools, boxes, tree trunks, folded tarpaulin.

'Welcome, welcome Captain!' Mayor Havilar said, with a low Casparan bow. 'We have the aid all ready, and the people who have volunteered to help.'

'Thank you,' Darrow said, returning the bow. 'We have brought some refugees for you to shelter for a while.'

He signalled to Balitoth, who led people off the ship. There were about thirty of them, mostly women and children, and three seriously injured. Havilar's face fell and a look of annoyance crossed his face fleetingly before he regained his composure. Three women came forward and took care of them, while the rest of the group started picking up the aid. Balitoth showed them where to stow it.

'Well, thank you again, Mayor,' Darrow said. 'You'll understand I'm sure we can't stay. Just until the aid and the volunteers are loaded. I'll go and prepare for takeoff.'

'Yes, yes,' Mayor Havilar said. 'I quite understand.' He bowed again and walked away with his guard.

Darrow joined Balitoth in seeing the cargo was secure and the volunteers distributed around the ship. Some of the men rushed together to the mess hall, and two people already there were told to leave. Darrow frowned at such behaviour but everybody settled down so he gave it no more thought. The behaviour of the volunteers would be Mayor Ludim and Governor Resen's problem. He was determined not to get involved in colony politics. The Kestrel took off and set course back to Westtown.

When they arrived back in Westtown it was late in the day. Chambers' shuttle was already there, landed to one side to leave space for the Kestrel. People were unloading and carrying boxes and blankets away. The aid the Kestrel had originally brought was all moved too. It was good to see progress.

There was quite a crowd waiting for them when they landed, men with shovels and picks in their hands. Darrow presumed the tools were for the volunteers he had brought to get straight to work. He was piloting the Kestrel, so he closed down the engines and opened the cargo bay doors. Balitoth could keep an eye on things until he got there.

He turned away from the view and left the bridge. In the corridor he met eight men, the volunteers from the mess hall. But they were not heading for the cargo bay, they were facing the bridge, facing him.

'Hello, gentlemen,' he said, 'the way out is that way.'

He pointed behind them and they grabbed him.

'No Captain,' one man said, 'this ship is our way out. We're not staying here waiting for the next earthquake.'

Taken by surprise, Darrow had no time to fight. He managed to smash one man against the corridor wall, but as one man let go of him another took his place. Darrow squirmed and twisted, but they all hung on tight. They struggled down the corridor a little way.

The sick bay door opened behind Darrow.

'What is going on out here?' Nefar said, appearing in the doorway.

He took in the scene and didn't waste a second,

grabbing Darrow and pulling him backwards into sick bay. Darrow fell through the door with three of his captors and Nefar banged the panel to close the door and locked it. He kicked one colonist in the head and grabbed another one by the throat and squeezed. Darrow took advantage and punched the third man in the jaw.

Dragging the man he had by the throat, Nefar opened a drawer and pulled out a sedative which he slapped on the man's neck. Letting him fall, he grabbed a second sedative and administered it to the man he had kicked. Darrow grabbed the third man.

'Not this one Doctor, I want to know what's going on. But first, I must secure the Kestrel.'

Darrow passed his captive to Nefar and went to the computer console. He locked all doors and computers to his and Nefar's access only. Looking over Darrow's shoulder, Nefar raised his eyebrows.

'Don't worry, Doctor, you won't have to do anything. In fact, it's better if you don't do anything. If I lock out to my access only and something happens to me, the crew can't get in. You're the backup, just in case. To be honest, I'd forgotten you were on board with the casualties. You came in handy there.' He turned back to the captive. 'Now, you, what's going on? And make it quick!'

The man looked up defiantly. 'We want to go home.'

Chapter 35

When Reuel heard the Kestrel arriving, he set off to take Tanner to Dr Nefar. Tanner didn't seem to be badly hurt, but Hoy insisted he get checked over. Hoy didn't want to risk him at the hospital in case his abilities were discovered. Hoy continued to dig for survivors.

On the way to the rise where the Kestrel had landed, Reuel and Tanner met Chambers, who was not long back himself. As they walked Chambers told them about the trouble at Easttown. They saw the cargo doors opening and Balitoth leading the Easttown volunteers out. They were met by a crowd of Westtown colonists, some carrying picks and shovels.

As the two groups greeted each other, some of the Easttown people were led away by a couple of Westtown men, presumably to give them assignments. The other Westtown men carried on into the cargo bay and joined the remaining Easttown men. Reuel frowned. Surely if you were going to unload, you wouldn't carry digging tools?

The scene changed in a split second, as one of the men hit Balitoth over the head with a shovel and the group ran into the cargo bay. Reuel shouted and he and Chambers dashed to the ship, leaving Tanner to aid Balitoth.

By the time Reuel and Chambers reached the cargo bay, the men had disappeared into the ship. They scrambled after them, and as they reached the corridor they heard the doors locking. Reuel's heart sank.

'The captain's on the ball,' Chambers said, 'but it means we can't get into things either.'

They heard footsteps on the stairs so they ran aft to

the staircase. Reuel stopped at the foot of the stairs and signalled to Chambers to go quietly. They crept up the stairs and along the aft corridor until they could see into the upper deck corridor. A crowd of men were there, about half with tools.

Reuel couldn't understand all the Casparan, but he got the gist of it. They were saying they had tried to get on the bridge but the doors were locked and they couldn't force them. The captain was in sick bay, judging by the gestures. Reuel signalled to Chambers and they descended the stairs and moved a little way along the corridor.

'The captain has locked himself in sick bay and the colonists can't get on the bridge,' Reuel whispered. 'There are a lot of them, but the corridor is narrow. Do you think we can fight them on our own?'

Chambers shook his head. 'Not without weapons, they have those tools, but the door to the cargo bay will be locked too, so we can't get out for help.'

'Can we open any door?' Reuel asked. 'We need to hide if we don't want to fight.'

'Quick, under the floor!' Chambers lifted a hidden latch and pulled open a hatch.

They leaped in and dropped the hatch just as the men came back down the stairs, looking for a way out. There wasn't much room under the floor, certainly not for two. Reuel had trouble keeping his spines out of Chambers' face. They held their breath and listened.

The men reached the cargo bay door and, finding it also locked, used the manual override to open the door. This time they were successful. The moment they ran out, Chambers and Reuel pushed open the hatch and climbed out.

'Go and let the captain know they've got out,'

Chambers said, and ran after them.

Reuel ran to the sick bay door. 'Captain! The men have got out. They manually opened the cargo bay door.'

The door opened, Reuel glimpsed three men unconscious on the floor before he followed Darrow as he ran out. In the cargo bay Reuel moved out to the open edge, where he stopped short. The captain was outside facing men with not just tools, but weapons.

Tanner and Balitoth were on the ground to the right, a man standing over them with a gun. Chambers was held to the left, his hands in the air with a gun trained on him. The Resistance group stood in a semi-circle facing the ship, three armed men in the centre facing the captain.

Reuel sized up the situation. The guns were too far apart to attack, unless it was co-ordinated, and he didn't know how Tanner and Balitoth were. A crowd of other colonists stood behind the Resistance group but were watching, not interfering. Did they want the Resistance to win? Was that it? Were they willing to see the Kestrel crewmen killed? Perhaps they were, if this was their only chance of getting home.

'You!' one of the Resistance group shouted. 'Come out here!'

Reuel reluctantly stepped out of the cargo bay. He wished he had stopped sooner and not allowed himself to be seen. The man who had shouted came forward and grabbed him by the arm, training his weapon on him.

'Captain,' the man said, 'we do not want to kill anyone, but this whole colony is in danger now. We will do what we have to in order to get our families home to safety.'

'There is no need for violence,' Darrow said. 'Surely your leaders -'

'Hah!' said the man, and there was a rumble from the watching crowd. 'Our leaders are useless, hanging on to their jobs only because no one else wants them.'

Reuel, growing increasingly agitated with a weapon pointed at him, realised all was not well in this colony even before the earthquake. But what could the Kestrel do? His mind searched for possibilities, but he knew, even if the captain sympathised, his first duty was to the Kestrel and his crew.

'I would be glad to carry a message for you to Caspar,' Darrow said, 'but you can't have my ship.'

The crowd started to rumble again, when Balitoth regained consciousness with a cry. The cry distracted the men with weapons, and Tanner struck. Every man dropped his weapon. Tanner grabbed the weapon of the man standing over him. He didn't know how to fire it, but he kept hold of it with one hand while he comforted Balitoth with the other one.

Chambers and Reuel grabbed weapons, Darrow dashed forward to try to reach the three men in front. But he was not quick enough, the distance was too great.

The three men in the centre of the Resistance group retrieved their weapons and faced Tanner, Reuel and Chambers. Three against three. Stalemate.

There was the sound of an engine, a shuttle engine, coming in fast.

Commander Parks! Reuel thought. *Right on cue.*

As everyone looked up, a laser scorched the ground between the two groups. The crowd fell back, and the shuttle circled low over their heads.

'Put down your weapons,' Darrow shouted, loud

enough for the whole crowd to hear. 'Tools as well, pile them up here.' He pointed to his feet.

There was a moment's hesitation, then one man moved to drop his weapon. Resolve crumbled, and one by one, weapons were given up. Tanner gave his weapon to Darrow and went back to help Balitoth stand. They both went into the ship, presumably to Dr Nefar. Chambers signalled to Reuel and they moved into the crowd to check for more weapons or tools.

The arrival of the shuttle and the sound of the laser had attracted attention and more people were arriving to see what was going on. They were also made to hand over their tools. Hoy arrived and Darrow called him over.

'Take a weapon and stand guard in the front of the cargo bay, where you're further back from the crowd,' he said.

Resen and Ludim arrived, together with the five armed men wearing green sashes. Reuel watched, this was another potential flashpoint.

'Governor, Mayor,' Darrow called, 'will you join me?'

After looking around, the two men came forward, the crowd pushed apart by the green-sashed men. There was an angry rumble from the crowd. Reuel moved to the front, and towards Darrow, still with his weapon, and Chambers followed suit.

'Captain,' Resen said, drawing himself up to his full height, 'what is the meaning of this? Why are you holding weapons against my people?'

'Because I have just put down an armed attack on my ship, Governor. Would you like to explain why your people are desperate enough to do such a thing?'

Resen jumped as if Darrow had slapped him and

looked around at the crowd, who started booing. Mayor Ludim spoke to one of the green-sashed men, who gave an order and the five drew their weapons and trained them on the crowd. Darrow's face was like thunder. He looked up at the still-hovering shuttle and gave a signal. A laser beam struck the ground again. Resen, Ludim and his men recoiled and pointed their weapons at the shuttle.

'I don't advise that,' Darrow said. 'You really have no idea what you're doing, do you? Your men will surrender their weapons, the same as everyone else. Now!'

Ludim reluctantly gave the command, and the weapons were added to the pile. Reuel wondered what the captain would do next. He couldn't think of any way out.

'Right,' Darrow said, rubbing his hands together. 'We will now have two meetings. I will meet with my senior staff on board the Kestrel and discuss whether there is any more we can do here. You leaders will meet with anyone you want to consult - including at least two representatives from the Resistance - and decide the way forward.'

Darrow smiled. 'I am a friend of Prime Minister Barok. I will personally deliver any messages you like. You have one hour. Anyone comes near these weapons, my ship or my shuttles in that time, they will be executed. Understood?'

There was a murmur of 'Yes,' from the crowd.

Darrow called Chambers and Reuel and told them to stand guard over the weapons. He told Hoy to call Blackwell away from his work on the desalination plant and Tomos from the hospital, then called Hoy into the meeting. Parks landed the shuttle and joined them.

Chapter 36

Most of the senior staff were not aware of part or all of what went on, so Darrow's first command was for Parks and Hoy to reveal all they had learned, then he summarised.

'All is not well here,' Darrow said. 'The colonists are unhappy with the Governor and at least one of the Mayors. After the earthquake, the colonists are afraid that the planet isn't safe. Things got out of hand when the Resistance tried to take over the Kestrel.'

Blackwell defused the tension.

'I wonder if our ground scanner would pick up the earthquake fault?' Blackwell said. 'They could map it and know where not to build.'

'Good idea, we can certainly offer them that assistance,' said Darrow. 'How's the work on the desalination plant?'

'Finished. I was on my way back when Hoy called.'

Darrow turned to Nefar. 'What about the medical side, Doctor?'

Nefar shrugged. 'We could stay for weeks with regenerators fixing all the injuries, but I think we have dealt with the most serious cases. The body does heal itself, after all, it just takes a little longer.'

'So how soon would you be prepared to leave?'

'Within a few hours, I think.'

'Lieutenant-Commander, how's the digging going?' Hoy's turn.

'Very well, thanks to Tanu, sorry Tanner,' Hoy said. 'He can pick up emotions from survivors under the rubble, so he has been pointing out where to dig.

'There are two problems with that. First, it's strange we find so many survivors. People are starting to get suspicious. But you can't leave people buried when you know they're there. Second, Tanner's getting overwhelmed by the shock and grief. He's finding it hard to deal with.' He paused for breath.

'If that wasn't enough, he got buried in a cave-in, so Reuel was taking him to Dr Nefar, but I gather he never got there.'

'I have given Lieutenant Balitoth's head injury initial treatment,' said Nefar. 'I will check Tanner over as soon as this meeting finishes.'

'Thank you, Doctor,' Darrow said. 'Hoy, do you think we need to stay any longer?'

Hoy frowned. 'It's hard to say. I don't know if we've found all the survivors yet, and there are definitely more bodies to dig out. Does our mission specify help with clearing the rubble and rebuilding? That's a huge job.'

'We were only asked to deliver aid. I think we've done a lot more. I'll talk to the colonists and see what they say.' He turned to Parks. 'What about you Commander, what have you found out?'

Parks shook his head. 'In Easttown the Resistance is well organised, so there's trouble there. I came back the long way round and the smaller settlements north and south of here have varying amounts of damage, mostly from the tsunami following the first 'quake. I didn't land to speak to anyone, so perhaps we could drop off aid and helpers before we go.'

'Can you document that for me to pass on?' Darrow looked around the room. 'Any other comments before I go to speak to the colony leaders?'

Hoy spoke up. 'Now they've got clean water, but I

don't know what the food situation is like. Ensign Reuel helped a woman from a farm who said they lost their crops to the tsunami. They may have enough for the crisis, but what about the future?'

Darrow was making notes. 'Got that. Let's see what the colony leaders have to say. Dismissed.'

***

Darrow went to meet the leaders. As he walked through the cargo bay, the aid from Easttown was being unloaded. When he left the ship, he saw the logs were already being worked with to build a shelter. To one side, the Resistance men were sitting on the ground with their hands tied, guarded by the men with green sashes.

Darrow frowned and shook his head. Colony life was regarded as idyllic, a way to start society the right way and forget the errors of the past. The truth was, people were the same everywhere and they brought their sins with them.

The leaders' meeting was still going on, and as Darrow approached the group of chairs he could see things were getting heated. Governor Resen saw him and interrupted the discussion.

'Captain Darrow is here, sirs. Perhaps we can continue this discussion later.'

They turned to him, their faces telling their own stories: anger, despair, determination, stubbornness, fear. There was no chair for him in the group, so he was forced to stand and tower over them. *Perhaps that's just as well,* he thought.

'Don't let me interrupt if you haven't agreed on the things I need to know,' Darrow said. 'You can discuss government later. I have to decide whether the Kestrel can leave, and I need to know what messages you want taken to Prime Minister Barok.'

They all started talking at once. Darrow's heart sank. He raised his voice.

'Gentlemen! One at a time, please.' The men fell silent and looked at each other. 'Let me start with my report,' Darrow said.

'We were asked to deliver aid, which we have done.' He ticked things off on his fingers. 'We were asked to offer emergency assistance, which we have done. My engineer reports the desalination plant is repaired, so you have clean water again. The most serious medical cases have been treated and the hospital is no longer overwhelmed. Many survivors have been rescued and some work has been done clearing the rubble. We have also surveyed the other settlements and here is a report on the current situation.'

He handed over a data stick to Resen.

'A lot of crops were swamped by the tsunami, so you have to consider whether you have enough food for the future.' He paused for breath.

'Now, we could carry aid to the settlements before we go, and we could transport your dead to the burial place. My engineer has suggested a ground scanner may be able to detect the earthquake fault, so I am prepared to give you ours. If you can map the fault line, you can build in safer places and calm the fears of the colonists.

'We have done all and more we were asked to do here. We will leave you the scanner, we will take a message to Prime Minister Barok, but we will take no colonists with us when we leave. Now do you have messages for the Prime Minister?'

One of the Resistance men stood. 'Captain, please tell Mayor Ludim to release my men.'

Ludim cut in. 'You have broken our laws and sought to overthrow the government. That is a very serious matter.'

'If you were doing your job we wouldn't need a change in leadership --'

Darrow raised his voice again. 'Since you don't seem to be able to answer my question, I'll leave you to continue your discussion. The Kestrel will prepare to leave.'

He turned on his heel and walked away. *These people!* he thought. *It's a wonder anything ever gets done. The sooner we get out of here, the better.*

He felt a tap on his elbow, and turned to see one of the Resistance representatives from the meeting.

'Captain, I have a question. How did my men's guns come out of their hands?'

Oh curses! Darrow thought. *I thought we'd got away with that one. Think quick.* 'My men disarmed them in a coordinated attack.'

The man shook his head. 'Not all of them. Even the ones with no attacker dropped their guns. How did you do it?'

'Why do you assume it was me?' Darrow said. 'I had nothing to do with it. I'm sorry, I can't help you.'

Darrow bowed and walked away. After a few paces he glanced back to see the man still standing there with a puzzled look on his face. *Tanner needs to be more careful,* he thought.

Chapter 37

Eventually a tentative peace was formed, though discussions continued. The colonists stopped arguing long enough to draft two messages for Darrow to take to the Prime Minister - one from each side. The Kestrel did a few last jobs for the colonists and was able to leave. Darrow gave orders for a parking orbit round Sabteca and called the crew together.

'First of all,' Darrow said, 'well done all of you, we've had a rough time the last couple of weeks. We've left Sabteca rather abruptly because I wanted to get away from the local politics, but we'll stay in orbit until you've all had the chance to clean up properly and rest.'

There was a murmur of laughter as the crew looked at each other still in their scruffy uniforms.

'There will be no duties until we leave orbit, except a watch on the bridge of course. At 1800 the junior crew will have dinner, and the senior crew at 1900. We leave orbit at 0800 tomorrow morning, ship's time, so we can all get a good night's sleep. Dismissed.'

It was a much happier crew that set to their duties the next morning, clean, relaxed and fit. Hoy was at the helm and Darrow ordered him to lay in a course that took them to Caspar. Everyone got on with writing reports for the mission log, and to give to the Casparans regarding the current situation on Sabteca and future aid requirements. Darrow had promised to deliver the colonists' messages personally, so they landed, to a much better reception after their mercy mission. He got a much better reception when he visited Prime Minister Barok too.

Darrow had sent a message ahead asking for only five minutes of Barok's time, and this time they were expecting him. Barok was grateful, not just for the aid mission, but for helping the colonists to start talking over their problems. Barok kept Darrow almost a hour. He wanted his impressions of the situation and the leaders in particular. Darrow tried to be diplomatic.

When he got back to the Kestrel he gave the whole crew two days' leave and stood watch himself. He wasn't entirely alone, since it was too dangerous for Tanner to show his face, but Tanner was grateful for the respite from everyone's emotions. An empty ship was bliss to him. Darrow also enjoyed having the ship virtually to himself. It was like an old friend, and it was nice to put down the burden of command for just a while and relax with her.

Tomos found it hard, though, on Caspar, as the last time he was on leave there he was with Roy Stubbs. They were only just getting to know one another and Tomos smiled when he remembered how useless Stubbs was with girls. He would never improve now. Tomos wandered aimlessly until he found himself in the park, heading for the very bench where they had sat and talked to Birsha and Emim through the bush. He sat down and put his head in his hands and cried for a long time.

***

Darrow used some of the time off to think about his crew. They were a mixed bag, but he was proud of them all. Young James Tomos would need nurturing after his recent experiences, but he had great potential. It was a shame really that he was determined to leave at some point and take over his parents' cargo ship. Reuel had caused some concern for a while, Darrow still wasn't sure what happened, but he seemed to be back to normal. *No*, he thought, *better than before*.

The only question that remained was what to do about Tanner. He had proven himself to be benign and had helped on Sabteca in many ways. Darrow considered he had saved the ship, for the second time.

But what to do with him?

Regulations stated anything found should be sent to headquarters, but Tanner wasn't a thing. As soon as the authorities became aware of him, they would want to experiment on him as the Bokans and Casparans had done and/or persuade him to work for them.

Darrow had strong reasons for keeping the regulations. He broke the rules when he was a young Lieutenant, and a friend died. Rules were made for a purpose. But it felt wrong to hand Tanner over. In the end, Darrow decided to call a crew meeting and discuss it with them. Maybe they would come up with an idea.

Once everyone reported back from leave, and before they took off from Caspar, Darrow assembled the crew in the mess hall.

'I won't keep you long,' Darrow said, 'but I want to hear everyone's ideas on Tanner's future.' He turned to Tanner. 'Do you have any plans or preferences?'

'No, Captain,' Tanner replied, 'but I want to thank you for letting me help on Sabteca. That's the sort of life I always imagined.'

'The trouble is,' Hoy said, 'every time you use your powers, you're going to give yourself away. Sooner or later you're going to get caught.'

'Perhaps we should follow regulations,' Blackwell said, 'and hand him over. PACT will protect him from other, more malign influences.'

Fear contorted Tanner's face.

'But what will PACT do to him?' Reuel asked. 'We do not know, we cannot be sure.'

Darrow smiled to see Reuel defending the man he was once so afraid of.

Balitoth said, 'If he went to a big city, he could disappear into the crowd.'

'Surely you don't want to live in hiding?' Parks asked Tanner. 'That's no life.'

'And he would still have to earn a living,' Hoy said. 'Where would he work? I don't see how he can be inconspicuous - he's bound to use his talents at some time, maybe without thinking.'

Blackwell raised his finger for attention and gave a slow smile. 'What if he joined the crew?' There was a general gasp. 'We could get him some papers - say his old ones were taken by the Bokans, and he would get paid. He'll be out of the way of the authorities most of the time, and can relax using his talents among us. He has already shown his talents can come in very useful,' Blackwell paused, 'and we are two crewmen short.'

There was a stunned silence. Everyone looked from Tanner to the captain and back again.

'But surely, Captain, your crew are appointed by the Planetary Alliance?' asked Tanner.

'Not always,' replied Darrow. 'We're not military, captains are given a lot of scope to make their own choices. Most of the missions the Kestrel gets sent on would be compromised by what would be seen as a military force. You might call us the diplomatic service,' he gave a slow grin. 'Though we're not often very diplomatic.'

'He hasn't been through the Academy though,'

Tomos said. 'He can't join the crew without qualifications.'

'Tabitha Enns did, even though we called it work experience,' Chambers put in. 'He can learn on the job. There's still a shortage of available crew.'

'I think it's a brilliant idea,' said Parks. 'How about it Captain?'

Darrow thought for a minute. 'I agree.' He stood up straight and turned to Tanner, his stern expression softening. 'Mr John Tanner, would you like to join the crew of the Kestrel?'

Tanner stood and bowed. 'I accept, with pleasure.'

Darrow turned to the rest of the crew. 'Crew, may I introduce you to John Tanner, our Special Operations Officer.'

###

Thank you for reading this book. I hope you enjoyed it.

Reviews are an author's lifeblood. If you enjoyed this book, please go online to Amazon and leave a review.

FREE BOOK!
Join her mailing list and receive this free book and monthly updates
http://eepurl.com/bbOsyz

Flight of the Kestrel is a series of space adventures, so I hope you'll stick with it.
Other books in the series:

Intruders: Flight of the Kestrel book 1

Tabitha Enns is given work experience on board the Kestrel, on the adventure of her life, that will push her to the limit. When a hostile alien species are discovered, the Kestrel is sent to make contact, leading the crew – and Tabitha – into danger, and the crew have problems with their friends as well as their enemies.

Crisis of Conscience, Flight of he Kestrel book 3

Can Captain Joseph Darrow of the spaceship Kestrel commit theft and murder to save the lives of his crew? Is Second Officer Daniel Hoy right, that the ends justify the means? Are there some lines you must not cross?

Can they persuade the Zoan lizard woman Raven to tell them her father's secret?

Newly qualified Ensign Tabitha Enns steps straight into peril. Can she prove her worth?

And look out for book four *Planet Fail*